Sapper is the pen name of Her
at the Naval Prison in Bodmin,
Governor. He served in the Roya
as 'sappers') from 1907–19, being Cross
during World War I.

He started writing in France, ado pen name because serving officers were not allowed to write under their own names. When his first stories, about life in the trenches, were published in 1915, they were an enormous success. But it was his first thriller, *Bulldog Drummond* (1920), that launched him as one of the most popular novelists of his generation. It had several amazingly successful sequels, including *The Black Gang*, *The Third Round* and *The Final Count*. Another great success was *Jim Maitland* (1923), featuring a footloose English sahib in foreign lands.

Sapper published nearly thirty books in total, and a vast public mourned his death when he died in 1937, at the early age of forty-eight. So popular was his 'Bulldog Drummond' series that his friend, the late Gerard Fairlie, wrote several Bulldog Drummond stories after his death under the same pen name.

BY THE SAME AUTHOR
ALL PUBLISHED BY HOUSE OF STRATUS

ASK FOR RONALD STANDISH
THE BLACK GANG
BULLDOG DRUMMOND
BULLDOG DRUMMOND AT BAY
CHALLENGE
THE DINNER CLUB
THE FEMALE OF THE SPECIES
THE FINAL COUNT
THE FINGER OF FATE
THE ISLAND OF TERROR
JIM BRENT
JIM MAITLAND
JOHN WALTERS
MUFTI
THE RETURN OF BULLDOG DRUMMOND
SERGEANT MICHAEL CASSIDY RE
TEMPLE TOWER
THE THIRD ROUND

SAPPER

Bulldog Drummond

KNOCK-OUT

This edition published in 2001 by House of Stratus, an imprint of Stratus Books Ltd., 21 Beeching Park, Kelly Bray, Cornwall, PL17 8QS, UK.

www.houseofstratus.com

Typeset, printed and bound by House of Stratus.

A catalogue record for this book is available from the British Library and the Library of Congress.

ISBN 1-84232-554-X

CHAPTER 1

It is difficult to say what it was that first caused Ronald Standish to adopt his particular profession. Indeed, it is doubtful whether it should be called a profession in view of the fact that he worked at it for love and only when the spirit moved him. Case after case he would turn down because they failed to interest him: then, apparently quite capriciously, he would take one up, vanish for a space, and then return as unobtrusively as he had departed to his ordinary life of sport.

That these sudden disappearances proved a little embarrassing to his friends is not to be wondered at. Captains of touring cricket elevens, secretaries of golf clubs, were wont to raise protesting hands to heaven when sometimes, at the last moment, Standish backed out of a match. But having played for his county at cricket, as well as being a genuine scratch man at golf, they forgave him and continued to include him in their teams.

Had he chosen to take up the art of detection seriously there is no doubt that he would have attained a world-wide reputation. He had an uncanny knack of sorting out the relevant from a mass of irrelevant facts, and refusing to be diverted by even the most ingenious red herring. But as he worked for fun and not because he had to, his ability was known to a comparatively small coterie only.

It was on a certain evening in March that, in stage parlance, the curtain rose and discovered him in his rooms in Clarges Street. A cheerful fire was burning in the grate: a whisky tantalus adorned the table. Outside the wind was howling fitfully down the street, drowning the distant roar of traffic in Piccadilly, and an occasional scurry of rain lashed against the window.

The owner of the rooms was standing with his back to the fire, an intent look of concentration on his face. Balanced on one finger was a driver, and it was evident that judgment was about to be pronounced. It came at last.

"Too heavy in the head, Bill: undoubtedly too heavy in the head. You'll slice to glory with that club."

His audience uncoiled himself from an armchair. He was a lanky individual whose appearance was in striking contrast to the speaker. For Standish was, if anything, a little on the short side, and his lack of inches was accentuated by the abnormal depth of his chest. He was immensely powerful, but in a rough house suffered somewhat from lack of reach.

"Can anything be done, Ronald?" demanded Bill Leyton. "I've only just bought the blamed thing."

"You might try having a bit of lead scooped out at the back, old boy, but I'm afraid the balance will still be all wrong."

He put the club back in its bag, that profound look of awed mystery, without which no golfer can discuss an implement of the game, still present in his expression.

"Too heavy in the head," he repeated solemnly. "And you tend to slice at the best of times, Bill. Damn! Who's that? Answer it, old boy, will you, and if it's Teddy wanting me to play tomorrow tell him I've gone to Paris for a month and have given up golf."

The lanky being crossed the room in a couple of enormous strides and lifted the telephone receiver.

"Hullo!" he remarked. "Yes – these are Mr Standish's rooms. Who is speaking?"

He listened for a moment, and then covering the mouthpiece with his hand, turned round.

"Bloke by the name of Sanderson," he muttered. "Wants to speak to you urgently."

Standish nodded, and took the receiver from the other's hand.

"Hullo! Sanderson," he said. "Yes – Standish speaking. What now? My dear fellow – on a night like this... Hullo! Hullo! Hullo!"

His voice rose in a crescendo and Leyton stared at him in amazement.

"Can't you hear me? Speak, man, speak. Hullo! Hullo!"

He rattled the receiver rest violently.

"Is that exchange?" he cried. "Look here, I've just been rung up by Hampstead 0024, and I've been cut off in the middle. Could you find out about it?"

He waited, one foot tapping feverishly on the floor.

"You can't get any reply, and the receiver is still off? Thank you."

He turned to Leyton.

"It's possible that he was called away; I'll hold on a bit longer."

But a minute later he gave it up and his face was very grave.

"Something has happened, Bill; I'll have to go to Hampstead. Either he's ill, or..."

He left the sentence unfinished, and Leyton looked at him curiously.

"What was it you heard?" he asked.

"He had just asked me to go up and see him at once. The last words he said were – 'I've got...' He was beginning a new sentence, and he never completed it. I heard a noise that sounded like a hiss; then came a clatter which might have been caused by the receiver of his machine dropping on to his desk. And there's been nothing since."

He crossed to a small cupboard in the corner, and Bill Leyton raised his eyebrows. He knew the contents of that cupboard, and things must be serious if Standish proposed utilising them.

"If you're taking a gun, old lad," he remarked, "I suppose I'd better come with you. And on the way there you shall explain to me who and what is Mr Sanderson."

A taxi was passing the door as they went out, and Standish gave the driver the address.

"Tread on the juice," he added briefly. "It's urgent. Now, Bill," he continued as the car swung into Curzon Street, "I'll put you wise as to Sanderson. He is a man who occupies rather a peculiar position in the Government. Very few people have ever heard of him: very few people even know that such a job as his exists. He is of Scotland Yard and yet not of Scotland Yard; the best way to describe him, I suppose, is to say that he is a secret service man. Crime as crime is outside his scope: if, however, it impinges in the slightest degree into the political arena, then he sits up and takes notice. His knowledge of things behind the scenes is probably greater than that of any other man in England: information comes to him from all quarters in a way that it doesn't even to the police. And if he were to write a book the wildest piece of sensational fiction would seem like a nursery rhyme beside it. So you will see that he is a man who must have some very powerful enemies, enemies who would feel considerably happier if he was out of the way. In fact..."

He broke off abruptly, and leaning back in his corner lit a cigarette.

"Go on," said Leyton curiously.

"I was having a talk with him a few days ago," went on Standish. "And for him he was very communicative: generally he's as close as an oyster. It was confidential, of course, so I'm afraid I can't tell you what it was about now. We must wait and see what it was that caused him to stop so suddenly."

"So it was that talk that made you bring a gun," said Leyton.

"Exactly," answered the other, and relapsed into silence.

Five minutes later the car pulled up in front of a medium-sized detached house standing back from the road. A small garden with a few trees filled the gap between the iron railings and the front door; save for a light from one window on the first floor the place was in darkness.

Standish tipped the driver handsomely, and then waited till his tail lamp had disappeared before opening the gate. The rain had ceased, but it was still blowing hard, and by the light of a neighbouring street lamp Leyton saw that his face looked graver than ever.

"Look at that blind, Bill," he said, "where the light is. That's his study, and what man sits in a room with a blind flapping like that? I don't like it."

"Perhaps he's round at the back," suggested the other.

"Let's hope so," said Standish shortly, and walking up the steps to the front door he pressed the bell.

Faintly, but quite distinctly, they heard it ring in the back of the house, but no one came to answer to it. He tried again with the same result: then stooping down Standish peered through the letter-box.

"All in darkness," he said. "And a Yale lock. Bill, I like it less and less. Let's go round and see if there's a light on the other side."

There was none, and for a moment or two he hesitated.

"Look here, old boy," he said at length, "there's something devilish fishy about this show. Strictly speaking, I suppose we ought to get hold of the nearest policeman, but I have a very strong desire to dispense with official aid for a while. I'm going to commit a felony: are you on?"

"Break in, you mean?" said Leyton with a grin. "Lead on, old man: I'm with you. Which window do we tackle?"

"None: a child could open this back door."

From his pocket Standish produced a peculiar-looking implement, the end of which he inserted in the keyhole. For a moment or two he juggled with it, and then there came a click as the bolt shot back.

"Asking for it, most of these doors," he whispered, and then stood listening intently in the passage. A faint light filtered down a flight of stairs in front of them, coming from a street lamp on the other side of the house. On their left an open door revealed the larder: next to it the dying embers of a fire in the kitchen grate showed that the servants had been about earlier, wherever they were at the moment.

Cautiously he led the way up the stairs into the hall, where everything was plainly visible in the glare from the glass over the front door. And at the foot of the next flight he paused to listen again. But, save for the howling of the wind, there was no sound.

"Come on, Bill," he muttered. "Not much good standing here all night."

They went up to the first story: the room with the flapping blind was marked by the line of light on the floor. And with a quick movement Standish flung open the door, his revolver gripped in his right hand – a hand which slowly fell to his side.

"My God!" he cried. "I was afraid of it."

Seated at the desk with his back to them was a man. He was sprawling forward with his left arm flung out, whilst his right hand, crumpled underneath him, still clutched the telephone receiver. And from the edge of the desk a little stream of blood trickled sluggishly on to the carpet.

For a while Standish stood where he was, taking in every detail of the room: then he crossed to the dead man and very gently lifted his head. And the next moment he gave an exclamation of horror.

"Great Scott! Bill," he cried, "the poor devil has been stabbed through the eye."

It was a terrible wound, and with a shudder Leyton turned away.

"Let's get the police, Ronald," he said. "We can't do anything for him and this ain't my idea of a happy evening."

But Standish with a puzzled frown on his forehead seemed not to hear.

"What an extraordinary thing," he said at length. "Death must have been instantaneous, and therefore if it had been accidental – if, for instance, he had suddenly become dizzy and his head had fallen forward on to one of those spike things you skewer letters on we should see it on the desk. Now there is nothing there that could possibly have caused such a wound, so we can rule out accident. Suicide is equally impossible for the same reason: in any event, a man doesn't commit suicide in the middle of a telephone call. So it is perfectly clear he was murdered, or killed accidentally."

"My dear old boy, even I can see that," said Leyton a little peevishly. "What about my notion of the police? Let's ring up."

Standish shook his head.

"We can't do that, Bill. It would mean taking the receiver out of his hand, and everything must be left as it is. You can go to the window, if you like, and hail a bobby if you see one passing: personally I want to try to get at this. Go and stand behind his chair for a moment, will you."

Obediently Leyton did so, though he was clearly puzzled.

"What's the great idea?" he demanded.

"I'm trying to reconstruct what happened," said Standish, "and I wanted to see if that light in the wall over there made your shadow fall on the desk. As you notice, it does, which makes it even more difficult. Let's try it from the beginning. Sanderson was sitting in the chair he is in now, the receiver to his face and in all probability his right elbow resting on the desk. His conversation was perfectly normal: quite obviously he was completely unconscious of being in any danger. He begins a sentence – 'I've got,' and at that moment he is killed in a most extraordinary fashion. 'I've got' – what? That's the point. Was he going to say – 'I've got information of some sort'; or was he going to say – 'I've got so and so with me here'? If the first, it is possible that he didn't know the murderer was in the room: that he was stolen on from behind. But in that event a shadow would have been thrown, and Sanderson with his training would have been out of that chair in a flash."

"It's possible," put in Leyton, "that only the light in the ceiling was on."

"And that the man who did it turned on that one before leaving?" Standish shook his head. "Possible, admittedly, Bill, but most unlikely. Surely every instinct in such a case would be to turn lights off and not on. However, one can't rule it out entirely. Let's go on. Supposing he was going to say – 'I've got so and so here': where do we get then? We wash out in the first place the extreme difficulty of striking such an accurate blow blindly from behind. The man, whoever he was, could have been standing in front of Sanderson or beside him. But even so it's terribly hard to understand. If you try to stab me in the eye with a skewer I'm going to move damned quick. Even if the man was standing beside him, and did a sudden backhander with his weapon, it seems incredible to me that Sanderson couldn't dodge it. One's reaction, if anything is coming at one's eye, is literally instantaneous."

"The plain fact remains that the poor devil didn't dodge it," said Leyton.

"There is another very remarkable point about the whole thing, Bill," went on Standish. "Why did the man select the middle of a telephone conversation of all times to kill him? It seems the one moment of all others to avoid."

"That certainly is a bit of a poser," agreed Leyton.

"It's such a poser that there must be a good reason for it, and there's one that occurs to me. If a man is speaking into a telephone, even one of the desk type like this, he keeps his head still. And that was probably essential for the infliction of this wound. Well – I'm just going to have a look round and see if I can spot anything, and then we'll go for the police."

He glanced through the contents of a paper-rack: there was nothing save a couple of invitations and some bills. Then his eyes travelled slowly over the desk. There was not much on it: a tray containing pens; a calendar; an open bottle of Stephens' ink. In the middle were several sheets of blotting-paper folded together into a pad, one corner of which was stained a vivid crimson – the dead man's head had fallen there.

"His pockets we had better not touch," said Standish, "but possibly the waste-paper basket might reveal something."

But it was almost empty: a torn-up letter, and a small fragment of blotting-paper with an ink stain in the centre of it was the total bag.

"Nothing much in that lot," he continued. "Hullo! this ink is still damp. And there's the place on the pad where this bit was torn from. Cheer up, Bill," he added with a faint smile, "I've nearly done. By the way, I wonder where the cork of that bottle is?"

And Bill Leyton exploded.

"Damn it, Ronald, I don't know and I don't care. This room, with that poor blighter sitting dead there, is giving me the willies. What does it matter where the cork is? It probably was taken out of the bottle and fell on the desk and made a blot. Then that bit of blotting-paper was torn off to wipe it up with."

"And the cork was then thrown out of the window in a fit of pique," added Standish with mild sarcasm.

"But what can it matter, old boy?" said Leyton irritably. "The wound can't have been done with a cork."

And then he shrugged his shoulders: there had appeared on the other's face an expression he knew only too well. Standish was following up some idea in his mind, and nothing short of an earthquake would disturb his concentration. What possible importance could be attached to the fact that the ink bottle was minus a cork Leyton failed to see, but he knew the futility of arguing.

"You don't shake an ink bottle, Bill, before you open it," said Standish suddenly. "And that one is half empty."

"What the deuce?" began Leyton feebly.

"It's got this to do with it," said the other. "The cork would be dry when it came out. Therefore the ink that that little piece of blotting-paper was used to mop up did not come from the cork."

He stiffened abruptly.

"Listen," he whispered, "don't make a sound. There's someone moving downstairs."

The two men stood motionless, straining their ears. The wind had dropped a little, and in a momentary lull they distinctly heard the creak of a board in the hall below.

"Get behind the curtains, Bill," he muttered. "It may be that the murderer has come back for something."

They stood waiting tensely, one on each side of the window. Between them the blind, with a sort of devilish perversity, flapped more than ever, so that it was quite impossible to hear any noise in the house. And since the door opened towards the window the passage outside was invisible from where they stood.

Through a little chink Leyton could see most of the room: the dead man sprawling over the desk; the half-open door; the switches on the wall beyond. But it was at the door he was staring, fascinated: who was going to come round it in a few moments?

Suddenly he heard a stifled exclamation from outside, and glancing across at Standish he saw that he was standing rigid, his revolver ready in his hand. Then he once more looked at the door: the visitor had arrived. Seconds dragged on into minutes: the suspense was becoming unbearable when, happening to glance at the two switches, he saw a hand resting on them. And the next moment the room was in darkness save for the light from the street lamp outside.

He could no longer see the door itself, only the desk with its motionless occupant looking even more dreadful in the eerie half-light. But an unmistakable creak from the side of the room told him the unknown had entered. What was going to happen now? he wondered; and the next instant he knew. Some hard object struck him a crashing blow in the face and in the stomach, and he let out a shout of pain.

"Splendid," came a voice from near the wall, "I thought I wasn't mistaken. I've got you covered, so just step into the lighted area by the window and step darned quick, or the next thing that hits you won't be a table."

Leyton glanced across at Standish, and saw him give a quick nod. The game was clear: evidently the table thrower thought there was only one man behind the curtains. So he stepped out obediently and waited. His nose felt as if it was broken, and he was half winded, but those were trifles compared to the shock the other man was going to get in a moment or two.

"You look a bit of a streak of misery in silhouette, don't you," went on the voice. "Let's have a look at you in real life. Peter – switch on."

And then things happened. He had a momentary glimpse of a vast individual about four feet away from him, and another man by the door. And the next instant he was tackled round the waist, and went crashing backwards, knocking over Standish, who had come out from his curtain and was standing just behind him.

"Two of 'em, Peter," roared the big man, "and one's got a gun."

What the result would have been is doubtful: he was wedged in a struggling mass between Standish, who was on the floor, and someone who felt rather like Carnera on top of him. But the end came most unexpectedly.

"Quit it, Hugh," cried another voice, "there's some mistake. I know this bloke."

"What's that?" The big man scrambled to his feet. "A mistake. There was no mistake about the revolver I saw in his hand."

"It's Ronald Standish. I've played cricket with him."

"Good Lord! it's Peter Darrell. Well, I'm damned." Standish was sitting on the floor rubbing his head. "Who in the name of heaven is your pal?"

"Drummond, old boy: Captain Hugh Drummond."

"I'm most dreadfully sorry," said Drummond. "I seem to have bloomered badly. But I saw poor old Jim Sanderson dead at his desk, and I could just see through the crack by the hinges of the door that there was someone behind this curtain. I couldn't see the other one, and I jumped to the conclusion that whoever it was couldn't be up to any good. So I drew the fox by bunging a table at it, and then I suddenly realised I was looking down a gun, when it doesn't do to stand on ceremony. However, those are all trifles: what on earth has happened here?"

"The poor old chap has been murdered," said Standish gravely.

"I'm not altogether surprised," remarked Drummond quietly. "He told me today that he thought the ice was getting darned thin. You've no idea who did it, I suppose?"

Standish was silent for a few moments while he studied the other.

"None," he said at length. "May I ask what brought you here tonight, Captain Drummond?"

"Nothing can prevent you asking what you like, Mr Standish," answered Drummond affably. "And perhaps I'll tell you if you'll answer the same question yourself."

"Cut it out, you two," said Darrell. "I personally guarantee each of you to the other. And it seems to me it would be best if we all pooled our knowledge."

"Bravely spoken, Peter," said Drummond. "But as that may be a longish job, oughtn't we to do something about this first? I suppose it will be necessary to get the police."

Standish glanced at him sharply.

"Of course it will," he cried. "What an extraordinary suggestion."

"Peter – I believe he suspects us," said Drummond. "You must explain to him some time or other that in the past we have always tried to dispense with their help. And mark you, Standish, we're on something pretty big: his murder proves it."

He went nearer the dead man and bent over him.

"My God! what an awful wound. Shot clean through the eye."

"Not shot," said Standish, "or I should have heard it. He was telephoning to me when he was killed. That's what brought Leyton and me up here."

"Not shot," echoed Drummond. "Then how in the name of fortune was that wound made?"

"Exactly," agreed Standish. "How?"

"At any rate, Peter, we now know why we couldn't get any reply on the 'phone," said Drummond after a pause. "Which, if you want to know, Standish, is what brought *us* up here also."

But Standish was not listening: he was staring at something under the desk.

"The plot thickens," he remarked as he stooped down to pick it up. "There is a lady in the case."

He held in his hand a fine bronze hairpin.

"It was lying half hidden," he said, "and the light happened to catch it."

"And he wasn't married," remarked Drummond thoughtfully. "That certainly looks the nearest approach to a clue there seems to be. Of course, it may belong to one of the servants. By the way – where are the servants? We haven't been exactly silent, have we?"

And as if in answer to his question they heard voices in the hall below. A man was speaking, and then came a woman's reply. They stood waiting, their eyes on the door. Someone was coming up the stairs; someone who evidently had no idea that anything was wrong, for they could hear him whistling under his breath. There came a perfunctory knock on the half-open door and a man appeared, who halted in amazement as he saw the four of them watching him. Then his eyes fell on the motionless figure at the desk, and with a gasp he staggered back against the wall.

"What's 'appened?" he stammered. "In Gawd's name – what's 'appened?"

"Who are you?" said Standish quietly.

"Mr Sanderson's butler, sir. I've just come in."

"What is your name?"

"Perkins, sir. I've just come in with my wife, sir. 'Ow did it 'appen, sir?"

"That, Perkins, is what we want to try and find out," said Standish. "Try and pull yourself together, my man, because I should like you to answer a few questions. Was that your wife I heard you talking to downstairs?"

"Yes, sir. We've just got in from the pictures."

"And when did you go out?"

"Quarter to eight, sir. Mr Sanderson let us go before he finished his dinner."

"Was anyone having dinner with him?"

"No, sir. He was alone."

"Did he say anything to you about expecting anybody after?"

"No, sir – not a word."

"Now, Perkins, here's a hairpin. Can you tell me if that belongs to your wife?"

The butler shook his head decisively.

"No, sir. That I know it doesn't. The missus has black ones."

"Is there any other maidservant in the house?"

Once again the man shook his head.

"No, sir. My wife and I do all the work."

"And you're quite certain, Perkins, that Mr Sanderson said nothing to you about expecting anyone this evening?"

"Quite positive, sir. His last words to me were – 'Come back when you like and I hope you enjoy yourselves.' And seeing the light in the window, sir, I just came up to see if he wanted anything. What's 'appened, sir? Lumme – this will break the missus' heart. One of the kindest gentlemen I ever knew."

The man's grief was obvious, and Drummond laid a kindly hand on his shoulder.

"He's been foully murdered, Perkins," he said.

"Who's the swine what did it?" cried the butler. "Strewth! if I could get my hands on him he'd go the same way."

"That's what we all feel," said Standish. "And with luck we'll do it. But I want you now to do something. Go out and get hold of the first policeman you see, and bring him back here."

"Very good, sir: I'll go. As a matter of fact, there was one not far from the house when we came in."

With a last look at his master he left the room, and a moment or two later the front door slammed.

"There's no good interrogating the wife," said Standish. "The police can do that if they want to, and we've found out all we can from Perkins. By the way, Drummond – what made you say a little while ago that we were up against something pretty big?"

"I think that that had better keep," said the other quietly. "There are footsteps on the drive which must be Perkins returning with the necessary peeler. Tomorrow we can compare notes. But there is one thing we must settle at once. The mere fact that you were talking to him over the telephone is sufficient to account for you being here, but not for Peter and me. So until we've compared notes shall we have it that we were all playing a quiet game of push-halfpenny in your rooms and came together?"

For a moment Standish hesitated, and a faint smile flickered round his lips. He was beginning to remember one or two yarns Peter Darrell had told him on cricket tours in the past which concerned Hugh Drummond – stories which he had largely discounted in view of the obvious hero-worship of the teller. But now he began to wonder if they were exaggerated. As a pretty shrewd judge of a rough house he had to admit that Drummond was a past master and could give him points. A glance at the unfortunate Leyton's nose, which was now a rich blue, and the feeling of his own elbow from which every particle of skin had been removed were sufficient confirmation of that fact.

"Don't forget," continued Drummond quietly, "that unless you agree I shall have to give my real reason for being here. The mere fact that I could get no answer to the telephone is not enough. And that means that things will come out at the inquest."

He looked at Standish searchingly.

"Things," he went on, "of which I don't think you are in complete ignorance yourself. Do we want them in the newspapers – yet?"

Voices could already be heard on the stairs: Perkins, wild and incoherent – the other stolid and unemotional.

"Right," said Standish, making up his mind. "We were all playing bridge in my rooms."

"Would to Allah we had been," muttered Leyton ruefully. "Then I shouldn't be wanting a new face."

"This way, officer: here's the room."

Perkins flung open the door, and a policeman entered who, after a glance at the dead man, gave the other four a look of keen scrutiny.

"Good evening, gentlemen," he said. "This looks a bad business. May I ask what you know about it?"

"I'll tell you all we know about it, officer," said Standish.

The policeman listened attentively, making a note from time to time with a stubby pencil.

"Nine-forty, you say, sir, when you were telephoning. And there was no trace of anyone here when you arrived."

"The house was empty," said Standish.

"Then may I ask, sir, how you got in?"

"A very natural question, officer," remarked Standish. "Feeling convinced that something was very much amiss I took the law into my own hands and broke in."

The policeman shook his head gravely.

"That's an offence, sir: you had no right to do so."

"I am fully aware of that fact," said Standish. "And I will take full responsibility for it when the time comes. I may say my name is very well known at Scotland Yard."

"Well, sir – it's your affair, not mine. And while I think of it, I'd just like the names and addresses of all you gentlemen."

They gave them to him, and he wrote them down in his notebook.

"Now, sir," he continued, "do you know of anyone who had a grudge against Mr Sanderson?"

"I can't say that I do," said Standish. "But his job was one in which he would almost certainly have made powerful enemies."

The policeman nodded portentously, and then proceeded to examine the body. But after a short time he straightened up and shook his head.

"Well, sir, this is too big a job for me to handle: I must get the Inspector. Will you gentlemen be good enough to remain here while I go to the station. I shan't be long."

"All right, officer: we'll wait."

The policeman picked up his helmet, and a few seconds later the front door slammed behind him.

"You can wait downstairs, Perkins," said Standish. "Don't go to bed, of course, and you'd better tell your wife what has happened."

The butler left the room, and suddenly Standish began to laugh.

"Sorry, Bill: can't help it. Your face is one of the funniest sights I've seen for a long while."

"Glad you think so," grunted Leyton.

"I apologise, laddie," said Drummond. "I apologise profusely. But it's a dangerous hobby – hiding behind curtains. Look here, why don't you toddle off and get a raw steak on it: if you beat up a butcher he'll give you his whole shop as soon as he sees you."

"Not a bad idea," agreed Standish. "In fact, it's a good one, Bill. Luckily that policeman asked no questions, but the Inspector is bound to want to know what you've been doing. So you push off: I'll say you weren't feeling up to the scratch."

"And, Peter, you go with him," said Drummond. "I've got a hunch, Standish – may be right, may be wrong. But we're in a two-man show."

"What do you mean?" asked Standish, looking a little mystified.

"A show when it will be better for all concerned to move in couples," answered the other quietly. "There's every reason for Peter going with him if he's under the weather, and it would be a ghastly thing if he was knocked out properly before the fun begins."

"But you don't think…" began Standish.

"I do," said Drummond shortly. "The game has begun, I tell you, and Rule A is – Take no unnecessary chances. So get a move on, you two, or you'll be butting into the Inspector. And vet the taxi, Peter, if there's one loitering about near the house."

"You seem to have had a certain amount of experience in this sort of thing," said Standish when the other two had disappeared down the road.

Drummond gave a short laugh.

"Just a little," he confessed. "There have been times in the past when Fate has been very kind to me. And I'm thinking that she is still smiling. Tell me, Standish, did poor old Sanderson say anything important over the 'phone? Give you any names or information?"

Standish shook his head.

"Not a word. What about you at lunch today?"

"Nothing at all. He told me that he had been aware for some time of a big organisation in England which was definitely hostile to the country. Some of the smaller fry had been laid by the heels, but that until a few days ago he had had no idea who the big men were. He also said that things were getting very ticklish and that there might be something doing in my line."

"Which, I gather," said Standish with a smile, "is hitting first and talking after."

"Something of that sort," agreed Drummond vaguely. "I can push a feller's face in rather quicker than most."

"It's much the same as what he said to me," said Standish, growing serious again. "And I'm afraid I was rather inclined to laugh at the old chap. By Jove! there's not much to laugh at over this development."

"That's a fact," agreed Drummond. "Who the devil was here, I wonder. Can it have been a woman alone?"

"A woman do that?" Standish pointed to the dead man.

"Why not? I've known at any rate one in the past who'd do it and ask for more."

"It's the actual wound that staggers me, Drummond, as I was saying to Bill Leyton earlier. It was either the most astounding fluke that the aim was so accurate, or else his head must have been held from behind."

"Then," objected Drummond, "he would surely have bellowed down the 'phone. Anyway, one thing is clear: this organisation he was talking about is a reality and he had found out too much for their peace of mind."

"It looks like it, I agree."

Standish glanced at his watch.

"It strikes me that that inspector is a damned long time coming," he remarked. "The station is only about a quarter of a mile away."

"Do you know him by any chance?"

"Yes. A man called McIver: he's quite capable."

"Not old McIver?" cried Drummond. "Why, he and I are the greatest pals. We once chased an elusive gentleman called Peterson together, though I must admit that I did most of the chasing, and he didn't altogether approve of my methods. By the way, have you been through the drawers in the desk?"

"I haven't," said Standish. "Your somewhat unexpected arrival interrupted matters."

"We might fill in the time till the police come having a look, don't you think? There are his keys on that steel chain."

He gently removed the bunch from the dead man's trouser pocket, and unfastened it from the chain. The centre drawer they could not get at, as it would have entailed moving the body, but they went through all the side ones systematically. But save for one small scrap of paper they found nothing of interest. It had evidently been torn out of a cheap note-book, and on it was scrawled in an illiterate handwriting – "The day of the week backwards. If two, omit first."

The two men stared at it mystified.

"That's certainly not his writing," said Standish. "What the deuce does it mean?"

"Must be something important," remarked Drummond, "or he wouldn't have kept it. But it's got me beat."

"Same here," admitted Standish, and once again he looked at his watch. "Do you realise," he said, "that it's forty minutes since that policeman left? Even if McIver was out someone else ought to have come by now."

They looked at one another thoughtfully.

"Can't have done the policeman in, can they?" said Drummond. "No object that I can see."

"Well, I'm not going to stop here any more," cried Standish. "I'm going to the station myself. Will you come too?"

"Yes," said Drummond. "I will. I've still got that hunch about a two-man show, and I can't do any good here."

They relocked the drawers, leaving everything, including the mysterious scrap of paper, exactly as they had found it. Then with a hail to Perkins to tell him what they were doing, they left the house.

It was still blowing hard, and the road was deserted. Most of the houses they passed were in darkness: that district of London contains an early-to-bed population. And they had walked some little way in silence, when suddenly Drummond caught Standish's arm and the two men halted. On the other side of the street were four or five new buildings in various stages of construction, and it was at one of these that Drummond was staring.

"I thought I saw something move," he muttered. "Hullo! what's that?"

Quite clearly above the howling of the wind had come a peculiar noise which sounded as if a pile of bricks had fallen down. And it came from the half-built house opposite.

"The gale blown something over," said Standish, but Drummond was already crossing the road. And with a shrug of his shoulders Standish followed him.

The usual litter of planks and heaps of cement that accompany building operations made walking difficult, and suddenly Drummond swore under his breath. He had stumbled over something – something that he at first thought was a sack, but which immediately afterwards he realised was nothing of the sort.

"Standish," he called out. "Come here."

The other joined him, and Drummond flashed on his torch.

"Well, I'm blowed," he muttered. "Is the joker drunk?"

Lying on the ground breathing stertorously was a man. He had evidently just slipped down from a sitting position, for a number of displaced bricks were behind him. But the thing that made them both stare at him in amazement was his costume: he was clad only in underclothes and a shirt.

Suddenly Standish bent over him and sniffed.

"Drunk be blowed," he cried. "The man's been chloroformed. His breath reeks of it."

And then he in his turn caught Drummond's arm.

"Look at his boots, man, look at his boots. If those aren't police regulation boots I'll eat my hat. Great Scott!" he almost shouted. "I've got it. We've been fooled, my boy. The police station – and run like the devil."

And three minutes later an astonished sergeant woke up from a slight doze as two somewhat breathless men came dashing in.

"Has PC 005 made a report, Sergeant?" cried Standish.

The Sergeant gaped at him stupidly.

"No, sir. He's not been in here since he started out on his beat. A report about what, if I may ask, sir?"

"Murder," said Standish shortly. "Mr Sanderson's been murdered."

"What's that? Mr Sanderson murdered?" came an incredulous voice.

Inspector McIver had entered from another room.

"Hullo! Mr Standish. And you, Captain Drummond. What's this you say, gentlemen?"

"Come straight along with us, McIver," said Standish. "There is not a moment to be lost. He's been killed in his own house, but I want to stop at one of the partially built ones half-way there. Stabbed in the eye, McIver," he explained as they started. "It's one of the most amazing crimes of modern times, as you'll see for yourself in a few minutes. But first of all I want you to have a look at this. Now then," he said as he led the way over the rubble, and Drummond flashed his torch on the unconscious man, "who is that?"

"PC 005," grunted McIver. "What the devil is the meaning of this?"

"He's been chloroformed," said Standish quietly, "with the sole object of stealing his uniform. And the man who stole it calmly interviewed us in his role as a policeman in the room where Mr Sanderson was murdered."

"Quick," said Drummond, "darned quick. This is beginning to look like the goods."

"Why should he want to interview you?" demanded McIver.

"Lots of reasons. Perhaps he didn't know how many of us were there: I don't know what the butler told him. But he wanted to get back into that room unsuspected. And he did so. Then he found four of us..."

"Four," echoed the Inspector.

"Yes," said Standish. "You know Mr Leyton, don't you, McIver? A great friend of mine. Tall, thin man."

"And you certainly know Peter Darrell," remarked Drummond.

"Yes: I know most of your friends, Captain Drummond," said McIver grimly. "Are they at the house now?"

"No," remarked Standish gravely. "Bill Leyton felt – er – a bit ill, and he and Mr Darrell left about an hour ago."

"An hour," cried McIver. "Do you mean to say..."

And the words died away on his lips as he suddenly felt Drummond's vice-like grip on his arm.

"Not a word," whispered Drummond. "Look there."

They had reached the gate of Sanderson's house, and Drummond was pointing at the lighted window.

"Get back under cover," he muttered. "That's the room where the body is, McIver, and there are men in it. I saw their shadows moving."

CHAPTER 2

They crouched down in the shadow of some bushes, staring at the house.

"Three of 'em," said Drummond in a low voice. "The Lord has delivered them into our hands."

"Couldn't be the butler and your two friends, I suppose?" whispered McIver.

Standish shook his head.

"Most improbable," he answered. "And if they are, there's no harm done. The point is, how we're going to get into the house. The front door is bolted with a Yale lock, and if we ring the bell the element of surprise has gone. I've tackled the back door once tonight: what about trying it again?"

McIver grinned faintly, but made no comment, and the three men keeping close to the wall tiptoed round the side of the house. As before, it was in darkness and Standish frowned uneasily.

"Where are Perkins and his wife?" he whispered. "I don't like it."

For the second time he produced his peculiar-looking implement and inserted it in the keyhole, and once again McIver grinned faintly as the lock shot back.

"Quite a professional, Mr Standish," he remarked. "I didn't know that that was one of your accomplishments."

They crept along the passage only to stop suddenly as they came opposite the kitchen door. For the fire had been made up, and by its light they could see the motionless figure of a woman sitting in a chair. She was lashed to it with rope, and a cloth had been tied tightly round her mouth. But her eyes were open, and as she saw them an ominous glitter shone in them. Clearly Mrs Perkins was not in the best of tempers.

"We'll set you free in a moment, Mrs Perkins," whispered Standish. "But the first thing to do is to catch the swine. My God! what's happened?"

For there had suddenly come from upstairs a hissing, crackling noise, and shadows began to dance fantastically on the stairs. Then a great cloud of smoke eddied towards them, followed by a strong smell of burning.

"They've fired the house," shouted Drummond, dashing up into the hall. The other two were just behind him, and the next moment they were all sprawling in a heap on the floor. They had tripped over something, and the something was the unconscious body of the butler. And as they scrambled to their feet there came a mocking laugh and the front door slammed.

"Get Perkins and his wife out of it," cried Drummond. "I'm after 'em."

But when he reached the road all that he saw was the red tail-lamp of a car disappearing in the distance: the men had got clean away. Behind him the upper part of the house was like an inferno: flames were roaring out of the window of the room where Sanderson's body lay, and were rapidly spreading all along the story. Then McIver appeared dragging Perkins, and a few moments later Standish came round the corner of the house supporting his wife.

"Petrol," said the Inspector shortly. "The place reeks of it. If only we'd waited here a minute or two longer we'd have caught 'em."

"True, laddie," murmured Drummond. "But these two wretched souls would probably have been burned to death."

Windows had been flung up in the neighbouring houses, and McIver, going out into the road, hailed a man opposite and asked him to ring up the fire brigade. He had to shout, so great was the noise of the flames which, fanned by the wind, were now sending out showers of sparks into the night. And then at last from the distance came the clang of a bell and the fire engine arrived.

"I wonder what was the inducement that made them run such a risk?" said Standish thoughtfully. "We almost got 'em."

He was standing in the road with Drummond watching the firemen at work.

"Papers possibly," answered the other. "Don't forget the keys were in my pocket, and that was a very substantial desk. They may have decided it would take too long to force the drawers – they knew we must come back shortly – and so they fired the place."

"Doesn't quite work, old boy," said Standish. "Since they used petrol they must have gone there *with the intention* of firing the house."

"That's true," admitted Drummond. "I wonder if Mrs Perkins can throw any light on the matter?"

But that worthy woman was not much help. She and her husband had heard their hail as they left the house, and then very shortly afterwards had again heard voices upstairs. Thinking they had returned, Perkins had gone up to the hall, and the next thing she had heard was the sound of a fall. She had called out, and receiving no answer had been on the point of going to see what had happened when two men rushed into the kitchen and seized her.

"Would you recognise either of them?" cried Standish.

Once again they drew blank. The men had been masked, and save for the fact that one was tall and the other short she could give no further description of them.

"So it boils down to this," said Drummond thoughtfully. "The only one of the whole gang that we should know by sight again is the bloke who masqueraded as PC 005."

Nor was Perkins of any assistance: less, indeed, than his wife. He had gone into the hall where he saw the outlines of three men. And he was on the point of switching on the light, when he received a stunning blow on the back of the head, and remembered nothing more.

"All the more fun, old lad," said Drummond earnestly to Standish. "I don't like these little performances when they are too easy. And unless I'm much mistaken the next move will come from them."

"What makes you think that?" said Standish doubtfully.

"Because they can't be sure how much we know," answered the other.

The fire, by this time, was more or less under control. Some of the bottom story was still intact, but the whole of the upper part of the house was completely gutted. Naturally the end which had suffered most was the one in which Sanderson's room had been, and where the petrol had been poured. And even as they watched, the floor of his study gave way, and what was left of the desk and the rest of the furniture fell with a crash into the room below.

"Two hours at least, gentlemen, before anyone can get in," said McIver, joining them. "Are you going to wait?"

"I don't think there's much use," answered Standish. "Presumably we shall be wanted at the inquest, and you know where to find us. And if you come round and see me tomorrow I can give you full details, though I warn you they aren't very full."

"You said he'd been stabbed through the eye," said the Inspector.

"That's right. And it was done in the middle of a telephone conversation with me."

"Most extraordinary," said McIver. "Well, the post-mortem may reveal something if there's anything left after that blaze to hold a post-mortem on. Good night, gentlemen."

He turned away with a nod, and the two men pushed their way through the fringe of spectators that a fire alarm draws together no matter what the time or locality. And it was not until they had walked some way in silence that Drummond glanced sideways at his companion.

"Are you going to give him *full* details?" he said quietly.

"Confound you, Drummond," laughed Standish. "I know what you're driving at. But you've got to bear in mind that I'm almost in a semi-official position."

"But not quite. That's just the point. And don't forget one thing: even the police have been known to suppress evidence at an inquest when they think it undesirable for it to be made public. Laddie," he continued earnestly, "it would be nothing short of a crime to run the slightest chance of spoiling this show. I may say that as a fairly good judge I have seldom known one start more auspiciously."

"There are points about it, I agree, which promise well," conceded the other.

"Certain things, naturally, you will have to tell: the telephone conversation, the wound – all that does no harm. But as for his suspicions which he passed on to us concerning the existence of this organisation, what is the use of mentioning anything about it? You know nothing more than that he had suspicions..."

"Which have now been amply justified," interrupted Standish.

"Exactly. Which is all the more reason why we shouldn't let the other side know that we know they're justified. Lull 'em, old lad, into a false sense of security. Then when we finally get on to 'em, we'll shake 'em to the marrow."

He waved a vast hand at a passing taxi.

"Let's go to your place," he remarked, "and have a spot while we talk it over."

Standish sat back in his corner and lit a cigarette. There was undoubtedly something in what Drummond said. The case would inevitably cause a tremendous sensation in the papers: the details were so bizarre and extraordinary. But it was possible that if they kept their mouths shut over certain points public interest would die down after a few days, and as Drummond had said, the other side would be lulled into a sense of false security.

That the other side was not to be sneezed at was evident. Their actions that night proved that they were bold to a degree: also that there were several of them. But, however bold they were, he once again began to ask himself why they had run such a foolhardy risk in coming back to fire the house. It could not have been a question of papers, for another reason besides the one he had given Drummond. Whoever it was who had done the murder would have had ample time to go through all the drawers and get away at leisure. What, then, could have caused them to take such a well-nigh incredible chance? Was there some clue left behind in the room that he had overlooked, and which it was imperative for them to destroy: a clue which possibly the man masquerading as the policeman had spotted? One thing at any rate was certain. Whatever had been their reason for doing it, they had succeeded only too well. No vestige or shadow of evidence remained for investigation.

"Our last remaining hope, as far as I can see at the moment," he remarked as the taxi stopped, "is that PC 005 will be able to throw some light on the matter. Though," he added grimly, "I don't think it's likely. There is an atmosphere of thoroughness about these gentlemen that appeals to me."

"My dear fellow, they're the goods," cried Drummond. "And I sincerely hope you've seen the force of my arguments. Hullo! what's stung you?"

For Standish had paused in the doorway of his sitting-room and was staring at his desk.

"Somebody has been at my papers," he said quietly.

Drummond raised his eyebrows.

"Are you quite sure?"

"Absolutely certain. They are none of them in the same position as I left them."

"Your man, perhaps."

"He knows it's as much as his life is worth," grunted Standish. "And confound 'em, whoever they are, they've forced all the drawers."

Drummond let out a bellow of laughter.

"Gorgeous," he cried. "We very considerately gave them all our addresses and they've wasted no time."

"You'll probably find they've done the same to you," said the other.

"They're welcome to anything they can find in my rooms," grinned Drummond, "provided they don't take my book of stories. But they aren't going to worry about me – at any rate not at present. It was you he was ringing up when they got him, and it's you they're after at the moment."

Standish nodded thoughtfully.

"You're probably right there," he agreed. "Anyway, I see no vast reason against a drink."

He walked over to the cupboard and produced two glasses.

"You haven't perchance got a spot of ale, old lad?" said Drummond. "I'd sooner have it than whisky if it can be managed."

"Sure thing," cried Standish. "There are a dozen Lager in the corner. Help yourself."

He mixed himself a stiff whisky and soda, whilst Drummond opened a bottle of beer.

"Poor old Sanderson!" Standish sat down with his drink. "I can't get over it. By Jove! he'll be a loss to the country."

"A loss for which payment is going to be extracted in full," said Drummond grimly. "We'll get 'em, Standish: you can stake your bottom dollar on that."

He took a long drink of beer, and the next moment choked violently as a hand clutched his arm so suddenly that the contents of his glass were spilled all over the carpet. He swung round: Standish was swaying beside him. His eyes were half closed, and he seemed to be trying to say something. Then with a grunt he pitched forward on the hearth-rug.

For a while Drummond stared at the recumbent figure dazedly: what on earth had happened to the fellow? He was breathing stertorously: his cheeks were flushed, and at first it seemed to Drummond that he must have had some kind of fit. And then as he bent over him he distinctly smelt something strange about his breath – something that was certainly not entirely due to whisky.

He straightened up, and stood looking thoughtfully across the room. Drugged, and the drug was evidently no weak one. And if he hadn't been drinking beer they'd both be lying unconscious on the floor.

The first shock over, his brain began to work at speed. As always in an emergency his head became ice cool, and though at the moment there was nothing to be done it was his course of action in the next half-hour or so that had to be decided and decided upon quickly.

He went to the door and opened it cautiously: there was no sound of movement in the house. Clearly, therefore, Standish's fall had not aroused anyone. Then he returned to the fireplace and once more bent over the unconscious figure. The breathing was easier; the colour in the cheeks more natural: he had been caught with the most ordinary of age-old tricks. But why? What was the good of drugging Standish, merely for the pleasure of drugging him? To shut his mouth at the inquest? Absurd. Standish was the principal witness, and if he was unfit to give evidence the proceedings would be adjourned till he was fit. There must be some other more cogent reason than that, and as far as he could see there was only one that held water. The other side was going to have a shot at kidnapping Standish altogether. They had gambled on the fact that he would have a drink before going to bed, and they proposed at their leisure to remove him that night.

A grim smile flickered round Drummond's lips: it was a situation after his own heart. One obvious line of action stood out: to call the nearest policeman and await further developments. But as a stealthy glance through the window showed him the figure of a man lurking on the other side of the street a difficulty at once arose if he took that line. There would be no further developments. And since the policeman would inevitably assume that Standish was drunk and not drugged, it might prove a little hard to keep him there the entire night. He would insist on putting Standish to bed, and then departing about his lawful occasions. Besides, his every instinct rebelled against such a defensive policy. Here was a chance to get information, and not to miss it. The point to be decided was the best way to set about it.

The man outside knew that he was there. He must have been seen going in with Standish, and since there is no back exit from the houses in Clarges Street he could not have left. So would it be feasible to leave ostentatiously by the front door: call up some message from the pavement to Standish, and then return later? If the light continued for a couple of hours in the sitting-room they would assume that the drug had worked, especially if he made some allusion from outside to Standish having a night-cap.

But here another difficulty arose. The street outside was almost deserted, and it would remain so for the rest of the night. It would be next door to impossible for him to return to the house once he had left it without being seen. Further, there was no hiding-place where he could remain concealed and hope to find out anything worth knowing. So that scheme would not hold water.

What about going to ground somewhere in Standish's rooms: the bathroom or his bedroom? Again he dismissed the idea. The others, if they came at all, would be bound to search the place, when he would certainly be discovered. And though it might lead to a pleasing rough house, that was not what he wanted. It was information he was after: to see without being seen.

Suddenly the only possibility struck him. It was a risk, but taking risks was the main creed of his life. What made him hesitate temporarily was a doubt if he could pull it off, and if it was not successful he might get better results by one of the methods he had already discarded. Could he bluff them into thinking that he too was drugged? Remain in the room the whole time and see what took place: see who came; get a line on what they were up against. Could he act sufficiently well to deceive them? That was the crux of the matter.

Standish was now snoring peacefully, and he realised the decision must be made soon. And for a moment or two Drummond was even tempted to get a taxi and take him back to his own rooms. Then he dismissed the idea as unworthy of consideration: it was worse, if possible, than calling in the law. He would chance it.

Creeping on hands and knees lest his shadow should be seen from outside, he took his beer glass to the bathroom to wash it. Then still on all fours, he returned and half-filled it with whisky and soda. He took the chair facing the door and placed the glass on the coal scuttle beside him. Then he suddenly noticed the empty beer bottle, and once more he crawled across the carpet to hide it amongst its full brethren. There was nothing more to be done now except to sit and wait.

The sound of the traffic from Piccadilly was growing less and less, and he glanced at the clock on the mantelpiece. Nearly two: how much longer would it be? He dared not smoke for fear it might be noticed, and as the minutes dragged on he began to wonder if he was not making a fool of himself. Were they coming at all? Had he misjudged the whole situation completely?

Three o'clock, and his head began to nod. He pulled himself together: to be found asleep would wreck everything. The fire had died down, but to make it up would be fatal, though the room was getting cold. Everything must appear to be normally consistent with them both having been unconscious for a couple of hours at least.

And then suddenly there came a sound which made him wide awake in an instant. A car had drawn up just outside. He could hear the faint purring of the engine; the opening of a door; finally the noise of a key being inserted in the lock below. There was a muttered conversation on the pavement, and then the front door was quietly opened.

Now Hugh Drummond was about as free from the needle as any living man, but he felt his pulses quickening a little. Had he been able to meet these people – and every instinct told him they were coming to the room he was in – had he been able to meet them in the ordinary way as himself he would not have turned a hair. Two or four – numbers never mattered to him in the slightest. But to have to sit there pretending to be unconscious, unable to do anything whatever happened, was a very unfamiliar role.

He let his head sprawl back on the chair in such a position that he could see with the minimum opening of his eyelids. Then listening intently he waited. The door was just ajar: the landing outside was in darkness. And through his almost closed eyes he watched the black opening.

A belated taxi travelling at speed passed in the distance, and then, as the noise died away, there came the sharp crack of a board from just outside. And the next instant he saw a man's face peering into the room. It was their friend of earlier on, who had impersonated PC 005, and who was now dressed in his ordinary clothes.

The door was pushed open, and he came into the room.

"All right," he whispered. "They're both here."

Two other men entered, and Drummond studied them cautiously. His breathing was heavy and regular: his limbs were relaxed; and after one searching glance through almost closed lids to ensure that he would recognise them again he shut his eyes completely. Were these the three, he wondered, who had fired Sanderson's house?

Of the two new ones, the first who came in was small and looked like a ferret. He had a sharp nose and prominent teeth: his hair was sandy and his ears stuck out. Moreover, in sharp contrast to the other two his clothes were shoddy. In fact, he looked rather like a cheap bookmaker's tout.

The third man on the other hand was the exact contrary. A top hat was slightly tilted on the back of his head; his evening overcoat, complete with red carnation, was open, revealing a white waistcoat and boiled shirt. His features were aquiline: his eyes a strikingly vivid blue. But what might have been a very good-looking face was spoiled by thin lips and a sneering expression. His character was plain for all to read: cold and merciless to the last degree.

He approached Standish and turned him over with his foot, whilst the other two watched him: there was no doubt as to who was the leader. Then he crossed to Drummond, and lifting up one hand pinched it hard. But Drummond, who had anticipated something of the sort, gave no sign, and with a grunt the man turned away.

"They're both under," he said curtly. "Which is which?"

"The one on the hearth-rug is Standish," answered the bogus policeman, while the man like a ferret went to the window and peered out.

"Who is the big guy in the chair?"

"His name is Drummond: I can't tell you more than that."

"You said there were four of them in Sanderson's house."

"So there were, sir. I suppose the other two have gone back to their rooms."

There came the scrape of a match, and the man in evening clothes lit a cigarette.

"You've been through all his papers?" he demanded.

"Every one, and found nothing," answered the other.

"I didn't think you would. What he knows is in his head – if he knows anything at all. You say Sanderson was actually telephoning to him at the time."

"So Number Four told me."

"And that over the telephone at any rate no information was given?"

"That's so, sir."

The leader, having crossed to the desk, was going methodically through the papers on it, and once again Drummond cautiously opened one eye. Ferret-face was still by the window, the other two had their backs to him, and for a moment or two he was tempted to take them by surprise. There would not be much difficulty in laying the pair of them out, summon the police and have the whole lot arrested. But he hesitated. As yet he had heard nothing of importance. Apparently some mysterious individual known as Number Four had murdered Sanderson, but obviously he was not one of these three. And there was still a possibility that some remark might be made which would give some valuable information.

Evidently the man in evening clothes was one of the louder noises in the gang: possibly even the loudest. Apart from the "sir," his whole demeanour placed him in a different class to the other two.

"When did you get your orders?" he demanded suddenly.

"Number Four gave them to me after he'd done the job," answered the other.

"Did they include laying out that policeman?"

"No. But it was necessary to get into the house somehow."

"You're a fool, Gulliver," said the man in evening clothes softly. "The last thing you want to do in this country is to monkey with the police."

"How else was I to get in?" muttered Gulliver sullenly. "And my orders were to get all names and addresses, and find out anything I could."

For a while the other made no reply, but continued methodically going through the papers on the desk.

"Did you find out anything?" he demanded after a while.

Gulliver shook his head.

"Not a thing. But a man like Standish wouldn't be likely to say much to an ordinary policeman in any case."

"Where is Number Four now?"

"I can't tell you, sir: I don't know. He handed me my orders, and then got straight into the car and drove off. A lady was with him."

"What's that? A lady. What sort of a lady?"

The man in evening clothes had swung round, and his voice had risen.

"Couldn't see very well: she was all muffled up. Young, I should think; anyway, she had a very good figure. Golden hair, too: I saw that."

"Good God! it's impossible."

The other had risen and was pacing excitedly up and down the room.

"She promised me," he muttered. "Damn it! she promised me. Look here, Gulliver, was she with Number Four when he did it?"

"I can't say, sir," answered Gulliver. "They were together when they came to the car, but whether she was with him when it happened I don't know. Do you know who she was by any chance?"

"Mind your own infernal business," snarled the other. "What the devil has that got to do with you?"

He continued to pace the room, and when he next spoke his voice was calmer.

"It was completely successful, was it? Sanderson was killed instantaneously?"

"Clean through the eye, sir, just as if he'd been pole-axed."

"Good. I hadn't much faith in it myself, but evidently I was wrong."

The last remark was made almost to himself, and Drummond, half opening one eye, saw that the man called Gulliver was looking curious.

"What is it, sir?" he said. "Is it something new?"

"It strikes me, Gulliver," answered the man in evening clothes, "that you're going to get into pretty considerable trouble shortly. May I ask you to repeat Rule Number Three."

"No member shall ask the business or question the orders of any other member," quoted Gulliver sullenly.

"Don't forget it, my friend," said the other softly. "You get your reward in strict proportion as to how you do your work. How another member does his is nothing whatever to do with you. Curiosity is only one degree less dangerous than treachery. And lest you should doubt it, Gulliver, you will find if you search the papers tomorrow that there will be an account of a second murder in them. Not as important as Sanderson's: in fact, it will probably be tucked away in a back page somewhere. You remember Jean Picot, Gulliver?"

"Yes," said Gulliver, moistening his lips.

"Tomorrow you will read an account of his death in an East End brawl. Most regrettable, and I am sure that no one will trace any connection between it and the flamboyant headlines announcing Mr Sanderson's. Which is where everyone will be wrong, Gulliver. Jean Picot was ill-advised enough to try to run with the hare at the same time as he hunted with the hounds. So incredibly foolish," he continued even more softly, "as to give information to Mr Sanderson. Well! he will give no more, and Mr Sanderson will receive no more."

"You know I'd never split," muttered Gulliver.

"I don't think you will," said the other contemptuously. "You haven't the brains – or the guts. However – enough of this. Is the street clear, Jackson?"

"A peeler has just gone by, sir," answered the ferret-faced man at the window. "He's turned the corner into Curzon Street."

"All right. I'll just finish going through these papers, and then we'll get him into the car."

"What are you going to do with the big bloke, sir?" asked Gulliver.

"Leave him here," said the other indifferently. "He's not the sort of thing one wants as a pet."

Silence fell on the room save for the rustling of the papers on Standish's desk, and Drummond began to do some rapid thinking. He had got a certain amount of information, though nothing of much value. The existence of a criminal organisation had been confirmed, if confirmation was necessary, and he knew the names of two of the members. Moreover, the features of the man in evening clothes were stamped indelibly on his memory, even though he was still in ignorance of his name. But the point that now arose was what he was going to do himself in the next few minutes.

The advantages of remaining apparently unconscious were obvious: he possessed knowledge which the other side did not know he possessed. But dare he allow them to remove Standish? Murder seemed to mean nothing in their young lives, and he could not run the risk of allowing them to kill him. On the other hand, if they intended to do him in why had they not done so at once?

Had he been in Standish's place he would have liked to chance it, in the hopes of finding out something really important. But in view of their very brief acquaintance he felt he was hardly justified in assuming that Standish would feel the same way. And yet it went against the grain to sacrifice the advantage he had got.

Once more he half opened one eye, and the next moment he almost gave himself away. For Standish was staring at him, and had quite deliberately winked. He was still sprawling on the hearth-rug breathing loudly, but since his face was turned towards the fireplace neither of the men at the desk could see him.

Now what was the line of action? The effects of the drug had evidently worn off, and Standish had been playing the same game – lying doggo and listening. But it completely altered matters, for now there were two of them and they were both armed. It would be the simplest thing in the world to capture the lot.

Again he glanced at Standish, and this time he saw his lips move. And even to one who had no knowledge of lip language the message was clear.

"Do nothing."

He closed his eyes: Standish had sized up the situation in the same way as he would have done. He deliberately intended to allow himself to be abducted on the chance of getting to the heart of things. So now they could both work from different ends.

"Nothing here at all."

The man in evening clothes pushed back his chair and rose.

"What's the time? Four o'clock. Get him below, and don't make a sound. Then cart him across the pavement between you as if he was drunk. Just wait till I see it's all clear."

He went to the door and peered out.

"All right," he whispered. "Get on with it."

The two others picked Standish up, and Drummond could hear the soft creaking of their footsteps as they carried him down the stairs. Then the front door opened and he heard them cross the pavement: the engine was started, and a few seconds later the noise of the car died away in the distance.

He sat very still, conscious that the man in evening clothes had not gone himself. He was standing on the hearth-rug close by, and after a while it required all the will power he possessed not to open his eyes. It was nerve-racking to a degree to feel the other man so near to him and not know what he was doing.

Suddenly he realised that the man was bending over him: he could feel his breath on his face. Was it possible he suspected? For if he did Drummond was at a terrible disadvantage. At any moment Sanderson's fate might be his.

He stirred a little and muttered foolishly: movement of some sort was imperative. And still the other man bent over him in silence, while the perspiration began to gather on Drummond's brow with the strain.

He rolled over with his head hanging across the side of the chair so that his forehead should not be seen, but he knew that he could not stand it much longer. What was the fellow doing? What was he waiting for?

And then he felt the man's hand on his arm, and only by the most monstrous effort of will did he avoid clenching his fist. The man was feeling his muscles, much as a butcher might feel a piece of meat. And all of a sudden he began to chuckle softly to himself.

The sweat was almost dripping on the floor, and yet Drummond made no movement. Never in his life had he heard such a diabolical sound. There was madness in it: a sort of gloating anticipation. But of what?

The man's fingers, like thin bars of steel, were travelling up and down his biceps and still that evil chuckling continued. And Drummond felt he would willingly have given a thousand pounds to be able to jump up and catch him one straight between the eyes. But it would not do: he *must* stick it. And then, at last, to his unspeakable relief the man moved away from him.

But he still remained in the room: Drummond could hear him moving quietly about. Once or twice he knew the man was behind him, but in the position he had rolled into it was impossible to see anything even if he opened his eyes. Five minutes, or was it five years, went by, and at length the ordeal was over. He heard the man go down the stairs; the front door shut and his footsteps on the pavement died gradually away.

With a sigh of relief he sat up in the chair, and stared round the room. The fire was out: he felt cramped and stiff. But the fearful tension of the last quarter of an hour was over, and the reaction was incredible. Never in his life had he been through a period of such unbelievable strain. And even now he was not quite certain whether he had bluffed him or not. He felt that the betting was that he had, but what had that devilish laughter meant? Had it been the idea in his mind? Why, if he believed Drummond was unconscious, should it afford him pleasure to find out what sort of condition he was in?

He went over to the window, and keeping behind the curtain looked out. The man who earlier on had been on the other side of the road was no longer there: the street was deserted. He could go whenever he liked, and a desire for something stronger than beer was beginning to make itself felt.

At the same time it would not do to run any risk. It was possible that his own rooms were being watched, and if so a comparison of times would show that he had left Clarges Street very shortly after the man in evening clothes, a fact which would tend to confirm any doubts that gentleman might have with regard to his having been genuinely drugged. And so after due reflection he decided to wait at least another hour before leaving. Beer it would have to be, and worse fates have befallen man.

He poured himself out a glass and sat down at Standish's desk. There were one or two points that had to be decided in his mind, and the first was what he was going to say at the inquest concerning Standish's disappearance. One thing was obvious: he must stick consistently to the line he had started on. He had been unconscious the whole night, and knew nothing. Why had he been unconscious? He had been drugged through drinking Standish's whisky.

And at that stage in his reflections he happened to glance at the sideboard and his eyes narrowed. The tantalus was empty. He looked at the coal scuttle where he had placed his own half-empty glass: it had disappeared. So they had removed all traces of the drug whilst he had been in the chair with his eyes shut. Probably the man in evening clothes had done it after the others had gone: it would have been a simple thing to do without his hearing. Any proof, therefore, of having been drugged was gone as far as the authorities were concerned.

But did that matter? It was the opponents who were the principal factor to be considered. They *knew* that a drug had been placed in the whisky: they would at once suspect if he did not mention it, even if it were incapable of proof. The essential thing as far as they were concerned was that everything should be consistent with the fact that he had been genuinely doped, and knew it.

A further point also arose: even when talking privately to McIver the fiction would have to be kept up. The Inspector was a good fellow, but however tolerant he might be unofficially there was no getting away from it, their action that night was most reprehensible. They had had an easy chance of collaring three of the gang, one of whom at any rate had been guilty of a grave assault on a policeman. And they had not taken their opportunity, but had deliberately let it go. It was a bird in the hand with McIver, especially when, as in this case, the two in the bush were somewhat problematical.

However, rightly or wrongly they had done it, and having started on the line there was nothing for it but to carry on. On Standish's behalf he felt fairly confident: he struck him as being quite capable of looking after himself. It was a pity he had not been able to get the number of the car, but it could not be helped. It meant that Standish would have to play an absolutely lone hand unless he could trace him by some other means. And as he recalled the conversation he had listened to that night he had to admit that so far he had no vestige of a clue as to where they had taken Standish.

One thing, of course, had come out: the man in evening clothes was not the head. There was a bigger man behind him – the man who had given the orders for Sanderson's death. And for the death of – what name had they said? – Jean Picot. A Frenchman presumably, and a low-class one if he had been killed in an East End brawl. And yet he had been in a position to give information to a man like Sanderson.

One thing it certainly tended to show: the gang was a large one with wide ramifications. People from all sections of society seemed to belong to it. The three who had been in the room that night were fairly typical of the upper, middle, and lower classes. What was it Sanderson had said to him: something which bore that out?

"I've been finding clues in all sorts of unsuspected spots: in the Ritz and in a doss-house down in the docks. And they're connected, but I can't get the connection at the moment."

And now, poor devil, he would never get it. Or perhaps he had got it, and that was why they had done him in. There was some more of their conversation, too, that he recalled.

"The robbery of the Exminster pearls four months ago, and the pulling of Light Parade at Newmarket – not much resemblance between the two, is there? And yet I am as certain as I can be that the same brain planned both. One was big, the other comparatively small, though as a matter of fact a syndicate made a packet over pulling that horse. And there have been other crimes – just as widely divergent, where one gets a trace here or a trace there that points to one central control. The thing has been outside my scope up to date, but there are indications now that they are beginning to concern themselves with things political."

"You mean Communism?" Drummond had asked.

"Not exactly – though a bit of that may come in as a sideshow," Sanderson had answered. "Communism in this country is never likely to do much harm: we're too level-headed. But it's a pretty open secret that all is not too well with us financially, and that is a state of affairs which, under certain circumstances, can be exploited with great advantage by the individual."

Drummond rose and began to pace up and down the room. If only he had paid more attention at the time, and taken Sanderson's words a bit more seriously, the old boy might be alive now. He had hinted in that last conversation that he knew he was in danger, but then someone else had come butting in and Drummond had drifted off. And now he was dead, and any information he had got had died with him. Something might perhaps be found in his office in Whitehall, but anything like that would be kept to themselves by the police.

Moreover, from what Standish had said to him he knew practically nothing either: they were both starting completely in the dark. And their opponents were evidently men who did not let the grass grow under their feet, or, when they deemed it necessary, stick at anything. It was going, in fact, to be a game of no mistakes, and it was not the first time he had played under those rules.

The faint grey streaks of dawn were beginning to show over the roofs opposite, and he decided that it would be safe to go. So once again he took his beer glass to the bathroom and washed it. And it was as he was returning to the sitting-room that he saw a piece of paper lying on the floor of the passage.

He stooped and picked it up. It had been torn off a larger piece, and at first sight it seemed to be a mere jumble of capital letters. And then as he studied it closer he saw that there were two lines of writing – the top one in ink, neatly written, the bottom one scrawled roughly and almost illegibly in pencil.

BMSMQYLIRPQMLQCMT

GoTo SANDERSONS Ho

"Go to Sanderson's house."

It was not hard to supply the three final letters, and to realise what he held in his hand. Clearly it was part of the orders received by the man who had impersonated the policeman. He must have torn the paper up, put the pieces in his pocket and accidentally dropped one on the floor.

Drummond sat down again at the desk and studied the message carefully. The ink letters had presumably been written by the giver of the order: the pencil ones had been added by the recipient. And he wondered if messages were always sent in cipher.

It was a subject of which he knew next to nothing. He had a vague idea that E was the commonest letter in the English language and that A, T, I, and O came next. And assuming that "house" was correct he had the cipher equivalent of four of the five vowels. A was Y, E was R, O was M, and U was T. Only I was lacking. In addition to that he held the clue to seven of the commonest consonants.

He lit a cigarette thoughtfully: this was a valuable find. Unskilled though he was in anything to do with decoding, even he could see that, with his knowledge of eleven frequently used letters, four of which were vowels, it should prove a comparatively simple matter to read any further message that might fall into his hands.

Presumably an expert would have been able to solve the thing without the pencilled solution below, though he dimly remembered having heard that even the simplest cipher could defeat a man unless there was a good deal of it. Now if E was the letter that was used most frequently the solver would almost certainly have started on the assumption that M stood for it.

Inspired with enthusiasm, it struck him that he might find out still more. Was there some regular sequence in the cipher letters? For instance G was represented by B. Now G was the seventh letter of the alphabet, and B was the second. Was the cipher letter always five in advance of the real one? But a moment's inspection caused him to scratch his head mournfully. By no possible method could S be regarded as five in advance of T, and it was worse still when the little matter of A and Y cropped up.

"Blank, old sport," he murmured sadly, "blank as be damned. Solving these blamed things ain't your *forte.*"

He put the paper carefully in his pocket-book, and took one final look round the room. McIver would almost certainly insist on coming to see it, and he wanted to leave nothing inconsistent with his story. He remembered of old that the Inspector was a hard man to bluff, but he had done it in the past and he felt tolerably confident of doing it again. There was nothing, so far as he could see, to give the show away, so switching off the light he left the room.

He glanced searchingly both ways when he reached the street: no one was in sight. But Drummond was taking no chances, and the whole way to his house in Brook Street he walked as if he was slightly drunk. And when he finally let himself in he fumbled for an appreciable time with his latchkey. To the best of his knowledge only a watering cart was about, but there were one or two small mews where a man could stand concealed and watch.

He closed the door behind him: the game would begin in earnest shortly. But in the meantime he wanted sleep. And his last coherent thought after he fell into bed was to wish Standish luck.

CHAPTER 3

He awoke about ten o'clock to find Peter Darrell sprawling in an easy chair reading a morning paper.

"By Jove! old lad," he remarked as Drummond sat up in bed, "you ought to let yourself out as a foghorn. I've never heard such an infernal row as you were making in my life."

"Dry up," answered Drummond. "Those were my deep-breathing exercises. How's that long, thin, warrior's face?"

"Haven't seen it this morning, but it looked like a Turner sunset when I left him last night. How did you get on?"

Drummond swung his legs out of bed and lit a cigarette.

"Peter, old son," he remarked, "we had the hellova time. Is there anything in that rag about it?"

"Not a word that I can see."

"Nothing about them setting fire to the house?"

"The devil they did! No – there's nothing about it here."

"I suppose the fire was too late for 'em to get it in. Anything about a policeman running around London in his pants? Oh! boy, we had a wonderful time, which finished up with them kidnapping your pal Standish."

Darrell looked at him in amazement.

"Kidnapping Ronald! Why the deuce did you let 'em do that?"

Drummond went to the door and shouted for his man.

"Beer, fool, beer: I have already been awake for hours. Yes, Peter," he repeated, coming back into the room, "they kidnapped him. In fact, old boy, bar that and one or two other small trifles, they put it across us good and hearty last night. Thank you, Denny: turn on the bath, will you?"

"What clothes will you be wearing, sir?" asked his man.

"Something neat and tasty, Denny; something that will carry conviction at Scotland Yard, where presumably I shall have to repair shortly."

His servant left the room and Drummond took a long drink of ale.

"Do you mind explaining?" said Darrell resignedly. "You say – 'bar that'. Kidnapping Ronald doesn't sound to me a screamingly successful point to you."

"That, old lad, is where you are wrong. We did it on purpose – with eyes open. At least I speak metaphorically: in reality they were shut. Their first score, Peter, was the policeman who interviewed us, who wasn't a policeman at all. After you two had gone Standish and I waited and waited and nothing happened. No one came: for the very good reason, as we discovered later, that no one had been told to come. So at last we decided to breeze along to the station ourselves and pull out McIver, and on the way we ran into the soul-shattering sight of an unconscious and semi-naked man in large boots, who turned out to be the real policeman. Point one to them. They'd got our names and addresses and gained an hour of valuable time.

"However, we toddled back with McIver, and as we got to the gate we saw shadows moving in the room where Sanderson's body was. So thinking we'd nab them we beetled round to the back door and got in at just about the same moment that the men upstairs were starting the bonfire. And it was some blaze, believe you me. They had emptied a young reservoir of petrol over the place, having previously knocked out that old bird Perkins and lashed his wife up in the kitchen. They must have been waiting for Standish and me to go, because we weren't away for more than twenty minutes at the outside.

"Well, to cut it short, we just had time to get the two old fruits out before the place was blazing like a furnace."

"And the men got clean away?"

Drummond nodded.

"They had a motor handy which must have been standing up the road a bit without lights, because we none of us saw a car before we went into the house. So that was point two to them: any clue they might possibly have left has been destroyed, for even before Standish and I left, the house was completely gutted.

"Then came their next little effort. I went back with him to his rooms for a spot, and the instant he got in he noticed his desk had been tampered with. However, as he had nothing which could give anything away, that didn't amount to a row of pins, except that it showed rapidity of movement on the part of the opposition. Then came point three. Standish had a whisky and soda, while I lapped up a beaker of ale. And, Peter, my lad, they'd doped the whisky. Our one and only Standish went down like a pole-axed bull and passed clean out of the picture. And it was then that little Willie did a bit of thinking. What was the object of doping him unless they meant to come back?

"At any rate it was worth having a dip at. So I washed out the beer glass: half-filled it with whisky and soda and sat down to wait. I was going to sham being doped if they arrived, and see if I could find out anything. And that is exactly what happened, though I can't say I found out much. Three of 'em came about two hours later: a man in evening clothes who looked capable of murdering his mother for the gold in her false teeth; the bloke who had done the policeman trick on us and whose name is Gulliver; and a little sandy excrescence who looked like a ferret and answered to the name of Jackson."

"Do you think they were the three who had fired the house?" asked Darrell.

"The man in evening clothes, whose name I never heard, was not: that was clear from the conversation. With regard to the other two – I don't know: they may have been in the party. However, to get on with it: there was I playing 'possum in the chair and Standish stretched out genuinely on the hearth-rug. Well, it soon became evident that they intended removing him and leaving me, and I was just wondering if I'd have at 'em or not when I saw that Standish's eyes were open. The effects of the drug had worn off, and he was doing just the same as I was – playing 'possum.

"Well, now there were two of us and we were both armed. Moreover, the man in evening clothes and Gulliver were chatting on this and that by the writing desk, with their backs to us. So it would have been easy money to round 'em up. But your pal wasn't having any, and he got it across to me to do nothing. He'd decided, and I think he was perfectly right, to let 'em take him away.

"Of course I don't know how long he'd been foxing and how much he'd heard. But it was clear to me that though the blighter in glad rags was pretty high up in the list of starters, there were others who were even higher. And presumably it is into their august presence that Standish is to be introduced. I know it's a risk, but since he was on for it himself I think it was worth taking, don't you?"

Darrell grunted.

"I should think you'll be as popular as a skunk in a drawing-room when McIver hears about it," he remarked.

"But, my dear Peter," said Drummond in a pained voice, "McIver isn't going to hear about it. Hasn't your mind yet grasped the elementary fact that I was drugged myself, and know no more what happened than you do? I spent the night unconscious in one of Standish's armchairs."

"Well," said Darrell doubtfully, "it's done now, old boy, and that is all there is to it. But I can't help thinking you'd have scored a bit more if you'd pinched those three birds."

"Don't forget I know them," remarked Drummond, "and they don't know I know 'em. Except, of course, Gulliver – the sham policeman, who we all know by sight. But it's the man in evening clothes, Peter, that we're going to have a bit of fun with. The others called him 'sir,' and he's got some nasty habits. Which reminds me. While I have a tub, cast your eye through that paper and see if there is any mention of a man called Jean Picot, who was killed in a brawl down in the East End."

He wandered into the bathroom and Darrell picked up the paper. And after a few minutes' search he found it under "News in Brief":

> "A man named Jean Picot was stabbed yesterday afternoon in a fight in Mersey Street, a small slum running parallel to Whitechapel. He died before reaching hospital. The name of his assailant and the cause of the affair are unknown."

He read it aloud to Drummond, who listened thoughtfully.

"They're thorough, Peter," he said, "devilish thorough. I can't tell you the name of the assailant or his number, but I can give you the cause of the affair. Jean Picot had been giving information to Sanderson."

"You heard that last night?"

"I did. Also that a gentleman called Number Four murdered Sanderson with some patent weapon that was being tried out for the first time, and of the efficacy of which my friend in evening clothes was doubtful. Further, the hairpin we found belongs to a woman with golden hair and a good figure, who I should think means something in his young life."

He came back into his bedroom towelling himself vigorously.

"They seem to have chatted pretty freely," said Darrell.

"They did. Evening Clothes in particular at one period got distinctly shirty with Gulliver. He implied that a similar fate to Jean Picot's awaited anyone who started talking out of their turn.

So perhaps it's as well that he knows nothing about Gulliver's bloomer. Look in my pocket-book, Peter, and you will there find a scrap of paper which he accidentally dropped in the passage outside Standish's room."

"This piece covered with letters?"

"That's the one. Now Gulliver was given his orders by this mysterious Number Four, after Sanderson had been murdered. His orders were in writing and in cipher, and that bit of paper you're holding in your hand is part of them. Very considerately he has translated the cipher for us, so that it should not be a matter of vast difficulty for us to read any further message which may fall into our hands."

"How do you know these are Gulliver's orders?"

"Because when Evening Clothes was ticking him off for monkeying with the policeman his excuse was that his orders were to get into Sanderson's house. And as you see, the letters he has scribbled in in pencil bear that out. That HO at the end must be either house or home, and of the two I should think house was the more likely."

Suddenly Darrell gave a little exclamation and picked up the newspaper.

"I may be wrong," he cried, "but I believe I saw something in the agony column of the same sort. Yes: here it is. Now, is that from the same source? It's a long line of capital letters."

Drummond bent over his shoulder and studied it.

IPHDTMICITYOOTIUNYIUT
MNJICILPTNO

"There you are, old lad," he remarked complacently. "With a little care we'll solve it in our heads. Look at the key: wherever you see R put an E, which as you know is the commonest letter in the English language, and meanwhile I'll get dressed."

"All that you say may be correct," murmured Darrell a few moments later, "but there would seem to be one trifling difficulty. There isn't an R in the whole blamed sentence."

"Not an R." Drummond paused with his shirt half on. "There must be an R. It stands for E. You can't have a sentence without an E. Look again, Peter."

"I'm looking. Moreover, I've put in the other letters, and whoever wrote this has got 'em again."

DR ODHDUA UD AD UO DHDNRU

"You can't in common decency ask a man to Dhdnru."

"Don't be an ass," said Drummond. "You've probably got it wrong, you mutton-headed idiot."

"Try it yourself, old son," grinned Darrell. "But that's the solution, as far as it goes, if your key is correct."

"Damn it – the key must be correct," cried Drummond. "We know that, because it makes sense."

"Then this can't be the same cipher," said Darrell. "Even if what you say is right, and E is the commonest letter, we don't get any farther. That would mean that I in the message stood for E and you get UE and AE. No, laddie, much as I regret to say it, this is a wash-out completely."

"Cut it out of the paper anyway, Peter," said Drummond. "Somebody might have a brainstorm later. Hullo! who's that?"

He paused in the act of putting on his tie and listened.

"I believe it's McIver himself. Put that bit of paper away, old boy: there's no good mentioning it to him."

The door opened and the figure of the Inspector could be seen in the passage outside.

"Good morning, Captain Drummond," he said. "I fear I'm a little early, but the matter is rather important. Do you know where Mr Standish is?"

"Come in, McIver," said Drummond quietly. "I was expecting you. So Standish is not in his rooms?"

"I've just come from them. Not only is he not there, but his bed has not been slept in."

"I was afraid of it," remarked Drummond. "McIver – they drugged us both last night."

"Who drugged you and how?"

"Dope in the whisky in Standish's rooms. I had one when I got there, and so did he. And the next thing I remember was when I woke this morning in one of his easy chairs with a mouth like a tallow factory. Of Standish there was no trace. Of course I was a bit muzzy, and what I hoped was that he had come round before me and gone out for a walk to cool his head. But if he's not back there now it looks rather bad."

"Are you certain he drank a whisky and soda himself?"

"Quite: I saw him do it. And since both drinks came out of the same decanter it's pretty certain he was laid out the same as me."

"You saw nothing suspicious?"

"Immediately we got into his sitting-room Standish noticed that his papers had been tampered with," said Drummond. "But beyond that – nothing."

McIver frowned.

"This is the most perplexing affair," he remarked. "What the deuce do they want to kidnap him for?"

"Because they don't know how much he knows, McIver. They're afraid of what he might say at the inquest."

"And how much do *you* know, Captain Drummond?"

"Precious little," said Drummond frankly. "And I don't think Standish knew much more. There are one or two things that stick out a mile or so, of course. It's obvious that we're up against a powerful and utterly unscrupulous gang of criminals, and it's further obvious that Sanderson was on their tracks. In fact, he said as much to me the other day, though at the time I didn't pay much attention. Well, they've got him all right, and presumably because he was 'phoning Standish at the time they've removed Standish also."

"Did you see the wound in Mr Sanderson's head?"

"Both Mr Darrell and I did," said Drummond. "It was straight through the right eye, and death must have been absolutely instantaneous. It might have been done with some implement like a very fine stiletto, or with a very small-bore revolver, were it not for the fact that Standish would have heard the latter over the wire. By the way, has PC 005 sat up yet and taken notice?"

The Inspector grinned faintly.

"He's the sorest man in the London police force today," he answered. "But he can't tell us anything. All he knows is that he was suddenly set upon from behind just as he was passing the half-built house where we found him. There were two men in it, and before he could blow his whistle they'd got a cloth soaked in chloroform round his mouth and nose. And the next thing he remembers is coming to and being extremely sick."

"How long was it before they got the fire out finally?" asked Drummond.

"About an hour after you and Mr Standish left," said McIver. "But the whole of that end of the house is merely a shell."

Drummond looked at him thoughtfully.

"What do you make of it all, McIver?"

"Very much what you do, sir," answered the Inspector. "It's quite clear that we're dealing with a mighty dangerous bunch, and that Mr Sanderson knew too much for their liking. Or at any rate they thought he did. When he was talking to you about it did he say anything definite?"

"No. He mentioned two or three crimes that have taken place recently – one I remember was the Exminster pearl robbery – and said he had reason to believe that they were organised by the same brain."

"He mentioned the Exminster case, did he? That's queer."

"Why?" asked Drummond.

"Well, as you know, sir, most of the big burglaries are the work of one of perhaps half a dozen men. And each of them has a distinctive way of working. The police can almost always tell by the way a job is carried out which particular merchant has been on it. They may not be able to prove it, but that doesn't alter the fact that they know. Then they keep a very wary eye on the fence he usually employs, and sometimes get him that way. But in the Exminster case it was different. None of the familiar traces were about, and Andrews, who was on it, told me he was pretty well certain it was the work of a new man and an expert at that.

"And there's another funny thing about that case," he continued. "Lord Exminster offered an enormous reward for the recovery of the pearls. They are family heirlooms and he is a very wealthy man. And the reward he offered was considerably in excess of what the thief could get by selling them to a fence. In fact, it's doubtful if any fence in England would buy them at all: you can't cut pearls, and those stones are too well known. Moreover, his Lordship let it be known that if he got them back there would be no questions asked. But he has never seen a sign of them from that day to this."

"Possibly the thief is holding 'em and hoping for better terms," said Drummond.

"Maybe. But the reward was ten thousand pounds, which is good enough for the average burglar. No: I wonder if Mr Sanderson was right, and the burglar was acting under orders from someone else."

"Then it would seem funny that the someone else didn't pouch the reward."

"That depends on whether he wanted the pearls or the money most. With an average thief there would be no doubt about it – the money every time. But there have been cases – I admit I've never come across one myself – where the man behind the actual working criminals was so big that money didn't matter. He employed men to steal works of art, for instance, which under no conceivable circumstances could he hope to sell, or even display to his friends."

"You mean he merely gloated over them in secret," said Darrell.

"Just so, sir. He'd pay the man who did the job a lump sum down, through one or even two intermediaries, and the transaction was finished. And in all probability the actual criminal didn't even know who he was working for."

Drummond lit a cigarette, and strolled over to the window. What McIver was saying not only bore out Sanderson's theory, but also what he had observed himself. The allusion to other members of the gang by numbers – presumably if there was a Number Four there must be others as well; the giving of orders in cipher; the reprimand to Gulliver because of his curiosity with regard to someone else's business – all tended to prove that there was a controlling force and very rigid discipline. So rigid, in fact, that anything in the shape of treachery was punished with death – *vide* Jean Picot. And for the first time he began to feel uneasy over Standish. Had the risk been justified?

He turned round as McIver rose.

"What are we going to do about Mr Standish?" he said.

"I don't see that there is anything we can do," answered the Inspector. "He's a gentleman who is very capable of looking after himself, but I'm bound to admit I don't like it."

"I shall have to mention the drugging at the inquest."

"Most certainly, sir. There's no point in your not doing so. My hat!" he added with a short laugh, "this is going to supply the papers with some copy. Well, sir, I'll let you know when and where you'll be required."

"Will you want me?" asked Darrell.

"Yes, sir. And the other gentleman, too – Mr Standish's friend. The post-mortem is today, and the inquest will be tomorrow. And by then we shall know if there is anything in Mr Sanderson's office that throws any light on the matter."

"I doubt it," said Drummond as the door closed behind the Inspector. "Sanderson wasn't the sort of bird who committed things to paper: he carried them in his head. What about strolling round and seeing Leyton, Peter: he ought to be told what has happened to Standish."

"I'm with you," said Darrell, getting up. "But the more I think of it, old boy, the less do I like this stunt of his. Even if he does find out where their headquarters are he's not going to be allowed to get away with it."

Drummond grunted: the remark expressed his own thoughts rather too nearly for his liking.

They found Leyton eating breakfast very slowly and carefully, and Darrell's description of his face overnight still held. Every colour from bright red to deep indigo was represented, and he apparently found it necessary to assist the working of his lower jaw with his hand.

"Behold your handiwork," he remarked as they came in. "I should think that a year might see my recovery. You'll find cigarettes on the mantelpiece."

He uttered a sharp yell of pain.

"God! there's another bit of my face gone: I forgot I couldn't turn my head."

Drummond regarded him with a professional eye.

"As pretty a bit of furniture throwing as ever I did in my life, laddie," he remarked. "I mean, the fact that you were the victim does not detract from it as a work of art. Have you thought how you are going to account for it at the inquest? A slight tiff with the girl's brother, or what?"

"Take him away, Darrell," moaned the sufferer plaintively, "or I shall have a relapse. Where's Ronald?"

"Where, indeed," said Drummond. "Pay attention, old boy, because one or two things have happened since we parted."

And once again he ran over the events of the past night.

"So that's how it stands, Leyton," he concluded. "Peter thinks we were wrong, and I myself am beginning to wonder."

"You didn't even get the number of the car," said Leyton.

"I couldn't. Evening Clothes remained behind with me, so it was impossible to get out of the chair."

"Which means, then, that Ronald, in full possession of his senses, and with a revolver into the bargain, was really being guarded by two men."

"And the driver. Unless, of course, there was someone else in the car who didn't come upstairs."

"I don't think you need worry," said Leyton at length. "If he went into it as you say yourself with his eyes open, he'll come out of it OK. And McIver knows nothing of this?"

"Not a word. And it's essential that he shouldn't. He would be bound to insist on it being mentioned, which not only will not help Standish, but will also wash out the one big card we hold. It's obvious that the man in evening clothes is one of their star turns, who, as things stand now, will not be on his guard against me the next time we bump into one another. And if anything is said about this, that advantage is gone."

"The point is, are you likely to bump into one another again?"

"One can but look," said Drummond. "He had the expensive-restaurant appearance, and if the cause is good one is prepared to masticate a kipper in two or three of them nightly in the hope of meeting him."

"But what do you do then, old boy?" objected Darrell. "You can't toddle up to him and introduce yourself."

"Peter," remarked Drummond, "you pain me after all these years. You leave all that part of the programme to little Hugh."

"And in the meantime," said Leyton, "there seems nothing for it but to wait and hope that Ronald gets away with it."

"That's so," agreed Drummond, getting up. "I'll send you up a few more pounds of steak, and I should think you'd better say you impinged on a lamp-post when bottled. So long, old boy: you'll be all right again in a month or so."

He strolled out, followed by Darrell, and paused undecidedly on the pavement. And then his eyes suddenly narrowed, though he still swung his stick as before.

"We're being shadowed, Peter," he remarked, "as I rather expected we should be. Don't look round, but he's looking into a flower-shop window about twenty yards away. I noticed the same man as we came here."

"What are you going to do about it?" said Darrell.

"Have a little fun and laughter to pass the time," answered Drummond with a grin, walking towards a man in a blue-serge suit who was now engaged in lighting a cigarette.

"Lovely blooms, sir, are they not?" he remarked affably.

The man stared at him.

"What the devil do you mean, sir?" he cried. "I don't know you."

"A great love of nature should be a sufficient introduction to enable us to dispense with more formal methods," said Drummond earnestly. "And when a man stands gazing at the hydrangeas or what-nots for twenty minutes, till his nose resembles a pomegranate in hue, he is at once admitted to the noble brotherhood of wurzel growers. Tell me, my dear new friend, have you ever shadowed anyone before?"

"Do you want me to call a policeman, sir?" spluttered the other.

"Rather: I'd love you to. But let's finish our little chat first. Where were we? Ah! yes – this shadowing business. You know, my dear sir, you're quite incredibly bad at it. I watched you with the greatest interest the whole way from my house, and I should love to know if I'm to have the pleasure of your company for the rest of the day. Because, if so, I must insist on your going home to get an overcoat. Wait, you little rat, till I've finished."

The man writhed impotently, as Drummond's great hand closed round his arm.

"You see," he went on, "I'm going to my club in St James's Square, and I fear you'll find it somewhat cold waiting for two or three hours. And I don't think you'd be very popular as a temporary member."

He relaxed his grip, and in a flash the man was gone.

"Come on, Peter," he grinned, "let's go and have one. There is another of 'em we know, but I'm afraid the small fry aren't much use to us. What a pity Evening Clothes stopped behind last night: if he hadn't I might have been able to board the luggage grid of the car. But he's our hope, Peter, unless Standish pulls off the trick. You and I will have to spend our substance in riotous living until we bump into him again."

He stopped and bought a midday paper.

"Great Scott! they've got it all right. Look at the headlines."

AMAZING CRIME IN HAMPSTEAD
HIGH HOME OFFICE OFFICIAL MURDERED
HOUSE COMPLETELY GUTTED
POLICEMAN CHLOROFORMED

He skimmed rapidly over the letterpress: it was much as he would have expected. There was no mention of either Standish or himself, though Perkins, in an interview, had alluded to four strange gentlemen who had been in the house when he returned from the cinema – gentlemen whose names he did not know. But the account ran to two columns and finished up with the announcement that the elucidation of this unprecedented outrage was in the capable hands of Inspector McIver, and further developments might be expected shortly.

They turned into Drummond's club, and the first person they saw waiting in the hall was McIver himself.

"I must apologise, sir, for coming round here," he said, "but I went to your house to find you, and your servant said I'd probably catch you at your club."

"That's all right, McIver," said Drummond. "Come into this room and we shan't be disturbed."

"Now, sir," began the Inspector when they were seated, "a very strange development has taken place. Mr Standish has disappeared, and so I can't ask him direct, but you'll be able to tell me. He was quite positive, wasn't he, that he heard no sound, no report, when he was speaking to Mr Sanderson on the telephone?"

"That's so, McIver," said Drummond. "And that was why he was convinced that the wound was inflicted with an instrument."

"Well, sir," said McIver, "the post-mortem on what was left of the body has been carried out. It was charred, of course, beyond recognition, but a great part of the head remained. And in view of where the wound was it was on the head we concentrated."

He leaned forward impressively.

"Embedded in the brain, and not very far in, was found a bullet of very small calibre."

"Which knocks the stiletto theory out of court," said Drummond. "But if he was shot, why didn't Standish hear any report?"

"A compressed-air pistol," suggested Darrell.

"Or something fitted with a silencer," remarked McIver. "There are one or two very efficient ones on the market."

"Have you ever heard one being used, McIver?" said Drummond. "Because if you have you'll know that the term silence is only relative. They undoubtedly muffle the report very considerably, but not enough to prevent it being heard over the telephone."

"Supposing the man who was using it was some distance away from the instrument," suggested the Inspector.

"That would mean that he was some distance away also from Sanderson," cried Drummond. "And you can hardly expect one to believe that the murderer, whoever he was, drew a large cannon from his pocket and took deliberate aim at one of Sanderson's eyes. By the way, how did the bullet enter the eye – direct from in front?"

McIver nodded.

"Yes: straight from the front but a little upwards. Now it struck me that Mr Sanderson might have been leaning backwards looking up at the ceiling, as he was speaking into the receiver. Then he wouldn't have seen what the other man was doing."

"I see two objections to that theory, old policeman. I lay claim to a certain modicum of efficiency with most kinds of firearms, but just think of the accuracy of shooting necessary if the man was some distance away from Sanderson to plug him through the eye. Why, it's target shooting brought to a fine art. He would have had to take the most careful aim, and even if Sanderson was looking up at the ceiling, he would surely have seen the other fellow focusing the young field gun."

"Supposing he didn't focus it: supposing he took a quick pot shot which by luck got Mr Sanderson in the eye. What about that?"

"It's possible, McIver," agreed Drummond, "but I don't think it's likely. And I'll tell you for why. If the bullet is of very small calibre, and has only gone in a short distance, there can't have been much power behind it. Well, what was going to happen if he'd missed the eye, which was now more than likely with a quick pot shot. Damn it – he'd have done no damage at all. He might have chipped a bit off Sanderson's ear or peppered him on the cheek, but he wouldn't have killed him. And what possible object could there have been in doing that?"

He lit a cigarette.

"Just one moment before you speak," he continued, "because there is another thing that I think puts your theory down and out definitely. Death was instantaneous: so if he was leaning back when he was killed, why did we find him sprawling forward over his desk?"

"I admit all the difficulties, Captain Drummond," said the Inspector a little peevishly. "Nevertheless, the fact remains that a bullet was found in his brain, and it can't have been thrown there. Therefore he was shot by some form of gun, revolver, or air pistol, which amongst other things was so nearly silent that Mr Standish didn't hear it over the wire. But whether it was fired at a long range or from close to it seems at present impossible to say."

"Agreed," cried Drummond, "but I know which I'm betting on. Close to, McIver: I'd lay a fiver to sixpence on it. Incidentally there is one thing that I don't think Standish told you last night. We found a hairpin on the floor under the desk – a bronze hairpin which did not belong to Mrs Perkins."

"So a woman was there?"

"Well, old lad," said Drummond with a grin, "I believe even Watson would have deduced that."

"She may have done it," continued the Inspector unmoved.

For a moment Drummond hesitated: should he tell McIver all he knew? Better not: there was no point in altering the plan of campaign now.

"True," he said calmly, "she may have done it. Or she may have assisted in the deed. Or she may have been there earlier and left before it happened. I don't think it takes us much farther. All we know is that a woman with golden hair or auburn hair was in that room some time last night."

Inspector McIver rose with a grunt.

"At any rate that is one positive fact which is something," he said. "Have you seen the midday papers?"

"I have," answered Drummond. "They've let themselves go all right, haven't they?"

"Nothing to what they'll be after the inquest when you've given your evidence," cried the other. "You'll find yourself keeping reporters off with an umbrella."

"I've done it before," laughed Drummond. "So long, McIver: keep me posted if any fresh developments occur."

"I will. And that reminds me: I've circulated Mr Standish's description to every Chief Constable, though I doubt if it will do much good. His salvation is going to lie in his own hands, and no one else's. If they didn't stick at murdering Mr Sanderson, they're not going to stick at him either. And you'll probably be the next on the list."

"Mother's little ray of sunshine," laughed Drummond. "See that Scotland Yard sends me a wreath."

The door closed behind the Inspector, and Drummond's expression grew serious again as he turned to Darrell.

"There's a darned sight more in what he says than I like, old boy," he remarked. "Your pal Standish has got to pull through on his own in this show."

"I thought for a while that you were going to tell McIver about Number Four and the rest of it," said Darrell.

"If it would have helped Standish in the slightest degree I would have. But it couldn't have. He may literally be anywhere in the British Isles. There's one point though, Peter, that strikes me. I think it would be a good thing to see Leyton once again. He is the only available person who was really present at the time of the telephone call, though McIver doesn't know it. And now that we know he was shot and not stabbed, it would be just as well to find out for sure if Standish said anything at the time which throws any light on it. Because the more I think of that wound the more amazing does it seem to me."

"I agree," said Darrell. "And so did Standish if you remember."

"Let's have a stoup of ale and then go round and see him."

They found him applying fresh steak to his face, and told him the new development.

"And what we were wondering," said Drummond, "was whether he said anything which would help."

"Let me get things in order," said Leyton thoughtfully. "I answered the telephone, and spoke to Sanderson. At least I assume it was Sanderson: he said it was. But as I never knew him it may have been somebody speaking for him. I then gave the receiver to Ronald, and he certainly spoke to Sanderson, or if it wasn't Sanderson it was to someone who could imitate his voice sufficiently well to deceive Ronald. And Sanderson asked Ronald to go up and see him. Ronald said, 'My dear fellow! on a night like this.' Then Sanderson answered 'I've got' and never completed the sentence. Instead there came a noise which Ronald said sounded like a hiss, and the clatter of what was probably the receiver hitting the desk. That's all I can tell you."

"Noise like a hiss," repeated Drummond. "That seems to point to a compressed-air weapon of sorts, doesn't it?"

"Well, it completely defeated Ronald," said Leyton. "Of course, he didn't know about the bullet being found in Sanderson's brain, and thought it was a question of stabbing. But he got deuced excited over a bottle of ink without a cord, and a piece of blotting-paper in the basket with damp ink on it."

"What was the great idea?" said Drummond curiously.

"Ask me another, my dear fellow. The only thing I can tell you, and Darrell will bear me out in that, is that when Ronald sits up and takes notice over anything, however apparently trivial, there's generally some reason for it. But as far as I'm concerned I don't quite see that it matters vastly. From what you overheard, Drummond, when you were foxing they evidently tried out some patent brand of new weapon. And the damned thing succeeded only too well. They killed the unfortunate Sanderson, and that's all there is to it."

"Not quite all," said Drummond quietly. "In fact very far from it. And it's this point that I know was worrying Standish. Don't you see the almost inevitable conclusion that Sanderson must have been in ignorance of the fact that it was a weapon at all?"

The other two stared at him.

"The bullet went in from straight in front," continued Drummond. "And as McIver sapiently remarked, it can't have been thrown in. It must have been propelled along a barrel of sorts. And that barrel Sanderson must have seen in front of him, pointing at his eye for an appreciable time before the shot was fired. Now do you mean to tell me that anyone, particularly a man like Sanderson, is going to continue sitting calmly in a chair telephoning when he's looking down the wrong end of a gun? Therefore he didn't know it was a gun."

"Even so," said Leyton after a pause, "I don't see that it matters much."

"The devil you don't," cried Drummond. "Well – I do. If in addition to being up against a gang who don't stop at murder, we have also got to compete with a weapon which is unrecognisable as a weapon until it is too late, the dice are loaded pretty well against us. Sanderson was no fool, and I don't think that any of us can flatter ourselves that we would spot a thing that he didn't. Hullo! old boy, you have a visitor."

Leyton swung round: a small and excessively dirty street Arab was standing in the doorway.

"How the dickens did you get in, my lad?" he demanded.

"Through the door, guv'nor," piped the urchin. "Are you Mister Leyton?"

"I am."

"A bloke give me this 'ere note to tike to yer. Give me 'alf a crown, 'e did, and 'e said you'd give me anuvver."

He produced a crumpled piece of paper from his pocket and handed it to Leyton, who gave an exclamation when he saw it.

"Good Lord!" he cried, "it's from Ronald."

"Hold hard a moment," said Drummond. "Now, my stout-hearted young sportsman, can you give us a description of the gentleman who gave you this note?"

"Medium-sized bloke, sir: bit red in the face. Broad 'e was though."

"What was he dressed in?"

"Blue-serge suit, sir; wiv mud on it."

"And where did you meet him?"

"Dahn in Bishop Street, near the Elephant and Castle."

"Sounds all right so far, Leyton. May I see the note?"

In silence the other passed it to Drummond.

"Tell Drummond to come as soon as he can. 34 Lower Wood Street. Disguise if possible."

"You are sure this is in Standish's writing?" said Drummond.

"If it isn't, it's a very fine forgery," answered Leyton.

"Tell you one thing, guv'nor," chipped in the urchin eagerly, "the gent wot give me the note looked to me as if 'e was dodging for 'is life."

"What made you think that, infant?" demanded Drummond.

"Way 'e was looking over 'is shoulder all the time. Just like wot one sees at the pictures."

"Good. Well, here's half a dollar for you, and just listen to me for a moment. When you get into the street I shouldn't be at all surprised if somebody or other speaks to you and asks you what you've been doing up here, and what we've been talking about. And if anyone does, tell him to go to hell."

"Right-'o, sir!"

A grimy finger was raised in salute, and the next moment the little Arab had disappeared.

"I thought so," said Drummond, who had gone to the window. "A man has stopped him. Damn it! the little blighter is taking money from him."

He peered through the curtains, and then suddenly grinned.

"OK," he remarked, coming back into the room. "He pocketed the money, and then cocked a snook at the donor. Now then, chaps, this requires thinking out a bit. I feel pretty sure in my own mind that that note is genuine. If it was a forgery with the idea of trapping me, surely they would have sent it direct to my house. But Standish, even if he remembered my address, which I doubt, knew that the surest way of getting me would be through Leyton, who is, so to speak, on our list of distinguished invalids."

"Confound you," laughed Leyton. "But to come back to the note; I'll swear that's his writing."

"At any rate we're going to act on the assumption that it is genuine," said Drummond.

"Can you manage the disguise part of it?"

"Can I manage my foot? That's easy, old lad. The slight difficulty at the moment is the undoing of the gentleman outside. He has got to be shaken off, and any friend of his who may be about. So we'll try the simplest method first."

He went to the telephone and dialled a number.

"Hullo! is that Smith's hotel? Put me through to the hall porter, please, Dover Street entrance, at once. Is that you, Robins? Captain Drummond speaking. I want you to have a taxi waiting for me with the flag down and the engine running in a quarter of an hour from now. Tell the driver that the instant I get into the car he is to start at once without waiting for any orders, drive down Hay Hill and into Berkeley Square, where I'll give him further instructions. Got that? Good. And, Robins – get a good machine."

"What's the great idea?" said Leyton as he hung up the receiver.

"As old as the hills, old boy," answered Drummond, "but it often comes off. Smith's has another entrance in Albemarle Street."

CHAPTER 4

"By Jove! Peter, that note from Standish has taken a load off my mind," Drummond remarked, as ten minutes later he and Darrell turned into Piccadilly. "I wonder what he's found out."

He stopped for a moment to look into a shop window, and make sure the follower was not lost.

"He's better than the other one, I think, but that ain't saying much: anyway, he's still there."

"What about a gun, Hugh?" said Darrell as they resumed their walk.

"I'll borrow one from Aaronstein," answered Drummond. "Whom, by the same token, Peter, I want you to ring up for me. Tell him I'll be down in three-quarters of an hour, and I'll want some lunch. Any rig will do which will not attract attention amongst the denizens of Lower Wood Street."

"Do you know where it is?"

"Not an earthly. But old Aaron has a very good map."

"Shall I come into Smith's with you?"

"Yes, please, old boy. And should the gentleman behind smell a rat and try to follow me, stop him some old how."

They turned up Albemarle Street, with their attendant about ten yards behind them.

"Shall I let McIver know we've had this note?" asked Darrell.

"Leave it for a bit, Peter, until we know what Standish's game is. Maybe he wants to lie doggo, which would be impossible if McIver once hears he's free again. And as far as I'm concerned don't worry if you don't hear from me tonight, but at the same time stand by to act on any message you get. To prove it's genuine I'll sign it 'Cuckoo.' Here we are, old boy: keep your eye skinned on that bird. He may not know the architecture of Smith's, but on the other hand he may."

The two men swung into the hotel and parted at once, Darrell remaining by the Albemarle Street entrance whilst Drummond walked rapidly along the passage that led to the Dover Street one. And it soon became obvious to him that the man did know the plan of the building and had spotted the trick. From behind came Darrell's voice hailing him as a long-lost friend, and glancing round for an instant he had a glimpse of the man's face distorted with anger, dodging wildly from side to side whilst Darrell dodged in time. Then he was in the taxi which was off in a second. And he was the other side of Berkeley Square before his infuriated pursuer finally shook off Darrell and dashed out into Dover Street.

"A quid if you'll tell me where that taxi went," he shouted to the porter.

"What, that taxi that's just gone?" said Robins blandly. "With the big gentleman inside?"

"Yes, you fool," snarled the other. "Quick – I'm police."

"Are you now?" remarked Robins with a wink at Darrell. "Well, that being so, you ought to know that divulging the destinations of taxis is strictly forbidden in the regulations laid down for hall porters."

But the man had seen the wink, and with a venomous look at Darrell, who was grinning broadly, he disappeared.

"The Captain up to his old games, sir?" asked Robins.

"Can't keep him off 'em," laughed Darrell. "Thank you, Robins: you worked it splendidly."

"The best machine I could get, sir, and I know the driver. He's a good man. Thank you, sir: though it's a pleasure to help the Captain at any time. He's clear away this time."

And though Drummond was even then thinking the same thing he was far too old a stager to leave anything to chance. The Park had been his first order, and he followed it by doing a little tour of the less-frequented roads in Bayswater. And not until the machine had remained stationary for five minutes in an almost deserted road did he feel absolutely confident that he'd got away with it.

"Dodging the wife, sir, or treasurer of a slate club?" grinned the driver.

Drummond laughed.

"Seems a bit like it, doesn't it? We will now go to the nearest tube station."

"Right, sir. Queen's Road."

His destination, the emporium of Samuel Aaronstein, lay in the purlieus of Whitechapel. It was a peculiar shop, in which everything from a bootlace to a grand piano could be obtained, and one of the principal side-lines was the sale of second-hand clothes. It was that that had first attracted him there, coupled with the fact that old Samuel had the invaluable gift of holding his tongue. Many times in the past had Captain Drummond of Brook Street vanished into a private room at the back of the shop to emerge later in one of Samuel's outfits as Mr Jones of Houndsditch.

Moreover, the old Jew was perfectly honest, as he had often proved. It was quite safe to leave money or valuables in his charge for any length of time: everything would be accounted for to the uttermost farthing.

The shop, as he had anticipated at that time of day, was not very full: the evenings are the rush hours in those parts. And with a quick nod to Aaronstein he walked straight through into his own particular room behind, where he was immediately joined by the proprietor.

"Morning, Samuel," he said. "Has Mr Darrell telephoned?"

"Half an hour ago, sir. I've laid out three different rigs that vill fit you."

"Good for you, Sam," cried Drummond, beginning to undress rapidly. "What are they?"

"Ordinary vorking man, Captain; commercial traveller; seafaring rig."

"Do you know anything about Lower Wood Street down Elephant and Castle direction? I'm going there, and I want the most suitable of the three."

"I'll go and ask young Joseph," said Aaronstein. "That boy knows every district in London."

He returned in a couple of minutes.

"Not the seafaring one, sir," he said, "but either of the other two. There are shops there and tenement houses, so vhichever you decide upon it von't be conspicuous."

"I'll chance the commercial traveller," said Drummond after a moment's thought. Number 34, he reflected, might be a shop or it might not: if it was he could do the traveller act, if it wasn't he could pretend to be looking for a room.

"And I'll want a revolver, Sam: no good saying you haven't got one, you old devil, for I know you have."

The Jew shook his head dubiously.

"Vell, Captain Drummond," he said, "you vill be careful, von't you? If the police knew I had firearms in the shop..."

"They won't, Sam: if any question arises I'll say I got it out of a Christmas cracker. Then I want a good map of London, and that lunch which I trust Mr Darrell ordered."

"Certainly, sir; certainly. The lunch vill be ready in ten minutes: Rebecca is cooking it now. I vill go and hurry her up."

Over his meal Drummond studied the map. From Standish's note it was clear that he thought he had been followed, otherwise there seemed no object in suggesting disguise. And it was therefore in Lower Wood Street that danger was to be anticipated.

Drummond marked its position clearly in his mind: the fewer questions he had to ask the more likely was he to be taken for a local resident. And the great thing was to attract as little attention as possible. For though his ability to make up was considerable there was one thing he could not disguise – his size. And it seemed to him to be more than likely that anyone who was keeping Number 34 under observation would have been warned to keep a look-out for a big man going in there.

"Marvellous," said Aaronstein, returning half an hour later to remove the lunch. "Your own mother vould not know you, Captain."

"Not bad, Sam," agreed Drummond. "Give me the gun, and I'm off. Keep my things for me as usual."

The old Jew's praise was deserved: Drummond was a commercial traveller to the last button. A moustache completely altered his face, and by walking with a pronounced stoop he managed to conceal his height. And though he knew for certain that he had not been followed to Aaronstein's shop, he assumed his proposed role at once. No mistakes was the order of the day, and the stoop wanted practice.

Lower Wood Street proved to be one of those depressing localities which abound in outer London. It was long and straight and featureless: two rows of drab houses, each one exactly like its neighbour. At one end were a few cheap shops, and half-way along some stalls almost blocked one of the pavements. As usual the houses on one side were even numbers, on the other odd, and deciding that any watch that might be kept on Number 34 would probably be from opposite, he chose the odd side for his first survey.

The numbers at the end of the street where he had entered were high ones: his goal therefore was some distance off. And his plan was to walk right to the other end of the street, giving Number 34 a preliminary inspection as he passed; then return on the even-numbered side and begin playing his part.

The road was fairly crowded, particularly near the stalls, a state of affairs that cut both ways. It made him less conspicuous, but the same thing applied equally to any possible watchers of Number 34. And one of his main objects was to try to spot those watchers if he could.

He reached the stalls: the house numbers had now reached the fifties. And at the last one he stopped, apparently listening to the proprietor bawling his wares. But his eyes were busy searching the bit of road in front of him. Some children were playing in the gutter: two or three women were gossiping by an area railing. But so far as he could see there was no one about who looked in the smallest degree suspicious.

He walked on slowly until he was almost opposite his goal: then he stopped, and pulling a packet of Gold Flake out of his pocket he lit a cigarette. Was it his imagination, or had the curtain in the sitting-room of Number 34 quivered slightly?

He strolled on: one thing seemed sure. Whether it had moved or whether it had not, there was no one in the street who was watching the house. He reached the end of the road, crossed over and retraced his steps. And at Number 20 he began to act his role. Specimens of table linen were his stock-in-trade, and fortunately none of the good ladies in any of the houses he called at evinced the slightest interest in them.

At last he reached Number 34 and rang the bell.

"Good afternoon, missis," he began, as a buxom, homely faced woman opened the door.

But he got no farther: to his unqualified amazement she flung a pair of ample arms round his neck and kissed him.

"Why, it's Arthur," she cried. "Blessed if it isn't little Arthur come to see his old Aunt."

And simultaneously from a room behind came Standish's voice: "Play up, old boy."

Drummond needed no second bidding: he dropped his case of samples and kissed the old lady heartily in return.

"Aunt Marie," he exclaimed. "Well, I never did. To think of that now. When did you move here?"

"A year ago, Arthur. George," she called loudly to someone at the back of the house, "here's Arthur. He's coming to have a cup of tea."

Drummond followed her inside and she shut the front door.

"Well done, Mrs Bordon," said Standish, joining them in the passage. "I don't know whether we've bluffed 'em or not, but you couldn't have acted better."

"Where are they?" asked Drummond.

"In the house opposite. Two of them. Jove! old man, I'm glad to see you."

He led the way into a back sitting-room.

"Not half as glad as I was to get your note," answered Drummond quietly. "I had the needle badly all this morning. You spotted me as I went up the other side, did you?"

"Yes. The instant you stopped to light that cigarette. And then, knowing you were coming here, I fixed that little performance with Mrs Bordon. She was my old nurse. This isn't the only house you've been to, is it?"

"No. I called at seven others. I'm touting table linen."

"Excellent," cried Standish. "Any fresh news from your end?"

"I see you've got the midday papers," answered Drummond, "so you've read the official story. But there's one thing that will surprise you: I heard it this morning from McIver. Sanderson was shot: they found a small bullet in his brain."

"The devil he was," said Standish thoughtfully. "I did hear a faint hiss."

"So Leyton told me. But that will keep: let's hear what you've been doing. For I don't mind admitting that we've all been damned uneasy. You see, the devil of it was that that blighter in evening clothes stayed on after the other two had taken you off and I couldn't even get the number of the car."

"You know who that was, don't you?" said Standish.

"I don't: do you?" cried Drummond, sitting up abruptly.

The other nodded gravely.

"Yes," he said. "I do. And when I saw him last night I very nearly gave the whole show away I was so dumbfounded."

"I don't know when you actually came to," said Drummond, "but he didn't know you. He had to ask which of us was which when he came in."

"No: he wouldn't know me. I was but a humble guest at the City dinner at which he was the guest of honour two or three months ago."

Drummond stared at him.

"Guest of honour! Then who the deuce is he?"

"Sir Richard Pendleton."

"Pendleton – the surgeon," cried Drummond in amazement; "man – you must be mistaken. What on earth would he be doing mixed up with that outfit?"

"Exactly what I've been asking myself all day," said Standish. "I tell you I nearly gave it away last night when I realised who he was. I'd been awake for quite a while before you spotted it, and I'd heard his voice. That sounded familiar, but of course I couldn't turn round and see who it was. So I possessed my soul in patience till the other two picked me up, and then I risked a peep. And there's no doubt about it, old boy, it was Pendleton."

"But it's incredible," said Drummond. "I've never happened to meet him, but he dines out all over the shop. Half the women in London sit on his doorstep."

"I know all that," agreed Standish. "And there is only one possible explanation to my mind. It's a case of Jekyll and Hyde in real life. Mark you, there are quite a number on record. It's a peculiar form of perversion, that's all."

"Well, if you're sure it was Pendleton, there's no more to be said," remarked Drummond. "Let's hear what happened after they took you off."

"They dumped me in the bottom of the car and we started. And after a while Mr Gulliver – the police impersonator – began to snore. A little later his friend Mr Jackson followed his example, and the situation became rather amusing. There was the prisoner wide awake with a gun, whilst the guard slept peacefully. The driver was the only other occupant, and he was separated from us by a partition. The car was going fast, but I couldn't tell in what direction until the sun suddenly rose, and I realised by the shadow we were travelling south. I didn't dare move to see if I could recognise the country, because I was afraid of waking them, in which case it would have been necessary to act at once. My object, of course, was to find out where they were taking me without letting them get me there. It struck me that wherever my destination was it would be easier to get in than to get out."

"Exactly what struck us," said Drummond.

"Then came an extraordinary piece of luck: the car stopped and they both woke up.

" 'The damned gates are shut,' said Gulliver, and I heard the driver get out of the car. The Lord had delivered 'em into my hands."

Standish grinned at the recollection.

"I had already taken the precaution of removing my gun from my pocket, so I plugged each of 'em through one foot – a painful but most efficacious proceeding."

"Gorgeous," cried Drummond. "Man, it's a pleasure to hunt with you."

"I then got out of the car and had a look round. The din from inside was indescribable: the driver, with his eyes popping out of his head, was standing with the gate half open staring at me. And then the silly ass decided to have a dip himself: he let the gate swing to and came for me. That was short and sweet: a poor fighter. I got him one on the point of the jaw, and he departed into a ditch that must have been very wet, judging by the splash.

And after that I decided it was time to hop it: the band inside the car was now playing *fortissimo*. I took a glimpse through the gate, and saw a big house in the distance: then having put a shot into both front tyres I went off at a steady double up the road.

"I didn't know where I was – the country was quite unfamiliar – but I'd found out all I wanted to. Sooner or later I must come to a village, when I should be able to get my bearings. The danger was that I should be pursued before I could reach it. I'd delayed that particular car, but it was almost certain there would be another one available. And if my supposition was right and I'd found their headquarters, it was not going to be long before that other one was on the road. Moreover, our friends struck me as being of the type that would not hesitate to use a rifle if necessity arose.

"The gates were now out of sight, and the road stretched straight in front of me for half a mile. In the distance I could see the South Downs, but what was far more to the point was that there was a small but thick copse about a hundred yards away on my right. And I decided to sprint for that. I knew they must overtake me if I stuck to the road, and then I was for it. So I dashed across a field and went to ground in the undergrowth – just in time. For I had hardly disappeared in the bushes when I heard the roar of a racing car coming from the direction of the house. A big yellow Bentley came madly round the corner, and for a moment or two I thought it was going on. But the people inside were no fools: they knew I couldn't have got away up the road in the time. The car halted about two hundred yards beyond the wood and six men came tumbling out, each one armed with a shot-gun. And what was a darned sight worse, they had evidently spotted the wood as my most likely hiding-place, and they made a bee-line for it.

"The next few minutes were not too pleasant. I knew darned well that if they caught me they'd shoot on sight, and as they were forming into a line of beaters the chances were all Lombard Street to a china orange that they would catch me.

"The undergrowth was the sort that looks dense from outside, but turns out to be quite thin when you're in it. So little Willie did some pretty rapid thinking. I was close to the edge of the copse, and by the mercy of Allah I noticed a shallow ditch with a hedge beside it that ran almost to the road. And keeping on the blind side of the hedge I left that wood at speed.

"I could hear the men behind me going through the undergrowth and I knew that if one of them happened to break covert I was a goner. But no one did, and I reached the road OK. And then came the dangerous moment: get across the road I must, or they'd spot me as soon as they left the wood. Once again my luck was in: the ditch I'd been following went under the road through a small culvert. And so did yours truly: it was a bit of a tight fit, but I managed it.

"Now came the point. The road was above the level of the field the other side, but there was no trace of cover. They would be bound to see me when they got back to the car. Should I stop in the drain or what? Well, I didn't like the idea of that drain at all. They would almost certainly spot it, and that meant being plugged sitting. So there was only one chance, and it had to be taken at once. Crouching down, I hared as fast as I could towards the car."

"Priceless," cried Drummond. "As I said before, you're a pleasure to hunt with."

"Well – it worked. There was no one in the car, and I've driven a Bentley since the year dot. Of course they heard the engine start, and two of 'em came crashing out of the wood and let drive. But the range was far too great, so I waved 'em a tender farewell and trod on the juice.

"I drove for about a mile when I saw a village in front of me. And at that juncture I decided it would be safer to leave the car and walk. It was probably well known in the neighbourhood, and I wanted to run no risk of the local policeman asking me how I came to be driving it, especially as I didn't even know where I was, which would make it seem all the more suspicious.

"The village turned out to be a place called Fastington – one of those sleepy little Sussex places that lie round the foot of the Downs. The nearest railway station they told me was at Pulborough, and with that I got my bearings. I'd played a lot of golf there last summer, and knew a retired naval officer very well who lives close to the links. So I hired an ancient Lizzie, and drove to his house to see if he would send me up to London in his car.

"I found him in his garden dreaming of new and damnable bunkers to be added to the course, but when he descended from these realms of pure thought I got a set-back. His Lancia was *hors de combat*: I should have to hire or go by train. So I decided on the latter, and then asked him if he knew the name of a man owning a large yellow Bentley who lived near Fastington.

" 'There's a parson comes from there with a pronounced hook on all his drives,' he told me, 'but I think he's only got a baby Austin. And I did hear that some new tenant has taken the Old Hall, but I don't know if he plays golf or not.'

" 'Is the Old Hall a big house standing some hundred yards from the road in its own grounds?' I asked him.

"I gathered it was, and then departed for the station. And here is where the bad luck came in, for I am convinced it was a sheer fluke. I got on the train, and it was just moving when, happening to look out of the window, who should I see but the chauffeur I had knocked out early that morning. He gave a violent start: evidently he was just as surprised to see me as I was to see him. But the devil of it was that he did see me, and bolted out of the station like a scalded cat. I couldn't get out: we were almost clear of the platform. I could do nothing till we got to the first stop, Horsham, at any rate. You see, I had hoped that I'd completely shaken 'em off, and as I had no intention of returning to my own rooms in Town, I had intended to work secretly from an unknown hiding-place. And now if this damned chauffeur got through on the 'phone it might be possible for them to get someone on the train at Horsham. Which, I regret to state, is precisely what happened. That blasted engine positively crawled, and when we finally crept into the station there were two of the men who had been after me that morning. At least I recognised one for certain.

"Well, I was in a carriage by myself, and had no intention of having their company to London. So I was out like a flash and into a full third non-corridor. It may seem a childish precaution to you, but I think we've got to get one thing pretty firmly in the grey matter. We're dealing with a bunch who will no more hesitate to shoot openly than the 'on the spot' brigade in the States."

"I agree," said Drummond quietly.

"That stung 'em as far as London, and then the fun began. I'm no slouch at covering tracks, but those two had me beat. And, of course, they had one big advantage. They knew that I knew they were shadowing me, and so they didn't trouble to disguise the fact. But at last I really thought I'd shaken 'em off in one of those small streets north of the Elephant. I was making for here the whole time, and I scribbled that note the urchin gave you. But I'd reckoned without my friends: they had picked up the trail again. And five minutes after I'd come in here I saw the blighters the other side of the street."

"Is there any bolt hole at the back?" asked Drummond.

"Only by climbing the wall and going through somebody else's house," answered Standish. "And as the old girl here doesn't know the people it belongs to, it's a bit awkward."

"Washing out the birds opposite for the moment," said Drummond, "what are your ideas for the near future?"

"A closer investigation of the Old Hall," said Standish promptly. "Tonight, if possible. And I hoped you'd come with me."

"It would take a machine gun to prevent me," grinned Drummond.

"But," continued Standish, "it's imperative to dodge those two blighters."

"We'll fix that: don't you worry. We've got just the same advantage as they have: no finesse is necessary. And now that there are two of us I suggest that we draw 'em from their lair: then go straight up to 'em and knock 'em out."

"Simple and direct," said Standish with a smile.

And even as he spoke his eyes narrowed as he stared through the windows into the area at the back.

"Duck," he yelled suddenly, and both men hurled themselves on the floor as the glass shivered to pieces and a china ornament on the other side of the room split into a thousand fragments.

Simultaneously the door swung open: in the passage a man was standing with a revolver in his hand.

"Against the wall, both of you," he said curtly. "Put your hands above your heads."

And Drummond gave one short laugh. As Standish said afterwards, it was the most amazing piece of shooting he had ever seen, especially in view of the fact that the gun was a strange one. Drummond fired from the hip, and with a fearful curse the man let his revolver fall from a hand which now had a shattered wrist. And then he ceased cursing. Something that seemed like the buffer of an express engine hit him in the face: he was lifted bodily off the ground into a hat-rack behind him, and collapsing into its debris he lay still.

"So much for Number One," said Drummond quietly. "But I fear Number Two has escaped us for the moment. By Gad, Standish, you're right about these toughs: they go for the big thing. Never wanted to shoot quite so openly."

"They'll do anything to get us," answered Standish. "Lucky I saw that swine outside in the dusk. Come on, old boy: let's leg it now. If Number Two is round there the coast is clear in front."

He gave a hail to Mrs Bordon, and the next moment the two men were in the street.

"This way," said Standish. "If that fellow who fired is coming back he'll take the shortest route. And as I live, there he is rounding the corner now."

"We'll out him," said Drummond briefly.

The man had seen them, and for a moment he stood hesitating. And that moment was fatal: a fox in the middle of a pack of hounds would have had more chance. The two of them were on him like a flash: came a thud and the sound of a breaking jaw; then oblivion. And stopping only to snatch what looked like a heavy walking-stick from the unconscious man in the gutter, Drummond and Standish disappeared at speed into the gathering darkness.

"As tasty a five minutes as I can recollect," laughed Drummond, hailing a taxi. "That's larned 'em, old boy."

"Why Whitechapel?" cried Standish.

"To meet my old friend Aaronstein and become myself again."

Drummond was examining the stick as he spoke with a professional eye.

"A very pretty weapon," he remarked, passing it to Standish. "A spring gun and about the most powerful I've handled."

"Can it have been this they did poor old Sanderson in with?"

Drummond shook his head.

"McIver said the bullet was of very small calibre and only just inside the brain. This thing would have blown the back of his head off."

Standish nodded.

"That's true. That weapon, whatever it was, defeats me."

"So it does me," said Drummond. "But what defeats me even more is what you tell me about Pendleton."

"I grant you, it's amazing. But there's no possibility of my being mistaken."

"I wonder who the yellow-haired lady is," remarked Drummond thoughtfully.

Standish stared at him.

"What yellow-haired lady?" he demanded.

"Were you still unconscious when they were talking about her last night? Gulliver mentioned her as having been with Number Four just about the time when the murder was committed. The hairpin must have been hers. And Pendleton seemed quite upset when he heard about it. By the way, to go back to the weapon they murdered him with, I can tell you this much. It's something new that they were trying out for the first time, and Pendleton admitted he was doubtful as to whether it would be a success."

But for the moment Standish's thoughts were not on the mysterious weapon: he was trying to recall a piece of scandal he had heard recently in his club.

"Is Corinne Moxton a blonde?" he asked suddenly.

"The film wench?" said Drummond in some surprise. "Very muchly so, I believe. As a matter of fact, I was asked to a cocktail party this evening to meet her. But why the enthusiasm?"

"Because I heard her name coupled with Pendleton's the other day," answered Standish. "A fellow in the club was talking, and mentioned *en passant* that the gentleman had a pretty expensive taste in women."

"Even so," remarked Drummond, "I don't quite see the relevance."

"I was wondering if perchance she was the owner of the hairpin," said Standish.

"She's a fairly hectic mover, so I gather," answered Drummond, "but that's not saying that she is tantamount to being a murderess. If you like, I'll go to this bally party – much as I loathe 'em – and vet the lady."

"Who is giving it?"

"Some darned woman in Park Lane. I've got the card in the pocket of my clothes at Aaronstein's."

"You don't know if she knows Pendleton?"

"I don't. But she's the type that knows everybody one ought to know."

"I wish you'd chance it, old boy," said Standish. "It really would be rather humorous if you ran into Pendleton himself. I'll stay at the place you're changing at."

"Right you are," cried Drummond. "I'll go and lower some of the old girl's gin. And here we are at Sam's. Follow me straight through the shop."

He paid off the taxi, and led the way to the room at the back. The shop was crowded, but he caught Aaronstein's eye and beckoned to him to come too.

"All vell, Captain?" asked the old Jew.

"Quite, Sam, thank you. This is Mr Standish, who is going to remain here for a time."

Aaronstein bowed obsequiously.

"Pleased to meet any friend of yours, Captain," he said.

"About tonight," continued Drummond to Standish. "Disguise or not?"

"Not," said Standish. "If by chance they catch us a disguise is no good, and if they don't it isn't wanted."

"Make it so," said Drummond. "Sam, send out that young scoundrel of a son of yours for a gallon of ale. I've got a mouth like a lime-kiln. Here's the card," he continued as the Jew left the room. " 'Mrs Charles Dingle – to meet Corinne Moxton. Do come – angel man,' written in the corner. '6.30–9.' Ever heard of her?"

"No, thank God," said Standish. "By Jove! old boy," he cried in genuine admiration as Drummond peeled off his shirt and vest, "you have got some muscle on you."

"Not bad," said Drummond modestly. "I keep pretty fit, this way and that."

He paused, struck by a sudden thought. Standish's words had brought back those ghastly minutes that morning when the man he now knew to be Pendleton had run his fingers up and down his arm, and he heard again that devilish chuckling laugh of gloating anticipation.

He retailed it, and Standish listened in silence.

"Interesting," he remarked after a while. "It may be that he hopes you will be involved in some trial of strength at which he will be a spectator. It bears out that Jekyll and Hyde theory."

Drummond continued dressing as young Joseph entered with the beer.

"And there's another thing I haven't told you about," he said, "which will keep you amused while you're waiting here. Are you an expert on ciphers?"

"Pretty fair," said Standish.

"Then have a dip at this," cried Drummond. "The torn-off scrap was dropped by Gulliver in your rooms, translation and all complete. The other came out of the *Telegraph* this morning, and it struck me that it might be the same code. Unfortunately it makes absolute gibberish."

"I'll have a look at it when you've gone," said Standish. "What we've got to fix now is where we meet tonight. We'll want a car, and mine is in the garage close by my rooms."

"Which are being watched for a certainty," remarked Drummond. "We'll take mine: the garage is a quarter of a mile from my house. But I don't think it's wise to bring her down here: she's one of those super-charged Mercédès and might seem a bit out of place in Whitechapel. Tell you what, old boy: you and I will go independently by train to Epsom – it's on our road.

We'll dine at the Crown, and I'll 'phone my warrior to take her there. How does that strike you?"

"OK, baby," said Standish. "I'll be there about eight."

"Good. I doubt if I'll manage it by then, but I'll make it as soon as I can."

Drummond sank a final pint of beer, and sighed.

"Now for Dingle's pestilential party," he remarked. "If the cursed woman 'angel man's' me in a corner Charles will be a widower. I only hope I recognise her."

And had it not been for the fact that she was standing just inside the door as he entered the drawing-room he certainly would not have done so.

"My dear," she cried, "how utterly toothsome of you to come. I expect you know everybody, but it doesn't matter if you don't. Do keep an eye for me on young Henry over there: I think he's going to be sick."

"Is he the pale-green thing in the corner?" asked Drummond languidly. "If so, the catastrophe seems imminent."

"Corinne hasn't come yet," she continued. "Don't you think she's too utterly ravishing?"

"Incredibly utterly," murmured Drummond, drifting away and leaving a new arrival in the place of honour. In a far corner he had espied a man he knew slightly and he now proceeded to join him.

"Evening, Rogers," he remarked. "What an infernal crush."

"Didn't know you patronised this type of entertainment," said the other. "I don't myself as a general rule, but my wife was crazy to see this Moxton woman, and dragged me along."

"What's she like to look at?"

"I've only seen her on the films, but she looks a fizzer on them. By the way, what an extraordinary affair this Sanderson business in Hampstead is, isn't it?"

"Amazing," said Drummond, and at that moment a sudden stir by the door saved him the necessity of further elaboration. The guest of the evening was arriving.

She was a strikingly beautiful woman, with a well-nigh perfect figure, and she moved with an unconscious grace that was one of her principal charms. In one hand she carried the smallest Pekingese he had ever seen, and he was on the point of remarking on it when Rogers chuckled.

"I thought as much," he said. "He's never out of her pocket."

Drummond glanced at the door: Sir Richard Pendleton had just come in.

"Who is never out of her pocket?" he said indifferently as he lit a cigarette. A bit of acting was going to be required in a few moments, and until then casual conversation with Rogers would help.

"Pendleton – the surgeon. That thin-faced blighter who has just come in. Charges you a thousand quid to do the simplest thing, and from what I hear he'll want it all. The lady has somewhat expensive tastes."

"Is there a Lady Pendleton?" asked Drummond.

"Not so that one would notice," said Rogers with a grin. "I believe there is one, but one never sees her. Hullo! you seem to have attracted the gentleman's notice: he was staring quite hard at you, but he's looked away again now. Do you know him?"

"Never met him in my life," answered Drummond, taking a cocktail from a tray which a footman was presenting to him.

He looked casually across the room: Pendleton was whispering something in the actress' ear. And a moment later her glance travelled slowly round the people present: met his indifferently and passed on. But she had spotted him, and he wondered what the next move was going to be.

It came fairly quickly in the shape of his hostess.

"My dear," she cried, coming up to him, "Corinne wishes to meet you. Come and be introduced."

A bit blatant, he reflected, as he followed her across the room, but presumably Pendleton regarded himself as perfectly safe. And the next moment he was bowing over the film-star's hand.

"An honour," he murmured, "which I have often dreamed of in the silent watches of the night, but never imagined would come true."

"Say, big boy," she said, "you're talking boloney. Have you two never met? Sir Richard Pendleton – Captain Drummond."

"Good evening," said Drummond. "Charmed to meet you, Sir Richard – unprofessionally."

The other smiled.

"From what I can see of you, Captain Drummond, I don't think you're ever likely to meet me in any other capacity."

"Say, Cora's thrown a swell party," said the actress, and for an instant or two Drummond studied her face. Beautiful: more than that, lovely: hair the colour of spun gold. Her eyes had a strange tint in them that was almost green. Her complexion was flawless; her skin perfect. But – there was something: something he could not put his finger on that was wrong. And suddenly he realised that she was looking at him, and in spite of himself he felt his pulses quicken a little. There was no mistaking the message in those extraordinary green eyes, though it was only there for the fraction of a second, and for a moment he almost forgot the part she had played in Sanderson's murder. For Standish was right: she must be the woman in the case.

"They certainly seem to be making whoopee all right," he remarked, putting down his empty glass. "Personally I'm not very fond of crowds of this sort. Two seems to me to be the maximum number for pleasure."

"Come and see me some time, you big man," she murmured, "and we might fix one of your parties."

Again came the invitation direct and unmistakable: then she moved away as Sir Richard came up.

"Extraordinary, this case of poor Sanderson, isn't it?" he remarked. "I see they've got a lot of fresh evidence in the evening papers."

"And they'll have some more tomorrow," said Drummond, "when I've given mine."

"Yours!" echoed the surgeon, amazed. "Why, what do you know about it?"

"A lot, Sir Richard," answered Drummond quietly. "I was up there when it all happened."

"My dear fellow, you don't say so," cried the other. "Were you one of those four unknown men the butler talks about?"

"Sure," said Drummond. "There was a lot of fun and merriment last night, I assure you. And not content with murdering Sanderson, I'm damned if the blighters didn't drug the whisky in the rooms of a pal of mine who was also there. I know I drank some, and passed out till six o'clock this morning."

"Astounding," cried the surgeon. "And what took you up there in the first place, Captain Drummond?"

"Vulgar curiosity, Sir Richard," said Drummond quietly, "which is always reprehensible."

A footman was again bringing round a tray of drinks, and if Pendleton appreciated the snub he showed no sign of it as he took a glass.

"Was your pal also drugged?" he asked.

"I should imagine so. At any rate, he had disappeared when I recovered."

"Amazing: quite amazing. One doesn't expect to hear of things of that sort in England. I wonder who the miscreants are. Is this for me?"

The butler had come up to him with a letter on a salver.

"It's just been brought, Sir Richard," he said. "Urgent, the messenger said."

"Of such is a doctor's life," remarked Pendleton. "Will you excuse me?"

"Of course," said Drummond, moving away a little. How very sure the man was of his own safety, and of the efficacy of the drug in the whisky! And at that moment, happening to glance at the surgeon's face, he realised that the note contained news that had upset its recipient pretty considerably. Every drop of blood had left his face, and his teeth were bared into a snarl. Then in a second the mask was replaced, as he put the note in his pocket.

"No answer, thank you," he said, and the butler moved away.

"Not an urgent call for your professional services, I trust," said Drummond affably.

"No: not this time, fortunately," answered the surgeon.

His voice was completely normal: it was the look in his eyes that gave the show away. For they were fixed almost questioningly on the other's face, and Drummond knew, as surely as if he had read it, that the note referred to the Sanderson affair even if not to him personally.

"Fascinating job yours, Sir Richard," he remarked. "I've always envied people who can use their hands for such delicate work."

"There is a fascination in it," agreed the surgeon. "But we can't all be constructed alike. Your *métier*, for instance, I imagine is more of the sledge-hammer variety. To use a fishing metaphor, you would go after tarpon where I go after trout with a dry fly."

"Perhaps you're right," said Drummond. "Though, talking of fly fishing, I remember on one occasion going out with an expert. He was one of those merchants who could cast backwards and sideways between his legs, whereas when I wield a rod I generally connect with the next bloke's ear."

"And what was the result of your day?"

"I caught the fish."

"Beginner's luck?"

"Possibly: or perhaps the value of the unexpected. The crack of my line behind me so amazed the little fellows that they came to the surface to see what had happened, and I then stunned them with the fly."

"I fear you would not repeat the performance," remarked the surgeon.

"Once is sufficient for so many things in life, Sir Richard. The means of achieving one's end cease to be unexpected the second time."

"A philosopher, I perceive, Captain Drummond."

"In a mild way. But principally a believer in straightforward hitting as opposed to guile. I stunned my fish: the poor little thing couldn't believe I was such a fool as to throw a fly so badly. Whereas my wily companion was so full of cunning that he defeated his own ends."

"Almost might one think that you speak in metaphors," said Sir Richard softly.

"Good Lord! my dear chap," cried Drummond affably, "you flatter me. I'm not nearly clever enough for that. Ah! Miss Moxton, here's Sir Richard telling me that I'm a brainy fellah, whereas my strong point is pushing a bloke's face in."

The actress who had joined them smiled.

"I guess it's a very useful accomplishment, Captain Drummond," she drawled. "Some day you must let me see you do it. Don't forget that little party we're going to throw together."

"It is graven on my heart," said Drummond.

He bowed and went in search of his hostess.

"I trust young Henry has succeeded in keeping his lunch down," he murmured. "A wonderful party, my dear – but forgive me if I run away."

He lounged through the room, and Corinne Moxton's eyes followed him.

"If you don't fix that, Richard," she said quietly, "I'll never forgive you."

And had Drummond seen her face at that moment he would have known what that something was that was wrong. For it might have been used as a model for the quintessence of cruelty.

The expression faded and she looked at her companion sharply.

"Say – what's stung you? You've got a dial like an English Sunday."

"Standish has got away," he said briefly. "I've just had a note to say so. And with him was a big man dressed as a commercial traveller. A big man," he repeated thoughtfully, his eyes on the door by which Drummond had just left.

"You don't mean," she began.

He shrugged his shoulders.

"I mean that I would very much like to be able to read Captain Drummond's mind," he answered softly. "Very much indeed."

CHAPTER 5

Standish was half-way through his dinner when Drummond arrived at the Crown.

"I didn't wait for you, old boy," he cried as Drummond joined him, "because I began to feel deuced peckish. What luck?"

"It's the fair Corinne all right," said Drummond, after he had given his order to the waiter. "And what is more, she has extended to me the order of the glad eye. Why, I don't know, but she was very much come hither."

"Was Pendleton there?"

"He was. And I had a long talk to him. He struck me as being a nasty bit of work. He pointed me out to her just after they arrived."

Standish looked at him thoughtfully.

"He pointed you out, did he? And after that she got friendly."

"Mine hostess took me up specially to be introduced to the little dear."

"So that it is just possible," said Standish with a faint grin, "that the fact that she has apparently fallen for you might have some ulterior motive."

"Laddie," remarked Drummond gravely, "your intellect staggers me. And so in order to assist her I suggested a little party *à deux* at some future date."

"And you don't think that Pendleton has the slightest idea that we know about him."

"I don't think he can have; in fact, I'm convinced he hasn't. He may have nerve: he must have to be playing the game he is. But surely he couldn't have the unspeakable gall to have a long conversation with me in the middle of a large party if he thought I was wise to his movements last night. Oh no. He is absolutely confident in his own mind that we know nothing about him personally; but he is not so confident as to what we know about other things. He got a note while I was talking to him which upset him considerably. And it struck me that he began to look at me in quite a different way after he'd read it. I probably shouldn't have spotted it if I hadn't known about him, but that note concerned me or you or both of us."

Standish lit a cigarette, and was silent for a few moments: then he leaned across the table.

"Look here, old man, do you know what we *ought* to do?"

"Of course I do," said Drummond cheerfully. "Tell the police. Tell 'em I was lying when I said I was drugged last night; tell 'em all about Pendleton; put 'em wise to your doings this morning. But we ain't agwine to do it, boy."

"Why not?"

"Do you want little Willie to die of a broken heart? Do you want my last feebly breathed curses to ring in your ears through the long years to come?"

"You blithering ass," laughed Standish. And then he grew serious again. "You mustn't forget, old boy, that it's a question of murder."

"I don't," said Drummond. "But telling the police won't bring Sanderson back to life, and as far as finding the murderer is concerned, and other little points about our opponents, we are just as capable of functioning as old McIver."

"Confound you," said Standish with a grin, "it's all wrong. I admit quite freely that I'm of your way of thinking, but what's going to happen if we get scuppered tonight?"

"My dear old lad, it's all in the day's work. Must run the odd spot chance now and then."

"That's not quite the point. The devil of a lot of information is scuppered with us. And that really won't do."

"I get you, Steve," said Drummond thoughtfully. "And I quite agree with you. I've got an idea," he cried suddenly. "I'll go and 'phone Peter. He'll be mad as hell when he finds we're going without him, but that can't be helped."

"What are you going to say to him?"

"Tell him about Pendleton, and that we're going to do a bit of creeping in Sussex tonight. I'll tell him to stand by for a message, and say I'll use the word 'Cuckoo.' "

He glanced at Standish, and saw that he was weakening.

"Have a heart, old lad," he cried. "Peter gets the news and we get our spot of fun. So everybody's happy."

"Right-o!" said Standish resignedly. "We'll chance it."

"Stout fellah," cried Drummond. "Let's have a mug of port: then I'll ring up and we can push off. By the way, did you make anything out of that cipher?"

Standish shook his head.

"Nothing at all, beyond the obvious fact that the two keys are not the same."

"Do you think the one in the paper is from the same source as the other?"

"I should think it's more than likely. But it stands to reason that if they are using the newspapers as a means of communication at all frequently they are going to vary their code, otherwise any darned idiot can solve it. And now we'd better get a move on. There's no good our arriving there after they've all gone to bed. Always provided," he added, "there are any of them left to go to bed."

"You think they may have bolted?" said Drummond.

"I shouldn't be at all surprised. Whoever is running this show must know by now that those two beauties let us slip through their fingers this afternoon, and that we're at large. And their assumption would almost certainly be that the first thing we should do would be to go to the police."

"Perhaps you're right," said Drummond. "And yet I don't think that if I was the boss of the show I should bother to quit on what has happened up to date – police or no police."

Standish raised his eyebrows.

"Once granted that the Old Hall is their headquarters, which I am convinced it is, an official search of the house might prove a little awkward for them."

"And on what are you going to base your demand for an official search? The fact that you plugged two birds through the foot outside the lodge gate? The answer to that is, even if you get the warrant, that the owner hasn't the faintest idea what such a dastardly outrage has to do with him."

"We should find the two wounded men."

"Should we? Well, on that fact, old boy, I would definitely lay twenty to one against."

"And what about the six who came after me?"

"What about 'em? You have no proof that car-load came from the Old Hall. And, according to the owner, it most certainly did not. He again hasn't the faintest idea what you're talking about. Presumably some gentlemen out for a little early-morning bunny shooting were quite justifiably annoyed when they saw a man pinching their car, and proceeded to loose off a couple of barrels in an endeavour to frighten him. His line would be that though these dirty doings had happened to take place close to his house, he had no more to do with the matter than if they'd occurred in Northumberland. I'm going to get on to Peter."

He went through the smoking-room, and Standish lit a pipe. Viewed from that angle, he reflected, there was a good deal of horse sense in Drummond's remarks. Provided the men concerned, particularly Gulliver and Jackson, were not discovered, a flat denial on the part of the tenant of the Old Hall, that he was in any way mixed up in the affair, was perfectly feasible. And even if they were discovered he could always take up the line that the dictates of humanity demanded that when two wounded men were found outside his gates he should have them brought into the house.

"I've put old Peter wise to everything," said Drummond, joining him. "Told him where we're going, and all about Pendleton. I've also warned him to keep his mouth shut, unless we get done in. Now let's go and find the bus."

Standish glanced at his watch.

"Nine o'clock. With luck we'll be there by eleven. And we may as well take along that little toy we got this afternoon: there are still some rounds in it."

The night was fine with a few clouds scurrying across the sky. The moon was due to rise in an hour, and would be almost full, which was all to their advantage, as the drive up to the house was fringed with trees and undergrowth. Their plan was simple. They proposed to get off the car two or three hundred yards away from the main gate, and let Drummond's chauffeur take it on in the direction of Fastington. There were one or two by-lanes up which he could turn, and where he would be hidden from anyone passing along the main road. They would then scale the wall, and after that things would have to be left to chance.

Neither of them was under any delusions as to the risk they were running, and it was characteristic of them that the nearer they got the higher became their spirits. They were walking straight into the lion's den, and if anything went wrong their chances of coming out of that den alive were remote.

"We're nearly there," said Standish at length. "In fact, I think that's the wall in front of us."

Drummond pulled up, and handed the wheel over to his chauffeur.

"You know what to do, Mervyn," he said. "Go on straight past the lodge gates, and then wait for us. And you may have to wait quite a while," he added with a grin.

The road was deserted, and as the tail-lamp disappeared in the distance the two men approached the wall and examined it. It was about ten feet high, but fortunately there was no glass on the top, and in a moment Standish was on Drummond's shoulders and on top. He took a rapid look round: there was no one in sight. Then lying across it he held down his hands to Drummond, who joined him at once.

Some bushes lay beneath them, and they lowered themselves gently to the ground. Standish was carrying the rifle: Drummond's revolver was to hand in his pocket, and they started off steadily in the direction of the house. Fortunately the undergrowth was not thick, though blackberry brambles tore at their trousers. The moon was shining fitfully through the clouds that scudded by overhead: the trees were sighing and creaking in the wind. Otherwise all was silent.

Suddenly there came a sound which brought them both to a standstill. It was the deep-throated bay of a dog, and it was twice repeated. It came from in front of them and from some distance away.

"No Pomeranian did that," remarked Drummond thoughtfully. "And I didn't reckon on live stock, did you?"

"I did not," said Standish, "and it's a nuisance. If once the brute winds us it will give the show away, and we're to windward of it."

They went on a little more cautiously, and Drummond was now holding his revolver in his hand. The undergrowth was becoming thinner, though it still impeded their progress considerably. And then, but from very much closer at hand, the hound gave tongue once again.

They stood motionless, peering ahead. A small clearing lay in front of them, and they skirted round the edge, and took cover behind two trees. For something was moving twenty yards ahead. A cloud had obscured the moon, and it was impossible to see anything, but they could distinctly hear the sound of some animal crashing about in the undergrowth.

Suddenly the cloud cleared away, and the moonlight flooded the ground in front. And now they could see the movement in the bushes, though whatever it was that was there was still invisible.

"If it scents us," whispered Drummond, "you let drive first, old boy. That machine of yours is silent."

They waited, and now it seemed as if the brute opposite was waiting too. And then quite unexpectedly a huge mastiff came into the clearing and stood facing them, its head moving slowly from side to side. It was the size of a donkey, and Standish, the rifle cuddled to his cheek, steadied himself against a tree. It was not an animal it would be wise to miss the first time.

It lifted its head, and again the deep bay rang out into the night. Then it came towards them at a steady lope: it had spotted them.

"Now," muttered Drummond, and from beside him came a sharp hiss.

The hound paused for a second, only to come forward two or three steps. Then it paused again, and this time its legs slowly gave from under it. It collapsed in the centre of the clearing, and they watched it twitching convulsively: then it lay still.

"Shooting," said Drummond tersely. "A pity, too, because it is a fine dog."

They approached it cautiously, but it was quite dead.

"One I'd sooner have as my own than meet as somebody else's," said Standish. "But what I'm just wondering is what was causing all the excitement in the undergrowth there. It hadn't got wind of us then."

They plunged into the bushes, and it was Standish who spotted it first. Lying half concealed was the body of a man, and his throat had been completely torn out.

"Good Lord! it's Gulliver," cried Drummond. "Poor devil! What a death."

But Standish was looking at him queerly.

"I didn't see any blood on that mastiff's muzzle," he said.

Drummond stared at him.

"By Jove! you're right. There was no blood on him. What do you make of it?"

"If that wound had just been inflicted blood would still be flowing."

"It may have been returning to its kill," said Drummond.

"Gulliver was never killed here," said Standish decidedly. "There would have been far more blood on the ground. As you see, there is practically none. The thing was done somewhere else and the body carried here."

"And the hound found it again."

For a moment or two Standish stood frowning thoughtfully: then switching on his torch he again bent over the body.

"My God! Look at his eye," he cried suddenly. "The same wound as Sanderson's.

"So it wasn't the mastiff at all," he went on slowly.

"How do you mean, it wasn't the mastiff?"

"That tore his throat out."

"How do you know?"

"Because no one unless he was crazy would have shot him in the eye after he was dead. Therefore he was shot first."

"Granted," said Drummond. "But what of it?"

"This," said Standish. "No hound would ever touch a dead man."

"By Jove! you're right," cried Drummond. "I hadn't thought of that. Then if it wasn't the hound – what was it that went for his throat?"

"Exactly. What was it?"

"Queer doings," said Drummond thoughtfully. "What do you make of it?"

"Supposing that mastiff hadn't found this body and given tongue, do you think we should have found it either? The chances are a thousand to one against. It might have lain here for days undiscovered, and by that time it would have been almost unrecognisable. And when in the course of time someone did stumble on it the whole thing could then be put down to the hound: in other words, a ghastly accident. What is it?"

For Drummond had suddenly gripped his arm.

"I heard footsteps," muttered the other. "Quick – let's move from here."

Like a shadow he vanished, and Standish who followed had only an occasional glimpse of him as he dodged through the bushes with the uncanny silence of a cat.

"See and not be seen," breathed Drummond as Standish joined him. "That's the motto at present."

"It's about here," came a voice from the direction of the spot they had just left. "And mind that damned dog. He's queer – even with me. Brutus! Brutus! My God! Look there."

Two men came out into the clearing, and going over to the mastiff bent over it.

"He's dead! Shot!"

"Who by?" cried the other fearfully. "Here – this ain't no place for us. Hook it."

The speaker darted back under cover, followed more slowly by the other, and as the sound of their footsteps died away Drummond laughed.

"Wind slightly vertical," he remarked.

"Agreed," said Standish, "but it's a nuisance. They're hardly likely to keep the news to themselves. So if we're going to have a closer look at the house, old boy, we'd better get a move on."

"Spoken bravely, Horatio," cried Drummond. "Up and at it."

They pushed forward rapidly in the direction taken by the two men, indifferent as to whether they were heard or not. In a few minutes the inmates of the house would be bound to know that someone was in the grounds, so the vital need for secrecy was over. All that mattered now was that they should not actually be seen: the gun Standish carried was probably not the only one of its kind.

After about two hundred yards the undergrowth began to get thinner, and they slacked up a little. And a moment or two later they saw the outlines of the house in front of them. It was a large one, and to all outward appearances its occupants had blameless consciences. Two of the downstair rooms were brilliantly illuminated, and through the open front door light streamed out on to a big limousine standing in the drive.

For a while they crouched down watching. A man in evening clothes came to one of the windows and leaned out, and shortly after two others joined him. A weather conference evidently, for the first held out his hand to decide whether by chance it was raining, and then they all withdrew.

"Too far off to see their faces, blast it," said Standish. "Hullo! There they are in the hall."

The chauffeur had got down and was holding the door of the car open, whilst the butler helped two of them into their overcoats. And then for a space the three of them remained in earnest conversation just inside the front door.

"If we move a bit over to the left we might get a glimpse of the two who are going," said Drummond. "The inside of the car is lighted, and they may keep it so."

They skirted cautiously round the edge of the undergrowth until they were only a few yards from the drive. And they had barely taken up their position when the scrunch of wheels on the gravel announced that the car had started. They cowered down as the headlights swung round and passed over them: they peered eagerly out as the car came level.

Luckily the light in the back was still on, and they got a clear view of the two occupants. The one nearest them had a small pointed beard and was smoking a cigarette: his companion, a long, hatchet-faced man, had an unlighted cigar between his lips. And Standish, after one silent whistle of amazement, ejaculated – "Well, I'm damned."

"Who are they?" said Drummond curiously.

"The little man nearest us was Monsieur Julian Legrange, who occupies an almost unique position in French politics. He holds no portfolio, but his influence is enormous. Also, as one might expect, his knowledge of inside information is equally great. The other one is an Irish-American millionaire by the name of Daly – Jim Daly."

"What the devil are two men like that doing in this outfit?"

"I can't tell you, old boy. Though methinks the mystery of Sanderson's death is becoming a little clearer."

"But they couldn't be mixed up in that, surely?"

"Not directly, of course, though there is precious little Jim Daly would stick at if his pocket benefited, and he loathes England like poison. No, what I meant was that the political side of the matter is beginning to manifest itself."

"In the shape of the Frenchman?"

"In the shape of both. I grow more and more anxious to see their late host, for I'm thinking he must be an interesting individual. A man of many parts, who can entertain for dinner one of the most sought-after men in Europe, and at the same time carry on with the odd murder or two. I'm glad we came, old boy: a development such as that is the last I expected."

"Look at the house," said Drummond suddenly. "There are our two beauties running round in circles in the hall and telling the proud owner the worst about the little dog."

The two men were plainly visible talking agitatedly to a third whose shadow only could be seen. And the effect was rapid. The front door was shut, and the blinds were drawn down in the rooms, though the light still filtered out.

"Damn!" muttered Standish. "But we've got to see the gentleman somehow."

"And we will, old lad: at least I will. You can't."

"What are you getting at?" said Standish.

"Too many people in that house know you by sight," answered Drummond. "There are the birds that chivvied you this morning, to say nothing of the two this afternoon who may be there, when I luckily was disguised. None of 'em know me, so it's money for jam."

"But what do you propose to do?"

"Leave it to me, boy," said Drummond, grinning gently. "It's just the sort of show that Mother trained me for."

"It's madness, Drummond," said Standish uneasily.

"Madness your foot," remarked Drummond. "If there's anything at all in the visit of those two guys who have just left, it's something big and not too healthy. Now, there's no good kidding ourselves that the big noise in there is going to put his head out of the window if we go and sing a duet on the lawn. Therefore if we're going to do anything about recognising him when we next meet him it's got to be done and done quick. You can't help for reasons already stated: so I'll function. And for the purposes of this entertainment you aren't here at all: I'm alone. So stay put, laddie, till I join you."

He dodged on to the drive, and then without any attempt at concealment walked straight up to the front door and rang the bell loudly. That he was running a grave risk he knew, but trifles of that sort were not in the habit of deterring Hugh Drummond. And it seemed to him imperative that at any rate one person on their side should be able to recognise the opposing principal by sight.

After a considerable delay, during which he thought he could hear voices muttering on the other side of the door, it was flung open by a butler whose evening clothes left nothing to be desired – in fact, a man who looked a gentleman's servant.

"Yes, sir?" he remarked coldly.

"There has been a spot of trouble," said Drummond, "and I would like to see the owner of the house for a moment."

"At this hour, sir?" said the butler, even more coldly.

"Naturally," remarked Drummond genially. "Since I wish to see him now, it follows that I wish to see him at this hour. Does my reasoning seem faulty to you?"

"My master is not in the habit of receiving strangers without a previous appointment at this or any other hour, sir," answered the butler.

"And I am not in the habit of being made to run for my life by wild beasts," said Drummond curtly. "Nor am I in the habit of standing on the doorstep chatting of this and that with butlers. So get a move on, my lad, unless you want a belt in the jaw that will keep you on bread and milk for the next week. Tell your master that Mr Atkinson wants to see him, and that if, by chance, he does not want to see Mr Atkinson, the said Mr Atkinson will return in an hour or two with several members of the Sussex constabulary."

For a moment or two the butler hesitated, and then seeing that Drummond had already pushed past him and was glancing round at the heads that lined the walls, he closed the front door.

"Kindly wait here," he said.

"I intend to," answered Drummond, still studying the trophies. "Get a move on."

He heard a door open and shut behind him, and took a quick look round. From a room on the other side came the sound of voices, but except for that the house was silent. A big staircase occupied half one end of the hall: a door beside it led evidently to the kitchen quarters. Over the fireplace, in which some logs were blazing, hung a large oil painting of a man dressed in clothes of the Stuart period, and in the centre a big bronze bowl filled with ferns stood on a refectory table. In short, the whole atmosphere of the place was what one would expect in an ordinary English country house.

At length a door opposite opened and the butler reappeared.

"Will you come this way, sir," he remarked. "Mr Demonico will receive you."

The room into which he was ushered was in striking contrast to the hall. The heavy scent of hot-house flowers filled the air, and the heat was stifling. Moreover, the whole furnishing scheme was the very last one would have expected to find after what had gone before, especially in a room belonging to a man. Heavy brocades adorned the walls: glass cabinets containing enamel and other *objets d'art* stood in the corners, and on a table in the middle was a beautiful cut-glass bowl containing potpourri.

Seated in a chair on the other side of a roaring fire was a strange-looking individual, whose first and most dominant characteristic was his almost incredible baldness. He seemed to consist of a brightly polished white dome to which a body was attached as an afterthought. His eyes were concealed by dark glasses: he was clean shaven. But once over the hurdle of that hairless head it was the man's hands that attracted one's attention. Long and clawlike, the nails were manicured like those of a woman to the extent of being varnished pink, and on the third finger of each a magnificent ring glistened in the soft light.

For a few seconds Drummond stared at him fascinated. The butler had withdrawn: he was alone with this incredible apparition. And then he pulled himself together: Mr Demonico was speaking.

"I am at a loss to understand this intrusion, Mr – ah – Mr Atkinson," he said, "but my man tells me that you forced your way in after making some rambling remarks about the police. May I ask you to state your business with the utmost expedition, as your presence here offends me intensely."

His voice was soft and melodious, but in it there lay a note of deadly menace.

"Sorry about that, Mr – ah – Mr – sorry, but the old footman wilted a bit over the introduction, didn't he? However, my business is to speak to you in honeyed accents about your live stock. Are you aware that but for some fine agility on my part I shouldn't be here."

"Then I wish to God you were not quite so agile," remarked his host languidly.

"Not good, laddie," sighed Drummond. "I hoped for better things from you than taking such an obvious opening. To resume. Are you aware that I've been chased all over your confounded grounds by an animal that looked the size of an elephant?"

"May I ask what you were doing in my grounds at all?"

"Certainly; certainly. No secrets shall mar our friendship. Motoring along the road, carefree and with song bursting occasionally from a heart full of *joie de vivre*, there came an ominous spluttering: a pop or two: then silence. I realised I was out of juice. Now I had recently passed your place, and so I decided to walk back and see if perchance I could borrow sufficient petrol from you to get me to my destination, my dear old aunt's house near Pulborough. Still yodelling merrily I made my way up the drive, when to my horror a large animal which, as I say, seemed to me the size of an elephant, barred my path and began to yodel also. Moreover, it didn't seem a friendly yodel to me. And so, though I blush to admit it, I deserted the drive and plunged into the bushes, uttering shishing noises to tell it not to come too. Will you believe it, Mr – ah – Mr – well the same as before – that that stupid animal didn't understand my shishes: it followed me in a most tactless manner. Further, it ran much faster than I did, and it suddenly dawned on me that I had a revolver in my pocket. I drew it, and to cut a long story short, I regret to have to tell you that the elephant is defunct."

"How lucky for you," murmured Mr Demonico. "May I ask if you usually carry a revolver when visiting your dear old aunt near Pulborough?"

"Invariably," said Drummond. "She's deuced queer-tempered in the morning. She bit the butcher in the leg the other day."

"For heaven's sake spare me your childish attempts at humour," remarked the other, "and try to concentrate on one thing. What is your object in inflicting this tissue of lies on me?"

"Lies be damned," cried Drummond. "If you send out you'll find that that mastiff of yours doesn't think it a lie, and I wish to protest most strongly against such a dangerous brute being allowed to wander loose. If I hadn't been armed it might have killed me."

"An eventuality I could have contemplated with perfect equanimity," said Mr Demonico. "You have, however, not answered my question. What is your object in inflicting this tissue of lies on me? I do not allude to the death of the dog, of which I had already heard, but to the rest of the rigmarole."

He lit a cigarette from a small enamel box on a table beside his chair, and blew out a cloud of smoke.

"You see, Mr Atkinson," he continued, "your story crashes on one vital point. No one is allowed to pass my lodge gates under any pretext whatever without previous permission being given by me over the telephone. Therefore you must have climbed the wall. So will you be good enough to inform me, and at once, how you dared to be trespassing in my grounds at this hour of the night."

His voice had sunk to a whisper: his head was thrown a little forward, and the hand clasping his left knee seemed more talon-like than ever. And Drummond, watching him thoughtfully, realised that there was no good in prolonging the interview. His bluff had been called, but it had succeeded in so far as it had enabled him to do what he wanted – to see the man now sitting opposite him.

He rose, and lit a cigarette also.

"I fear your lodge-keeper must have been napping for once," he remarked. "Why on earth should I bother to climb your bally wall? However, since the dog is dead and did me no harm, I am prepared to overlook the illegality of your having such a dangerous brute loose without warning possible callers. But the least you can do is to ante up a tin of petrol."

He stiffened suddenly: from outside had come a shout for help. And it seemed to him that it had been the voice of Ronald Standish.

"Dear me," said the man by the fire softly. "Can it be that other people are visiting their old aunts at Pulborough?"

Without another word Drummond crossed to the door: if it was Standish who had called out, rapidity of action would be necessary. And the door was locked.

He looked at Mr Demonico, still motionless in his chair, and saw that an evil smile was twitching round his lips.

"Do you want me to break this door down?" he asked quietly.

"If you can, my friend, do so by all means. You appear to me to be a large individual. But I fear you may find, as others have done before you, that it is easier for the fly to get into the spider's web than it is for it to get out."

Drummond took a run and charged the woodwork with his shoulder, only to realise at once that it was hopeless. This was no ordinary door, but one that had been specially fitted, and he might as well have charged the wall itself.

"The window will serve equally well," he remarked, going over and pulling the curtains. And this time the man in the chair chuckled.

"So that's the game, is it?" said Drummond, as he looked at the steel shutter that stretched from floor to ceiling. "Well, laddie, what's the great idea? Do we sit here all night?"

"We sit here," snarled the other, "for exactly as long as I choose."

"And what happens if I wring your darned neck?" asked Drummond pleasantly.

"We sit here," repeated Mr Demonico, as if Drummond had not spoken, "until I satisfy myself as to who you are, and what you were doing outside there tonight."

A whistle sounded beside his chair, and he picked up a speaking-tube. And as Drummond watched him listening to the message, he saw his face change and realised instinctively that there was danger. But he said nothing, and having replaced the tube he pressed a button on the arm of his chair, and a moment later there came a clang in the wall. A small metal grille opened, through which Drummond could see two eyes looking into the room. The man in the chair gave a rapid order in a language which Drummond could not understand, and which to the best of his belief he had never heard before, and the grille closed again.

And now Drummond was doing some pretty quick thinking: if somehow or other they had caught Standish, the situation was undeniably serious. There was no hope of any outside help till the next morning, since there was little chance of Peter arriving earlier; until then they would have to rely entirely on themselves. And the devil of it was they were separated. Further, for all he knew Standish might have been knocked out, in which case everything depended on him.

The first thought that automatically came into his mind was that he was alone with Demonico and he had a gun in his pocket. Even without the revolver the man in the chair would be a child in his hands, and the possibility of using that fact as an asset for bargaining struck him immediately. Instinctively his hand went towards his pocket and Demonico laughed.

"You pain me, Mr Atkinson," he said. "I really wouldn't if I were you. Surely you cannot be such a complete imbecile as to imagine that I should have remained in here alone with you all this time without taking a few rudimentary precautions against such an action on your part. You have been covered by two of my men ever since you came into this room, and if you look carefully round the walls you will see where they are. The grille that opened is not the only one, believe me."

Drummond's hand fell to his side; he knew without bothering to confirm it that Demonico was speaking the truth.

"This is beginning to bore me," he drawled. "And the stink in this room is something grim. What is the next item in the programme?"

"One that I trust will not bore you, Mr Atkinson. In fact, I think I can guarantee that it won't."

"That's good," said Drummond. "Up to date this performance would have been given the bird by an audience of deaf mutes. I come here to ask for the loan of some petrol, and because I have the common civility to tell you about the death of your hound, you keep me here as a virtual prisoner."

"Virtual is a good word," remarked the other with a faint smile. "However, it won't be for long now."

Drummond stared at him.

"Before what?" he said.

"Before you get your tin of petrol, and resume your interrupted journey to your dear old aunt," answered Demonico pleasantly. "You see, Mr Atkinson, I am a great recluse, and I have to take precautions against strangers invading my privacy."

He rose and walked to a desk in the corner of the room, and once again Drummond's hand stole towards his pocket. Then he checked the impulse: what was the use? That Demonico was lying he was certain, but as things were, he was at a hopeless disadvantage. A glance round the room had shown him one of the two open grilles, with the muzzle of a gun fixed on him unwaveringly. He was a sitting target without a chance of escape.

If only he knew about Standish: it was that that was worrying him. Had that cry come from him? Had they got him somehow? If they had, someone in the house would almost certainly have recognised him. And if Standish had been spotted, did Demonico know that Atkinson was a false name? Did Demonico know that he was Drummond, and therefore mixed up in the whole affair?

The whistle in the speaking-tube sounded again, and Demonico crossed to it.

"Splendid," he said, as the voice finished. "Well, Mr Atkinson," he continued, replacing the tube, "your tin of petrol is all ready for you. I have thoroughly enjoyed your little visit, and I can assure you that there is no companion to poor Brutus to annoy you on your return journey. So that being the case, there will be no necessity for you to be armed. I must therefore request you to remove the revolver from your pocket and place it on the table beside you."

"Why the devil should I?" cried Drummond. "It's my gun."

"And it will be returned to you at the lodge gates by one of my servants," said the other gravely. "To be quite frank, Mr Atkinson, you seem to me to be a very excitable young man, and I have a rooted objection to excitable young men with revolvers."

"And what if I refuse?"

"Then it will be taken from you and not returned at the lodge gates. May I beg to remind you that you are still covered from two directions, so that even the great strength you so obviously possess will avail you but little. And one other point. When you take it out of your pocket hold it by the muzzle."

For a moment or two Drummond hesitated. He was convinced now that it was a trap, but what was he to do? He did not even know where the second grille was, so that the hope of getting a couple of shots through the two of them was not only forlorn but impossible.

"I trust you will not exhaust my patience, Mr Atkinson," continued Demonico. "I give you ten seconds to do as I tell you: after that you will be used as a target. My men are only awaiting my order."

"It's a most monstrous thing," cried Drummond with well-feigned indignation. "And I shall certainly complain to the police about it."

He threw the revolver on the table, and the other picked it up.

"Certainly," said Demonico smoothly. "I would if I were you. Though you may find it a little difficult to explain to them why you wished to shoot your aunt."

He paused suddenly, and stood listening: a car was coming up the drive. It stopped outside the front door, and into Drummond's mind there leaped a wild hope that it might be Peter. Demonico was frowning: evidently he was puzzled himself as to who was the late caller. And when the speaking-tube whistled again he picked it up quickly.

"Who?" he cried. "At this hour?"

And then a slow smile spread over his face.

"Ask them to wait in the drawing-room," he said.

He turned to Drummond with the smile still on his lips.

"The calls of business, Mr Atkinson, are indeed exacting. However, you would doubtless like to have your tin of petrol and resume your journey. Good night: you will have no difficulty with the door this time."

"What about my gun?" demanded Drummond.

"It shall be handed to you as I promised at the lodge gates. Good night."

He resumed his chair, and Drummond walked to the door. It was no longer locked, and he walked into the hall, which was empty save for a man by the front door. And he was at once acutely aware of one thing: someone using scent had just been there – the perfume still hung in the air.

"This way, if you please, sir," said a voice in his ear, and he turned to find the butler beside him. "The petrol is in the garage."

Should he bolt for it? A glance at the man near the door revealed an unmistakable bulge in his coat pocket: he had *not* been disarmed. And what about Standish? He must find out about him.

With eyes that took in every detail he examined the place as he followed the butler. Everything seemed normal, but with that uncanny sixth sense of his he knew that it was not. He knew that he was being watched by hidden eyes: he knew the house was alive with men. But no sign of that knowledge showed in his face: not for nothing was he known as one of the best poker players in London.

And now an intense curiosity was beginning to possess him: what was going to happen? That they were going to present him with a tin of petrol and let him go was inconceivable: if that had been the case Demonico would not have troubled to relieve him of his revolver.

They were now in a long passage with a door at the farther end. There were no windows, and it seemed to Drummond that it was a covered communication way between the house and some outbuilding. Could it be the garage? Could it be that, after all, he was wrong, and they were going to let him go?

The butler flung open the door, and he found himself in a room one side of which was occupied by a flight of wooden stairs. There was no light save that which filtered in from the passage they had come along, but by that he saw another door in front of him the whole appearance of which seemed very familiar. Again the butler opened it: there on the floor just beyond was a tin of petrol.

"There you are, sir," said the man, standing aside, and Drummond stepping forward picked it up. And even as he did so the second door clanged behind him and he found himself in darkness.

He stood for a moment cursing himself for a fool: then reaching out his hand encountered a smooth cold wall. He ran his fingers along it to find the door: all they met was a barely perceptible crack in the shiny surface. And he suddenly remembered his torch.

He switched it on, letting the beam travel round. And the first thing it picked up was a slanting red line above his head on one of the side walls; then the countersunk door he had just come in by. He was in a squash court: the wooden steps outside led to the gallery, and that was why it had all seemed so familiar.

He tried the door at once, but as he expected it had been bolted on the other side. And once again he began to do some rapid thinking. Escape was impossible: he could not reach the gallery with his hands even by jumping.

He took a step backwards, and nearly fell over the petrol tin, which he picked up and put against the wall. Then still trying to puzzle things out he commenced to walk about. Why had they taken the trouble to put him in a squash court? Was it just a prison, or was there some deeper motive?

There was no overhead glass, but at the back of the gallery he could see the faint outline of two windows. There lay a way out if only he could get there – a way out which short-circuited the passage back to the house. And then another idea struck him. Using his torch he went carefully round the four walls to find out if by chance there was another entrance. But there was no sign of one: the court was a genuine one, untampered with in any way.

Suddenly he stiffened and switched out his torch: someone was going up the wooden staircase that led to the gallery. He listened intently: more than one person was there. He backed into the centre of the court, his eyes fixed on the window across which whoever it was would have to pass. He counted three dim shadows: then came the sound of a chair being moved: the audience had arrived.

There was no doubt about it now: the court was not merely a prison. Something was going to happen which the three spectators had come to watch. And even as he arrived at that conclusion he got a whiff of the same scent that he had noticed in the hall. A woman was up there in the gallery – the woman who had just arrived by car. Could it be Corinne Moxton with Pendleton?

He stood undecided: should he call out to them and ask what the devil the game was? Or should he switch his torch on and endeavour to see them? And he was still trying to make up his mind when suddenly the court was flooded with light. But it was not the ordinary lighting which comes from the roof and illuminates the floor and the gallery equally. A powerful arc lamp had been fitted at the top of the back wall in the centre, with the result that the gallery behind it was in impenetrable darkness as far as he was concerned. Of the three spectators he could see no trace, though he knew they were there behind the light.

A pulse was beginning to beat in his throat, and he was white round the nostrils. Seldom in his life had Hugh Drummond been in the grip of such overmastering rage. His great hands hung clenched by his sides: his breathing had quickened. Was somebody going to plug him like that, a sitting target? Or what was going to happen? And the next instant he knew it was not the former. For the door in the back wall underneath the arc lamp was being slowly opened.

CHAPTER 6

The sight steadied him: if there was going to be a gladiatorial exhibition, the audience should have their money's worth. And it would not be his fault if the result proved different to what they expected. The door was still opening, but as yet he could not see who was outside. And it struck him that his present position was strategically unsound. In an instant he was across the court and standing by the door, so that when it was fully open it would be between him and whoever was coming in. At any rate they would start fair.

A board close to him creaked slightly, and he saw the shadow of a head just beyond the edge of the door which was now at right angles to the back wall. And at that moment came Demonico's voice from the gallery.

"Well, Mr Atkinson Drummond, let's see if you prefer this to the dog."

So he *did* know: that point was settled anyway.

"I'm sure I shall, you bald-headed old swine," said Drummond cheerfully, at the same time dodging back a couple of yards.

It was a sound move: thinking he had located Drummond the maker of the shadow was round the door like a flash. And for a second Drummond stared at his adversary aghast. He was a gigantic individual with the coarsened, vicious features of a low-down professional pug. But it was not at his face Drummond was looking, nor at the great torso and shoulders; it was at his hands. Encasing each of them was a canvas glove from which steel spikes stuck out front and back. The spikes were about an inch long and sharp-pointed, and after that one momentary pause Drummond moved, and moved quickly. The best method of dealing with this gentleman would have to be thought out, and until he had made up his mind anything in the nature of close quarters must be avoided.

The man had slammed the door, and with an ugly leer on his face he made a dash at Drummond, who quietly dodged. His brain was working at top pressure sizing up the situation. This must be the method by which Gulliver's throat had been torn out after he was dead, and he had no intention of letting the brute experiment on a living specimen. But he was under no delusions: once get to close grips and he was done for. The man was, if anything, longer in the reach than he: the instant those diabolical gloves were round his throat it was the finish.

Outfighting, too, was out of the question: one back-hander to his head that got home would lay him out. And still he dodged easily and methodically, keeping in the centre of the court, while Demonico's sneering remarks from the gallery kept up a running accompaniment. A gladiatorial exhibition it was, with a woman as a spectator! And as the amazing unreality of it struck him one of the gloves whistled past his face, missing him by the fraction of an inch.

He pulled himself together as Demonico laughed: that would not do. The devil of it was that the man, in spite of his low type, was almost, if not quite, as fit as he was, and the thing could not go on indefinitely. Besides, all his opponent had to do if he wanted a rest was to go and stand by the door for as long as he pleased.

The door! Was there a chance of opening it and getting out? It meant putting himself in a hopelessly unfavourable position for at least a second while he tried it to see if it was bolted. And once again a glove flashed past his face, grazing his cheek and drawing blood.

The blow roused him to fury, but it was the cool collected rage of the born fighter. He did nothing rash, which would have been playing straight into the other man's hands, but it made up his mind for him. He would take the offensive. And the first idea that came to him was the ordinary Rugby tackle. He knew he could bring the other down that way, but what then? Unless the man happened to be stunned by the fall, it would mean close fighting on the ground, which was every bit as dangerous as if they were standing.

And then suddenly his eyes fell on a small dark object against the wall – the tin of petrol. He had forgotten about it, and it dawned on him that there lay the germ of a plan. Still feinting and dodging he thought it out, and at last he got it cut and dried. A risk – but something had got to be done.

Little by little he began to breathe faster, and he saw a look of triumph gleam on the other's face.

"Getting tired, Pansy face," grunted the other. "Best give it up and come and take your medicine."

He did not answer: his knees seemed to sag a little; but every step took him nearer the door.

"He's going to try and bolt," yelled Demonico, and the man grinned sardonically. But no trace of expression showed on Drummond's face, though it was exactly what he wanted them to believe.

Out of the corner of his eye he was measuring his exact position: it was going to be a question of the fraction of a second. He was gasping now, and after each move he swayed a little.

At last he got to the spot he intended – half-way between the door and the tin and about a yard from the wall. And then he feinted in earnest. He made as if to spring for the door, and in the same movement went the other way. Completely deceived, the man, thinking he had him, sprang too. And Drummond had the tin by the handle, while the other, half off his balance, fell against the door. Came a grunt of rage: the tin was whirled round Drummond's head, as if it was a feather, catching his opponent fair and square on the nape of the neck. And without a sound the man crashed like a log to the floor and lay still.

Drummond seized him by the legs and swung him clear of the door: to get at Demonico was his only thought. But that gentleman had waited not on the order of his going: by half a second he had managed to get the bolt shot home on the other side of the door. And Drummond cursed savagely, but only for a moment. For though this method of finishing him off had failed, he was still a sitting target to anyone in the gallery.

Taking the unconscious man again by the feet he dragged him into one of the far corners of the court. He took off the spiked gloves and flung them away. Then if necessary he could lift the man up and hold him in front of his own body as a shield. It would be a tiring proceeding, but there was no other possible method that he could see of getting any cover, and even that would be totally inadequate if they sent an armed man into the court itself.

He stood listening intently: it was inconceivable that Demonico would allow him to get away with it. But the minutes passed and there was no sign of anyone. And then suddenly from far away in the distance he heard the faint sound of shouting. He took a few steps forward: the noise was increasing. And to his amazement he recognised Peter's voice, bellowing "Hugh" at the top of his lungs.

"Peter," he roared, "I'm in the squash court."

"Coming, old boy. Where's the blinking door?"

He was just outside and Drummond heaved a sigh of relief: the last half-hour had been a bit of a strain.

"The only way in is through the house," he shouted, "unless you break the window in the gallery."

"Right," came the answer. "With you in a moment."

Drummond heard voices outside, some of which he recognised: Algy Longworth's inane drawl; Ted Jerningham; Toby Sinclair. Peter had arrived with the old bunch, but why he had so providentially done so was beyond him. And where were all Demonico's men?

"Get on my shoulders, you blithering ass," came Peter's voice. "And don't put your dirty foot in my mouth."

"All right; all right," bleated Algy. "But I'm not a ruddy Blondin."

There was a crash of breaking glass, and Algy's voice again.

"I've been and gone and cut my new suiting. Hugh, old boy, be of good heart; little Algy is coming."

"Hurry up, you ghastly mess," shouted Drummond.

"Where's the door?" cried Algy, scrambling into the gallery.

"Where it usually is in a squash court," said Drummond resignedly. "You don't imagine it's in the roof, do you? By Jove! Algy," he added a moment later as Algy came into the court, "I never thought I should be glad to see you, but I am. What on earth gave you the brain-wave to come?"

"Peter will tell you," answered the other. "What's that in the corner?"

"Little Willie," said Drummond grimly. "And I think he's going to die. Anyway, we'll lock him in, so that he can do it in peace. Now we've got to move."

He bolted the door, and raced up the stairs to the gallery, followed by Longworth.

"Explanations can wait, chaps," he cried, as he landed on the ground outside, "though I'm damned glad to see you all. Follow me: we're going through this house with a fine-tooth comb."

He led the way round to the front door, with the others after him. And the first thing that struck him was that there was no car in the drive. So two members of his late audience had gone: what about Demonico?

The front door was bolted, but half a brick through a nearby window served equally well. And then in a body they poured into the house. The first room Drummond made for was Demonico's: it was empty. And it was then that Darrell spoke.

"Three of them – two men and a woman – bolted in a car just after we started to raise Cain," he remarked.

"Hell!" said Drummond. Clearly Demonico had got away too. But where were all the others? Room after room they went into: the house was empty. And at last they held a council of war in the hall.

"Got clear away – the whole bunch," muttered Drummond, "though the only three who matter are the ones in the car. The others have probably scattered in the grounds. My God!" he cried suddenly, "where's Standish? I'd forgotten about him."

"He's not in the house, anyway," said Darrell.

"Come on, boys," said Drummond, "though I'm afraid it's a forlorn hope. If he was all right he'd have joined us."

He made for the spot where he had left Standish: there was no one there. But the trampled-down bushes showed that a desperate struggle had taken place.

"They got him," cried Drummond savagely, "but what the devil have they done with him? Standish," he shouted, again and again, but there was no answer; and at last he gave it up.

"May Heaven help Mr Demonico when I get my hands on him," he said grimly. "All one can hope for is that the old lad's not dead. I heard him shout once, but I was in the house and couldn't get to him."

A sudden idea struck him.

"What sort of a car had they got?"

"Some sort of big American," said Jerningham. "And they were going all out down the drive."

"Any hope of catching 'em? They're bound to be making for London."

"Doubt it," said Darrell. "But we might have a chance, if we take your bus."

"It's down the road," cried Drummond. "Come on; let's hog it for home and Mother."

But the start was too great: no trace of the car they were after was seen. And as they drove into London Drummond slowed down.

"Tell me, Peter," he said, "what in the name of fortune brought you and all those warriors on the scene so providentially?"

"You'll see when you get to your house, old boy," answered Darrell, "provided she is still there."

Drummond whistled.

"She! We have a fairy in the place, then."

"And some fairy. I'll leave her to tell you the tale herself. But I'll explain the rest. About half an hour after I got your message from Epsom, your bloke Denny rang me up to say that a bird was on your doorstep asking for you urgently. So, knowing that you weren't available, I thought the best thing to do was to toddle round and interview her myself. She told me a long yarn, when she'd made certain that I was to be trusted, lots of which I couldn't make head or tail of. It mostly concerned Corinne Moxton, the film woman."

"Go on," said Drummond.

"I didn't know you even knew her," continued Darrell, "and I told this girl so. Her name, by the way, is Frensham – Daphne Frensham. However, she was very insistent about it all, and when she began talking about the Old Hall I thought it was time to sit up and take notice. So I roped in the lads and came down."

"Good for you, Peter. And I don't mind telling you, old lad, there is every indication of rare and refreshing times ahead. You told this wench to stop on at my place, did you?"

"That's the notion. As a matter of fact she seemed frightened to death. But she'll put you wise herself, and it's better for you to hear it first hand."

Drummond pulled up outside his front door, and told his chauffeur to take the car to the garage.

"Who have we got behind?" he demanded. "Great heavens! it's Algy. Life today has been one thing after another. However, since he's here I suppose he'd better come in."

"And this from the man whose miserable life I have just saved." Longworth got out of the car with dignity. "But I have no objection to sinking a pint."

Drummond produced his latch-key, but before he could use it the door was opened by his man.

"All well, Denny?"

"Yes, sir. The young lady seems quite comfortable."

"Good: lead me to her."

"There is one thing, sir. About half an hour ago a telephone message came through for you from someone who would not give his name. The message was this. OK Cuckoo."

Drummond stared at him for a moment in bewilderment: then light dawned on him.

"By Jove! Peter," he cried, rubbing his hands together, "that must be Standish. Can't be anybody else. I told him at Epsom that I'd arranged to use the word 'Cuckoo' with you as a proof that any message was genuine, and no one else but him could possibly know. Was it a trunk call, Denny?"

"I couldn't say, sir," said his servant. "The gentleman just asked who I was, gave that message, and then rang off."

"Splendid," said Drummond. "We'll larn these birds a thing or two before we're through with them. Now then – where is the lady?"

"In the study, sir. I have given her some sandwiches."

Drummond flung open the door. Seated in an armchair by the fire, fast asleep, was an extremely pretty girl. Her cheeks were flushed, and a mop of dark curls ran riot above a small, perfect face. She had taken off her hat which lay on the floor, and two silk-shod legs were tucked away underneath her in that mysterious attitude beloved of the female sex. The noise awoke her, and when she saw a complete stranger, for a moment fear shone in her eyes. Then Darrell appeared, and with a little exclamation of embarrassment she sat up.

"Just like me," cried Drummond contritely, "to make a fool noise and wake you."

"I had no business to fall asleep," she said. "Is it all right, Mr Darrell?"

"This is Captain Drummond," said Darrell with a smile. "Miss Frensham, Hugh. And the half-wit with the eyeglass is Algy Longworth."

"Oh! I'm so glad," she cried. "When Mr Darrell told me that you'd actually gone to the Old Hall I was afraid it would be too late."

For a moment or two Drummond looked at her keenly. Most certainly, if appearances were anything to go by, this girl was all right. But he was moving in deep waters, and he was far too old a soldier to take any chances.

"From the little that Peter has told me, Miss Frensham," he said quietly, "I gather you know Corinne Moxton."

"Why not tell him everything just as you told me," suggested Darrell.

"It's all so muddled and confusing, Captain Drummond," she cried. "I hardly know where to begin. Sometimes I feel the whole thing is some ghastly nightmare. You see, when Miss Moxton advertised for a secretary-companion I applied for the post, and much to my surprise I got it. I was overjoyed: I've always admired her on the films, and I thought it was going to be the greatest fun. The salary was very good, and it looked the most wonderful opportunity. I even wondered if, through her influence, I might perhaps get a job on the films."

"Take it easy, Miss Frensham," said Drummond gently. "We've got plenty of time: the night is yet young."

"It's four o'clock," she said with a shaky little laugh. "Well, my first shock came when Miss Samuelson – she was my predecessor – came back to the flat one day. She had forgotten something when she packed and had returned to get it. Miss Moxton was out, and Miss Samuelson and I had a talk. I thought she was looking at me rather queerly, and at last I asked her if anything was the matter.

" 'You'll soon find out what's the matter,' she said. 'I'm surprised you haven't done so already.'

" 'What do you mean?' I cried in amazement.

" 'What do you think of my late and your present employer?' she said.

" 'I've only been here a few days,' I reminded her, 'and I really don't know. She seems very nice so far.'

" 'Nice,' cried Miss Samuelson. 'Nice. My dear! there is no fiend in hell who is quite so fiendish as that she-devil in some of her moods.'

"At the time I didn't believe her. As you know, Captain Drummond, jobs are not easy to come by, and I thought she was jealous of me having taken hers. But a few days later I had reason to change my mind. I was sitting doing some work for her when there suddenly came a yelp of pain from the room next door, followed by a pitiful sort of moaning. Now, she has two dogs: one is a Pekingese, and the other is a dreadful little beast of a type I loathe. I rushed in to find out what had happened: evidently one of them had hurt itself somehow.

"I found Miss Moxton sitting in a chair by the window with the Pekingese on her lap. The sun was shining into the room, and from under the bed there came a little whimpering noise.

" 'I thought I heard one of the dogs crying out,' I said.

"And as I spoke I glanced at her face. Captain Drummond, I find it almost impossible to describe to you what her expression was like. Moreover, I watched it change: watched the mask that conceals her real nature replace the truth. And what was the truth? It was something so horrible, so diabolical that I almost cried out. It was a mixture of gloating joy and vindictive cruelty: it was dreadful, terrible, utterly evil. But when she spoke her voice was quite normal.

" 'Poor little Toto,' she said. 'I wasn't thinking what I was doing, and quite accidentally I burnt him with this.'

"And I saw that she was holding one of those big magnifying glasses in her hand."

Daphne Frensham paused for a moment, but none of the three men spoke.

"I pulled the poor little brute out from under the bed," she continued, "and there, on his head, was a nasty burn.

" 'I'll put some butter on it,' I said, and took the dog out of the room.

"Now all this may sound very trivial to you, but the thing I am getting at is this. I am as certain as I can be about anything that it was not an accident at all. You know how difficult it is to focus the heat spot from one of those glasses accurately, and that even when it is in the right place it takes some little time before a bit of paper catches fire. And this was quite a deep burn. I am convinced that she held that dog in some way and deliberately burned it in order to gratify some beastly side of her nature. I am convinced that she has in her some abnormal streak which can only be satisfied by the infliction of cruelty to something or someone. I do hope I'm not boring you," said the girl anxiously.

"I have seldom been so interested in my life, Miss Frensham," said Drummond quietly. "Please go on."

"Well, that happened about a month ago," she continued. "I tried to get it out of my mind, and persuade myself I'd been mistaken. And I'd almost succeeded when another incident happened. I was in her room one morning before she got up, and she was going through her letters. Suddenly we heard a commotion in the street, and I looked out of the window. There had been an accident: some man working on the house opposite had slipped and fallen on the pavement. The poor fellow was writhing with pain, and there was blood all over the place. It was a sickening sight, and instinctively I called out – 'Don't look: don't look.'

"In a flash she was out of bed with her nose glued to the window. And there she remained watching greedily till an ambulance arrived and took the injured man away. And it wasn't just morbid curiosity: it was something more fundamental. She enjoyed every moment of it: it satisfied that vile side of her nature. Can you believe it possible, Captain Drummond, that there are people like that?"

"Quite easily," said Drummond gravely. "I don't profess to be up in such matters, but I gather it is a well-known fact that cases of a similar description are by no means rare. If a person is abnormal anything may happen: it's only when it gets too bad or is dangerous to others that they push the bloke off to an asylum."

"And you don't think I'm exaggerating?"

"Far from it," Drummond assured her. "In fact, things are becoming considerably clearer."

"You see," she went on without asking him what he meant, "what I want to do is to try to show you Corinne Moxton as she really is and not as her public believe her to be. Otherwise you would think I was mad when you hear what comes next."

"Fire right ahead," cried Drummond cheerfully. "Your sanity is above suspicion."

"You met her yesterday afternoon, didn't you."

It was not a question but a statement, and Drummond nodded.

"I did."

"And Sir Richard Pendleton was with her."

"He was," said Drummond.

"And further, you were mixed up in the Sanderson murder."

"As a spectator only, I assure you."

His voice was lazy, but now his eyes were fixed like gimlets on the girl.

"Yesterday evening," she continued, "she came back with Sir Richard to her flat after the cocktail party you met her at. There is a small sort of closet place that leads out of her drawing-room, and I'd fallen asleep. It's becoming a habit with me, I'm afraid," she added with a smile. "Anyway, they didn't know I was there, and the first remark I heard as I woke up so dumbfounded me that my legs literally seemed incapable of movement. Corinne Moxton was speaking.

" 'You bore me, Richard,' she said. 'He was the first man I've ever seen murdered, and I wouldn't have missed it for the world. And anyway, that's all over. What you've got to concentrate your young life on is that big boy Drummond. I'm just crazy to see that guy up against it.' "

"Mother-love sure oozes from her," said Drummond with a grin. "And what did our Richard answer to that?"

" 'I'll fix that for you,' he said, 'but for God's sake, Corinne, be careful. Sanderson had to go, but don't forget bumping off isn't as easy in this country as it is in yours. And his death is going to raise hell all round.'

" 'Cut it out,' she cried contemptuously. 'His house is burned down: what shadow of evidence have they got? No, Richard, your life's work is Drummond. I'm not interested in the rest of your schemes, but that great stiff has me tickled to death. He's got to be put on the spot, and I've got to see it done.'

" 'He'll give us a run for our money, I assure you,' answered Pendleton. 'I felt his muscles last night. He's not as dangerous as that man Standish, but they'll both have to go. And if you like we'll go down to the Old Hall tonight and fix things up. Then I'll have to leave you to get him there.'

" 'Trust me,' she said. 'Now you get along, and come back later. We'll see about Sussex then.'

"And with that he left, and I sat on trying to think things out. I felt completely stunned. That she was cruel and had a horrible nature I already knew, but not in my wildest dreams had it occurred to me that she was as vile as that. And Sir Richard Pendleton! I hated him from the first moment I saw him, but that he, with his reputation, should be like it too simply knocked me flat. Of course, I'd read all about the murder of Mr Sanderson, and to find suddenly that my own employer was implicated in it was almost incredible. But there was no getting away from the evidence of my own ears, and I had to decide what I was going to do.

"One thing was clear: I should only be signing my own death-warrant if either of them had an inkling that I had overheard their conversation. So I waited till she was in her bath: then I crept along the passage and banged the front door as if I had just come in. She called out to me and I answered: all was well and good so far. But what to do next: that was the point.

"My first thought was the police, but I sort of funked it. I don't know anything about Scotland Yard, and I thought that if I went up to a policeman in the street and told him what I'd heard he'd think I was mad. And it was then that I had the idea of coming to see you, Captain Drummond. Your full name was in the papers, and I got your address from the telephone book. But I had to wait till Corinne Moxton had gone out.

"Sir Richard came back about an hour later to take her out to dinner, and from their remarks in the hall I gathered she had decided to go down to Sussex afterwards. So the instant they left I flew round here, never dreaming that I shouldn't find you. And then your servant rang up Mr Darrell."

"I got the message, Hugh, about five minutes after yours," said Darrell. "And when I heard what Miss Frensham had to say, I roped in the warriors and followed you."

"For which relief much thanks to all concerned," said Drummond. "Well, Miss Frensham, I'm most extraordinarily grateful to you. You completely saved the situation as far as I am concerned."

"But what do you make of it all, Captain Drummond?" she cried. "I mean, you don't seem as surprised as I thought you would be."

"Because, bless you, you haven't told me much that I didn't know already," he said with a grin. "What you say about the fair Corinne's character is most interesting: it explains a lot. Also you have confirmed the fact that it was they who were at the Old Hall tonight, and further, that they had no idea when they started that they would find me there. And it is interesting to know that she was actually in the room when they did in poor old Sanderson."

"But what are you going to do about it?" she cried. "We can't let the vile beast go free."

"She won't," Drummond assured her. "Life is going to be full of thrills for little Corinne before she's much older. But things are a bit deeper than even you think, Miss Frensham, and it isn't going to help matters if we rush our fences. Now in the course of your wanderings with your fair employer have you ever met a man with a head as bald as a billiard ball called Demonico?"

The girl shook her head.

"Never," she said decidedly.

"Because he is the bird who up till this evening presided at the Old Hall and who, unless I am much mistaken, is the principal noise on the other side. You've never heard her mention him?"

"No," she answered. "That conversation I overheard tonight is the only time I've ever even guessed that anything like this was happening."

"Well, chaps, we're up against something pretty big, and something that, at the moment, is mighty hard to get to the bottom of."

Briefly he recounted what had taken place at the Old Hall.

"Now, in view of what Miss Frensham has told us," he continued, "it seems pretty clear that the performance in the squash court was staged on the spur of the moment to please dear Corinne. And I'm sure I hope it did. But as she herself admitted, when she was talking to Pendleton, she's not interested in the rest of his schemes. I am, and so is Standish, far more interested than in that damned wench, much as she loves me. The whole of this elaborate organisation which killed Sanderson, burned his house down, and whose headquarters are, or at any rate were, at the Old Hall has not been got together for the sole object of letting Corinne see me killed. And so, people, it behoves us to take stock of our surroundings and see where we stand. Algy, you flat-footed son of Belial, take a piece of paper and stand by to make notes."

Algy Longworth roused himself from a slight doze and obeyed resignedly.

"Now," went on Drummond, "let's take points in our favour. First – Standish has got away with it: that message to Denny must mean that. We don't know where he is, but neither do the opponents. Second – we know about the fair Corinne's little peculiarities, but do she and the boy friend know that we know? I am inclined to think not, even after the episode of the squash court. Neither of them spoke – only Demonico did that. Their faces were in deep shadow: except that I could just make out that one of them was a woman I saw nothing at all."

He paused, struck by a sudden thought.

"By the way, Miss Frensham, won't Corinne smell a rat when she finds that you're not in the flat?"

"Oh no," said the girl. "I don't sleep there."

"That's good," said Drummond. "Very well then – point two: we know and they don't know we know. Point three: two celebrated financiers, Julian Legrange, a Frenchman, and Jim Daly, an Irish-American, are mixed up in the business, of whom the latter is known to be hostile to England. Any more points in our favour?"

"One, old boy," said Darrell. "Tonight's performance will have definitely put the Old Hall out of commission as far as they are concerned. That earth has been stopped all right."

Drummond nodded.

"That's so, Peter. Though, 'pon my soul, I don't know if that is in our favour or not. There are advantages in knowing where you can find your fox. Mark that as neutral, Algy, you chump. Now then – points against. One: they have at their disposal a mysterious weapon of the nature of which we have, at the moment, absolutely no idea save that it is some form of gun. Two: they evidently have plenty of money and a large and well-disciplined organisation. Three: orders are sent to members of that organisation by means of a cipher in the agony column of the newspapers, and we don't know the key to the cipher."

"Cipher," interrupted Daphne Frensham. "In the agony column? Wait a moment, Captain Drummond. About a week ago Pendleton was in the flat, and he had *The Times* on his knee. He was writing on a piece of paper as he studied it, and I thought he was doing a crossword or something. I noticed he was frowning as if he couldn't get it right, and then he suddenly said – 'Damn! I thought it was Tuesday,' tore up the paper, and began all over again quite happily. It sounds ridiculous, I know, but now you've said that about the cipher I'm sure he was decoding a message."

"Nothing is ridiculous in this show, believe me, Miss Frensham," said Drummond quietly. "Peter, I wonder if we've advanced a step farther. I wonder if that's why we couldn't read that message in yesterday's paper."

"Don't quite follow, Hugh."

"He said – 'Damn! I thought it was Tuesday.' From what Miss Frensham says he was frowning when he thought it was Tuesday, but as soon as he realised it wasn't, all was sunshine again. So I wonder if they have a different cipher for different days."

"There's a distinct air of possibility about that," said Darrell, "though I don't see that it's going to help us much. The messages are so short that unless one has the key it's hopeless to solve 'em. And if you're right we shall want seven different keys."

"Still, it's a point to bear in mind. Standish might make something out of it even if we can't. Because if we could read their orders we've got 'em cold. However, there's no use building on it. Well, chaps, any more points strike you?"

"Only one," said the girl, "and that's a small one. What excuse am I to make for leaving her?"

"But, my angel woman," cried Drummond, aghast, "you aren't going to leave her. It would be fatal. You'll be invaluable to us where you are: simply invaluable. Right in the heart of the enemy's camp. You mustn't go: you really mustn't."

"But she's practically a murderess, Captain Drummond."

Drummond waved a vast hand soothingly.

"I know; I know," he said. "Her habits place her lower in the scheme of things than a carnivorous slug. Nevertheless, you must suffer in the good cause, Miss Frensham. It's not pleasant, I know, to take someone's money and spy on them at the same time, but when that someone is a woman like Corinne Moxton it puts a different complexion on things. Of course, I wouldn't suggest it if I thought you were going to be in the slightest danger, but so far as I can see there can't be a breath of suspicion against you. And if you go on absolutely normally there never will be."

"All right," said the girl a shade doubtfully. "But what is it particularly that you want me to do?"

"Keep your eyes skinned," said Drummond promptly, "especially on Pendleton. You see, he fills a dual role. Not only is he running round with Corinne, but he's one of the big men in the other show. And early knowledge of his intentions should prove amazingly useful. Also see if by chance you can find out anything about this man Demonico. I can tell you nothing except that he is completely bald, and has a revolting-looking pair of hands with fingers like talons and highly polished nails. Tonight he was wearing dark glasses, but that may have been as a disguise. If Peter is right, and we've put the Old Hall out of commission for them, he will probably make his headquarters in London. And, of course, it would be of immense value to know where they are."

Daphne Frensham got up.

"Very well, Captain Drummond," she said, "I'll do it. But if I'm to turn up on time tomorrow I'll have to be getting along now or I shall get no sleep at all."

"Look here, Miss Frensham," said Drummond, "do you mind if I make a suggestion? I am not going to the window to see, but I'm quite certain that if I did I should perceive the same bloke lurking outside who was there when I came back. Now Denny can easily rouse his wife, and I'm sure she can rig you out for the night. Then tomorrow I will smuggle you out of the house at the back by an exit which even the wariest of watchers would miss. You see, I don't want to run the smallest chance of your being followed to your own place and then from there to Miss Moxton's flat. If that happened the whole show would be given away."

"But won't it be an awful bother?" she said.

"Good Lord! no. Denny is quite used to little trifles of that sort."

He rang the bell, and after a few moments his servant appeared.

"There you are, Miss Frensham," he said after he had given the necessary instructions. "Mrs Denny will fit you up with all you want. Good night, and tell her what time you want calling.

"A good girl that," he continued as the door closed behind her. "By Jove! you chaps, this is a funny show. I didn't enlarge too much on it in front of her, but there's no doubt we're dealing with something we've never struck before in the shape of Corinne Moxton. She's like one of those cases one reads about in abstruse medical treatises. Abnormal, and it takes 'em all ways. With her the obsession is to see ghastly sights. It's the only way she can get any excitement. Think of a woman watching that blighter with spikes on his hands trying to tear my throat out, as her evening's entertainment."

"The amazing thing to me is that the men should have stood for it," said Darrell. "They wanted you out of it, Hugh: why did they run such a risk?"

"The lady decided that she wanted her spot of fun," said Drummond. "In addition to that, they probably thought I hadn't a hope, and to be quite candid, but for that tin of petrol, I hadn't. Sooner or later we'd have had to come to close quarters, and then that blighter must have got me. And even after I'd laid him out, if you and Algy and the rest of the bunch hadn't turned up when you did I'd have been for the long drop. I was a sitting target for anyone with a gun in the gallery."

"It was the only possible thing to do, old boy, after hearing what that girl had to say," said Darrell. "Wake up, Algy, you hog, and finish your beer: it's time we pushed off. By the way, Hugh, I suppose you'll tell the police about the Old Hall?"

"I shall. And about Demonico. But I shan't mention Pendleton and Corinne. That card we'll keep up our sleeves. Night, night, chaps, and many thanks for rolling up."

He waited till the front door slammed behind them: then he went to the window and looked out cautiously. So far as he could see the street was deserted save for the two men who had just gone, but he stood watching for a considerable time to make sure. Then he returned and flung another log on the fire.

It was a peculiarity of Drummond that he wanted far less sleep than an ordinary individual, and at the moment he felt singularly wide awake. So, lighting a cigarette, he threw himself into an easy-chair, and picked up Algy Longworth's scribbled notes. They represented the situation as he saw it, but there was one characteristic omission which, being entirely personal, he had not mentioned. It was his own position in the matter.

In the course of his life he had made many mistakes, but under-estimating his adversary had never been one of them. And Drummond was under no delusions in this case. Whatever might have been his position relative to Standish at the time of the conversation overheard by Daphne Frensham, the events of the night had altered things considerably. *He* was now more of a menace to the other side, because he had seen Demonico and Standish had not. In any event, Standish for the time being had disappeared and was therefore safe, whilst Drummond had returned to his usual haunts in London.

He was so accustomed to taking his life in his hands that the thought did not worry him unduly. At the same time he had a rooted objection to being scuppered without getting a run for his money. And therein lay the danger. Given a large, well-disciplined, and absolutely unscrupulous gang it was not difficult to dispose of a man in London with complete safety. And as he saw it, getting him out of the way was so vital to them that they would not even worry about the complete safety. It was essential to Demonico that he should be silenced, and silenced before the inquest.

He grinned faintly, and lit another cigarette: this was like old times. And then the grin faded: there was one big difference that he had forgotten. If Standish was right there was more in this show than in those previous ones: there was a definite threat to the country. As against that Standish was free, and if anything happened to him Standish could carry on. But for all that nothing was going to happen to him if he could possibly avoid it.

The trouble was that he was moving in the dark: he did not know from what direction danger was going to come. It would not be from Demonico himself, or even from Pendleton: some underling would be deputed for the job. And that underling would know Drummond whilst Drummond would not know the underling. Dare he therefore run the risk of being killed before passing on his information to Scotland Yard? What about ringing them up now and asking them to send round one of their big men? If he said it was concerned with the Sanderson affair someone would be bound to come. And his finger was actually on the dial when a sudden sound behind him made him swing round.

Standing between the curtains was a man. He was tall and clean-shaven, and he was apparently unarmed, for both his hands were thrust in his trouser pockets.

"Good evening, Captain Drummond," he said quietly. "May I have a short talk with you?"

"How the devil did you get in?" demanded Drummond, staring at him.

"Through the open window," answered the other with a faint smile. "I thought it would attract less attention than ringing the bell and disturbing the house."

"You seem," said Drummond, "a moderately cool customer. What do you want to talk to me about?"

"The Sanderson affair, of course. Do you mind if I sit down?"

In silence Drummond pointed to a chair.

"If you've got anything of interest to say," he remarked curtly, "I am prepared to listen. Otherwise you'll leave by the way you entered, and the first thing that hits the pavement will be your ear."

"I think you will find it quite interesting," said the stranger, "I have come to tell you the name of the man who killed him."

CHAPTER 7

Drummond eyed him dispassionately. The man appeared to be a gentleman, and seemed perfectly at ease. He had crossed his legs, and was calmly leaning back in his chair as if his unusual mode of entry and his last remark were the most ordinary things in the world.

"That," agreed Drummond, "will undoubtedly prove interesting. But may I first ask why it is I who am thus honoured and not the police, and secondly, why you should choose this ungodly hour?"

"Certainly," said the other. "My reason for not going to the police is a very simple one. The police have no idea that I am in England at present, and to be quite candid, I prefer that state of affairs to continue. I have come to you because your name was in all the papers, and there is only one Captain Drummond in the telephone book, whereas there are several Standishes. Lastly, the ungodly hour is due to causes beyond my control. I couldn't come before, and it would have been dangerous for you if I had postponed my visit a moment longer than necessary."

"Dangerous for me!" echoed Drummond. "Why?"

"Because," said his visitor gravely, "a rat surrounded by terriers is a far healthier insurance proposition than you are unless you vanish and stay put. In fact, it was to make you realise that, almost as much as to tell you the other thing, that decided me to come and see you."

"Deuced kind of you," remarked Drummond. "And your simile is most edifying. You propose, I take it, to blow the gaff, an operation not unattended with danger to yourself. Why this touching solicitude for my safety?"

"Because there has been quite enough murder done," said the other. "I came into this show, for reasons into which we need not enter, but I did not bargain for wholesale killing. And you're the next on the list after tonight's effort down in Sussex."

"I confess," murmured Drummond, "that some such idea has already occurred to me. But before we go any farther, since we are having this heart-to-heart talk, what is this show into which you came?"

"All in due course," said the visitor, "though I will be as brief as I can. I've got to be away from here before it is light to ensure my own safety. Now, in the first place are you aware that the members of this gang communicate with one another by cipher?"

"I am," answered Drummond. "Do you know the key?"

"Of course I do," said the other, rising and going over to the desk. "If I may take a piece of paper I'll put you wise. Come over here, Captain Drummond, and you shall see for yourself. It's simple, but at the same time unless you know the trick it is well-nigh impossible to discover it."

He drew a fountain-pen from his pocket.

"Is that the *Sporting Life* over there? That will do: thank you."

He opened the paper out on the desk.

"Now take any pencil or pen," he continued, "provided the pencil has a sharp point. The first thing you have to do is to look along it, as I'm doing now, selecting the left-hand column of the centre page. Now use this pen of mine – I'll hold it for you – and look. Get your eye quite close to it."

And then occurred an amazing interruption, which left even Drummond gaping stupidly. He was just bending down to focus his eye to the pen, when the pen disappeared and his visitor, cursing dreadfully, leaped to his feet, wringing a hand from which blood was spouting freely.

"What the devil is it?" cried Drummond. "What's happened to your hand?"

But the other, like a man bereft of his senses, was staring at the pen lying on the carpet.

"I don't understand," he muttered. "I don't understand."

And at that moment there came from the pavement outside the sound of a laugh.

Drummond swung round and dashed to the window: a man was running up the street.

"Hi! you," he shouted, but the man took no notice and vanished round a corner.

"So," he said, coming back into the room, "it would seem that your visit here has been found out. And it strikes me, my friend, that you now join me in the rat and terrier parallel. Somebody got you through the open window."

The other did not answer: he was watching Drummond with terror in his eyes.

"Pull yourself together, man," went on Drummond contemptuously. "You've only been plugged through the hand. I'll get something to bind it up with: you're ruining my carpet. Stop over in that corner: you're quite safe. I'll have a look out of one of the other rooms and see if anyone else is there."

He crossed the hall, and going into the dining-room peered cautiously out of the window: the street was empty. Then, still marvelling at the extraordinary incident, he went upstairs for iodine and some clean handkerchiefs. Presumably the man had been followed, and had been shot as a traitor with one of the silent guns such as Standish and he had captured the previous afternoon. Luckily for him the firer had not killed him, but had only given him a very painful wound in the hand. It undoubtedly showed, however, that things wanted watching: there was a rapidity of action about the other side which was distinctly disconcerting.

"Here we are," he said, opening the study door, only once again to stand staring foolishly. For the room was empty: his visitor had gone.

"Well, I'm blowed," muttered Drummond to himself. "Have I dreamed the bally thing? Why's the blighter hopped it?"

But the question remained unanswered. A trail of blood leading to the window showed that he had left by the same way that he had come, but except for that no trace remained of his mysterious visitor. Even the pen with which he had been demonstrating the cipher had disappeared.

Drummond closed the window thoughtfully: the whole thing was beyond him. What on earth could have induced the man, knowing there was danger outside, to go and run his head into it deliberately? Had his terror temporarily unhinged his brain? Nothing else could account for such an act of suicidal folly. Just as things were becoming interesting, too.

However, it could not be helped. The man had gone, all his secrets untold: there seemed to be nothing for it now but to follow everyone else's example and go to bed. And his hand was actually on the switch of the light when the telephone bell began to ring. He picked up the receiver: was it his late visitor calling him up to explain his sudden departure? It was not: to his surprise he heard Standish's voice at the other end of the wire.

"Cuckoo," it came, "just to dispel any doubts. Standish speaking. I want you to obey me implicitly. Leave the house as soon as you can, and it is absolutely essential that you should shake off any watcher who may be there. *You must not be followed.* Make arrangements to remain away for at least a week, probably more. Get your servant to tell Darrell what has happened, in case we want to get in touch with him, so that he will be on the look-out. Got me so far?"

"I have," said Drummond.

"When you leave," continued Standish, "make your way to the Marble Arch, and walk along Oxford Street on the south side. It will be light by then, and you will see a stationary car facing west. Number ZZ 234: make, Bugatti; I'll be waiting for you inside. And, for God's sake, old boy, watch your step."

He rang off, and Drummond replaced the receiver. This was action such as he liked, but what was he to do about Daphne Frensham? She complicated matters to a certain extent, but the complication had to be faced, and faced quickly. He switched off the light: he would have to speak to her.

He went rapidly to Denny's quarters and beat him up.

"Denny," he said, "get your wife out of bed, and ask her to go and wake Miss Frensham. I don't want lights going on all over the house, so she'd better take a candle. She is to tell Miss Frensham that I want a few words with her. I'll be in my dressing-room. Tell your wife and then come upstairs to me.

"Now," he continued, when Denny rejoined him, "pay attention. I am disappearing for at least a week. Either get Mr Darrell round here and tell him, or go and see him yourself. Do not write it, or speak over the telephone to him. Do you follow?"

"Yes, sir. Any address, sir?"

"I can't tell you, for I don't know. Ah! there she is."

A knock had come on the door and Drummond opened it. Daphne Frensham was standing there with Mrs Denny behind her.

"A thousand apologies, my dear," said Drummond, "for pulling you out of bed like this, but further developments have taken place. I've got to leave here, and so you will have to do your get-away on your own this morning. Now it has suddenly dawned on me that it is Sunday: things have moved so hectically these last few hours that I'd forgotten the fact. I suppose you don't go to Miss Moxton on the Sabbath, do you?"

"No," said the girl. "I don't."

"Splendid: that makes it easy. In the first place you can have your sleep out. Then I want Mrs Denny to rig you up in some togs which will make you look as if you were the housemaid going for her day out. Can you do that, Mrs Denny?"

"Yes, sir; I can manage that."

"Your own clothes," continued Drummond, "can be done up in a parcel and posted to you on Monday by Denny. But you must appear to be one of the maidservants when you leave this house: that is essential. Another point arises. You are almost certain to be accosted by a man when you start off: at least, I shall be very much surprised if you are not. Do not be angry with him, or give him a clip on the jaw. Far from it: encourage him. And when he, as he will do, leads the conversation round to me, let him understand that, so far as you know, I have left suddenly for the Continent. Then shake him off – if he thinks you're one of the servants, he won't follow you – and make your way back to your own flat by a round-about route. Is that all clear?"

"Quite. But where are you going?"

"I don't know myself," said Drummond with a smile. "Now there's one thing more. If you find out anything in the course of the next week pass it on to Peter Darrell. Good night, bless you: sleep well. Things are moving."

He watched her cross the passage and go back to her own rooms; then he turned once more to Denny.

"Don't forget that: I've gone to Paris, except to Mr Darrell. Give me my razor and toothbrush, and I must be off."

Drummond took his revolver from the drawer and loaded it: then he changed rapidly into a rougher suit.

"And don't forget another thing, Denny. No telephone message purporting to come from me will be genuine unless you hear the word – Cuckoo."

He slipped the gun into his pocket and crammed a cap on his head.

"I'm going out the back way: lock up after me."

The passage led into some mews, and for a time Drummond stood in the shadow, reconnoitring. It was just dawn, and in the cold, grey light the place seemed deserted. After a while, skirting along under cover of the wall, he reached the street. Still he saw no one, and at length he decided that everything was all right. He turned and started briskly for the Marble Arch.

The morning was chilly, and he turned up the collar of his coat. So far as he could see he had made the arrangements fool-proof at his end. Provided that Daphne Frensham played up and acted her part well, she was safe. No one would worry over a maid on her Sunday out. Peter was fixed; Denny was fixed; everything, in fact, was all right except for that confounded interruption which had cost him the key to the cipher.

He swung into Oxford Street: a hundred yards ahead of him he saw the car. And immediately afterwards Standish got out of it and beckoned to him to hurry.

"I think it's OK," he said as Drummond came up, "but I shan't feel safe until we're well out of Town. Keep an eye skinned behind to make sure we're not followed."

They drove all out till they reached the Great West By-pass, and then Drummond gave the all clear: there was no sign of anything in sight.

"Where are we bound for?" he enquired.

"There is a pub I know in the New Forest," said Standish, "where the cooking is excellent and the port passing fair. Also it's not too far from London."

"Sounds good to me," said Drummond. "Well, well, old lad, I'm deuced relieved to see you. I was afraid they'd got you at the Old Hall."

"They darned nearly did," remarked Standish. "But nothing like as near as you ran it."

"What do you know about that?" said Drummond in some surprise. "You couldn't see what happened in the squash court."

"I'm not alluding to what happened in the squash court," answered Standish, "though I'd like to hear about that later. I'm alluding to what happened in your study not an hour ago. Sorry I couldn't stop when you shouted after me."

"What the blazes are you talking about?" cried Drummond, staring at him in amazement.

"Only that in another half-second Number Four would have got you just as he got Sanderson. By Gad! old boy, it was a close thing."

"But," Drummond positively stuttered, "was it you who shot him through the hand just as he was going to give me the key to the cipher?"

"Cipher my foot," said Standish with a short laugh. "I don't blame you a bit, Drummond: that's the way he must have caught Sanderson. Some clever conjurer's patter to get you to put your eye to the end of that so-called fountain-pen, which is really one of the most diabolical weapons that has ever been constructed. The ink on Sanderson's desk ought to have put me wise to it, because I've heard of this contrivance before. It's an American invention, and is, when you boil down to it, extremely simple. It looks exactly like a fountain-pen: it has a nib, and it can be written with. But instead of the ink reservoir there is a hollow steel tube covered at one end by a thin plug to make it appear solid. At the other end is a tiny cartridge and bullet, and the bullet is fired by operating the lever which in a genuine pen one uses for filling purposes. It is, in short, a tiny gun, but amply powerful enough to penetrate through a soft thing like an eye into the brain."

"My sainted aunt!" said Drummond slowly. "It would seem then, old boy, that I have to thank you for my jolly old well-being and all that sort of tripe."

"You have to thank the fact that I happened to be carrying that spring gun, and remembered about the pen just in time. Didn't you see how amazed he looked after I'd hit him, when he saw that the pen was still intact? The first thought that had naturally come into his head was that something had gone wrong with the mechanism of his beastly contraption, and that it had burst in his hand. Then he saw it hadn't, heard me laugh, and knew he'd been shot from outside."

"Great Scott!" cried Drummond, "that explains what was puzzling me. I thought he'd been hit by one of his own gang, and I couldn't understand why, that being the case, I found he'd bolted when I came down with handkerchiefs and iodine. Of course, *he* knew the shot had not been fired by his own people. But tell me, old boy, why didn't you shout out to me? I'd have nobbled the swine."

"I'll tell you frankly," said Standish gravely. "I was frightened."

"Frightened!" echoed Drummond. "What of?"

"Our not being able to disappear and hide. I'll go into that more fully later, but that was the reason. I dared not plug him through the head and kill him, though he richly deserved it, and with that weapon in his hand nothing would have been said if I had. But it would have entailed our remaining in London, and getting in touch with the police. The same objection applied if I called out to you, and we'd held him prisoner. Again, the police would have had to be called in, and we should have been detained in Town. And I didn't dare risk it. We'll get the swine later, but at present there are far more important things to tackle, and you and I have got to tackle 'em. And to do so successfully we've got to lie hidden for a time. For I tell you, Drummond, speaking with all seriousness, our lives at the present moment are not worth the snap of a finger. We have butted into an enormous coup. What that coup is I don't know, but we've got to find out. And it's coming off within the next week, so we haven't too much time."

"How do you know that?" demanded Drummond.

"From the scraps of conversation I overheard from my captors, while waiting my turn in the squash court," said Standish with a grin. "After you'd gone into the house I remained where you left me for a considerable time, until I began to get really uneasy. So I decided to go and investigate, and as luck would have it I ran full tilt into a whole bunch of them. It was hopeless from the word 'go,' but I gave a shout so as to let you know."

"I heard you," said Drummond, "but I was locked in and could do nothing."

"There was nothing to be done in any case, old boy: there must have been at least twenty of 'em. They trussed me up and gagged me, and chucked me into an outhouse, where three or four of them mounted guard. And it was from remarks they made that I gathered they none of them expected to be in England more than another ten days, which shows that the coup, whatever it is, is coming shortly. From their accents and conversation generally I put them down as American and Irish gunmen, and quite obviously they were a bunch of toughs who would stick at nothing. Every now and then a new one would drift in: your late visitor – Number Four – came in two or three times.

"About twenty minutes after they'd got me something occurred which evidently surprised them. Did any woman appear on the scene?"

"Corinne Moxton and dear Richard," said Drummond.

"I wondered if it was her. In any case her arrival caused a change of plan as far as you were concerned."

"Bless her kindly heart," said Drummond grimly.

"Something spicy was to be staged for her, apparently in the squash court. And what was more, as they were at pains to inform me, when you were disposed of I was to be the next item on the programme. What happened to you in there?"

Briefly Drummond told him and Standish whistled.

"A merry little piece of work – our Corinne," he exclaimed as Drummond finished. "What an extraordinary kink for a woman to have. However, the rest you know. I heard Peter and the boys arrive, and for a time there was some deliberation as to whether they should have a pitched battle or not. But orders must have come through from the boss, because the whole lot just vanished. Whether they scattered and lay doggo in the grounds, or what they did, I don't know: I was having a whole-time job trying to get free. Then I heard you shouting my name, so I knew that you had survived the entertainment in the squash court. But I was still gagged and couldn't answer. And then when at last I did get free you had all gone. Providentially, however, I found that a car had been overlooked by the opponents in their hurried departure, and getting into it I trod on the gas, stopping only to retrieve the gun which I had left in the bushes. Then I came round to see you and fortunately arrived in the nick of time. But what has been puzzling me is what was the reason of Peter's opportune arrival?"

"That had me guessing too," said Drummond, and then he told Standish of Daphne Frensham.

"Are you sure she is to be trusted?" remarked Standish when he finished.

"As sure as one can be over anything in a show of this sort," answered Drummond. "And the fact remains that but for her getting into touch with Peter neither you nor I would be sitting in this car at the present moment."

"That's true," agreed Standish.

"There's another thing too," went on Drummond. "She doesn't know where I'm going to: I didn't know myself when I left. But she's all right, old boy: I'm certain of it. And she should prove an invaluable ally sitting, as she will be, right in the heart of the enemies' country."

"This man Demonico – you say he was bald."

"As a billiard ball. With repulsive hands manicured like a woman's."

"I'm trying to tape him," said Standish thoughtfully. "I've got a fairly extensive acquaintance with international crooks, but he seems a new one on me."

"A dangerous customer, if I'm any judge," remarked Drummond.

"My dear fellow, they're a dangerous gang. I think you're perfectly right about Corinne Moxton: she's in it simply to gratify her sadistic tendencies, and is, in reality, the least dangerous, even if the most unpleasant, of the whole bunch. Pendleton is on a different footing. He – if what Miss Frensham told you is correct – is obviously mixed up in their bigger schemes. In fact, that was clear when they drugged me. I wouldn't be surprised if he isn't second-in-command, with this man Demonico the boss. But what is agitating my grey matter at the moment is what sort of a coup they can be proposing to pull off that necessitates keeping a young army of low-class riff-raff about the place. If one could only get a line on the type of thing they've got in view. It can't be high-class burglary: all those men are capable of is smash-and-grab or a hold-up in a shop. If it's political, as poor old Sanderson said, what do they want 'em all for? They're not the slightest use for any delicate work."

"I suppose it couldn't be a question of abducting someone: kidnapping him, and holding him prisoner," said Drummond thoughtfully.

"That's certainly a possibility. There are quite a number of people who would like to see the Prime Minister out of the way, and Legrange and Daly are two of them. At the same time, even if they were planning such a fantastic scheme as kidnapping Dermot, what can they want that number of men for? There's another thing too that I gathered from their remarks: a lot of them have only just arrived in the country. Recently arrived: leaving in a week. It all points, old boy, to some very big coup for which these ruffians have been specially brought over. And the devil of it is I can't even begin to imagine what it can be."

"We've got to solve that cipher somehow," said Drummond. "By the way, did I tell you that Daphne Frensham has a hunch that it may be something to do with the day of the week. Apparently Pendleton... Great Scott!"

He broke off suddenly, and Standish glanced at him.

"What's stung you?" he asked.

"Do you remember," answered Drummond slowly, "that bit of paper we found in Sanderson's desk? Wait a minute: I'm trying to get it exactly. 'Day of the week backwards. If two, omit first.' That was it, wasn't it?"

"As near as makes no odds," agreed Standish. "What about it?"

"Only that that also points to the key being dependent on the day of the week. Pendleton's annoyance when he found he'd been trying to solve a Wednesday message under the impression it was Tuesday: the fact that we made complete gibberish of yesterday's message, which was Saturday, simply and solely because we were using letters obtained from Friday's code; and last but not least, that apparently nonsensical sentence in Sanderson's desk – surely those three things taken together make it almost a certainty."

"I believe you're right, old boy," said Standish thoughtfully. "It undoubtedly supplies a meaning to what you say was a nonsensical sentence. At the same time I don't know that it puts us much forrader."

"I know," said Drummond gloomily. "That's what Peter said. Still, it's something to be on the right lines: it might help you. Personally I'm hopeless. The simplest crossword sends me into a muck sweat, and a child can outwit me with the most footling riddle. But a brainy feller like you ought to be able to cough up something."

"I'll have a shot," said Standish, "but I won't promise anything. And if I can't make it out I know a bloke in London who probably can. The devil of it is, you see, that the messages will almost certainly be short ones. Further, since the majority of the members of the gang have only recently arrived, not many are likely to have been sent. And so, even if we got a lot of back papers, you would be lucky if you found more than two Tuesday codes, or two Fridays. Which is awkward. For though it is quite true that any cipher invented by man can be solved by man, it is essential to have a lot of it to work on. And that is just what we shan't get. Still – we can but have a dip at it."

They drove in silence for some miles. A watery sun that gave no heat gleamed fitfully through the flying clouds, and a strong desire for breakfast grew in both men.

"Eggs and bacon, laddie," said Drummond cheerfully. "Lots of coffee, and then little Willie proposes to hit the hay."

"Only about another twenty miles," cried Standish. "And I can do with a bit of shut-eye myself. Do you think you killed that blighter in the squash court?"

Drummond grinned happily.

"I'm afraid I did," he said, "because I should very much like to have had a further chat with him. I wonder whose great brain thought of those spikes. Demonico's presumably. By the way, did you hear any gup about Gulliver? Why did they do him in?"

Standish shook his head.

"No: I didn't hear his name mentioned. Talking out of his turn, I suppose, or a small token of their respect and esteem for letting me get away."

"There's another point that arises," said Drummond after a while. "What about this inquest tomorrow? We are two of the principal witnesses."

"Leave that to me, old boy. I'll fix it with McIver and Co.: the police can be very discreet when they want to. Tomorrow's affair will be merely a matter of form, and then an adjournment for a week. I shall tell 'em about the Old Hall, of course, and your pal Demonico."

"What about that swab Pendleton and Corinne?"

"I think it's best to put all the cards on the table: they can be trusted not to act precipitately. We must do it, old boy: it would be unpardonable if these swine pulled their game off because we said nothing about them."

"As a matter of fact," said Drummond, "I was on the point of ringing them up myself just as Number Four arrived."

"I shall tell McIver that you and I are going to lie doggo for a while. And I'll tell him why. He's a sensible chap, and if I give him the situation from our point of view he'll see it at once."

"It goes against the grain running away from that bunch of toughs," said Drummond gloomily.

"I agree: it does. But it would go a darned sight more against the grain to get plugged from behind by some unknown man. And that, old lad, would have been our portion for a certainty if we'd stopped on in London."

"I suppose you're right," agreed Drummond, as Standish swung the car off the road up to the entrance of an hotel. "Anyway, let's hope the staff is up: my stomach is flapping against my backbone. What's this pub? The Falconbridge Arms. Seems good to me."

And it is not too much to say that the sum of ten thousand pounds would willingly have been paid by the occupants of a room in Sir Richard Pendleton's Harley Street residence for the information contained in Drummond's last few sentences. It was the doctor's consulting room, and Sir Richard himself was seated at his desk. Opposite him Number Four, his hand bound up, sprawled sullenly in a chair: whilst, huddled over the fire, crouched a figure whose completely bald head proclaimed him as Demonico. And the prevalent atmosphere was one of tension.

"It's no good putting that stuff over on me." Number Four was speaking. "I tell you I had that sucker as stone cold as I had Sanderson. He was just putting his eye to it when that pal of his got me through the window."

"You've said all that before," snarled Demonico. "The plain fact remains that you bungled the thing hopelessly."

"I bungled, did I?" answered the other, white with anger. "What about you down at the Old Hall? That was a pretty piece of work, wasn't it? A howling success, I should say. You had 'em both for the asking, and then you let 'em get away, just because you wanted to put up a peep-show for that blasted woman."

Pendleton's fist crashed on the desk.

"If you make another remark like that," he said thickly, "I'll smash your face in."

"Will you indeed, Sir Richard Sawbones?" snarled Number Four. "I agree it's about all you are capable of – hitting a man with one arm. I tell you – I'm fed up with this. Who has done all the dangerous work up to date? I have. And what have you done, you damned pill pusher? Gone messing round the place to little parties and things with that tow-haired..."

"Stop!"

Demonico's imperious command rang out, and the two furious men pulled themselves together.

"This is no time for childish squabbles," he went on sternly. "The stakes are altogether too great. We must co-operate – not fight."

"Sorry, Doctor," said Number Four sheepishly. "I didn't mean to hurt your feelings."

Pendleton accepted the apology with a curt nod.

"Now," continued Demonico, "let's get back to the beginning. Who is this man Standish that Sanderson should have telephoned to him particularly?"

"I can tell you that," said Pendleton, "for I've been making enquiries. He was a friend of Sanderson's, and is apparently a sort of amateur dabbler in crime with very distinct detective ability."

"That's right," said Number Four. "That's what Sanderson said. Miss Moxton and I had been codding him up about the cipher – the same as I did Drummond, and he suddenly decided to ring up Standish. And I couldn't miss the opportunity. His head was steady: he suspected nothing when I pretended to fill the pen."

"So much for him," continued Demonico. "Now what about Drummond?"

"As far as I can make out he's a friend of Standish," said Pendleton. "He and the other two were playing bridge when Sanderson telephoned. But to my mind Drummond is the most dangerous of the lot. He's immensely powerful, as we have found out to our cost, and he knows you."

"He won't the next time we meet," said Demonico quietly. "That is, if there is a next time. The point is not, however, whether he knows me, but whether he knows anything of our plans."

"He knows we use a cipher, boss," remarked Number Four, "but he doesn't know what it is."

"It might be advisable to change it," said Pendleton uneasily.

"Impossible, so late as this," answered Demonico decisively. "It would result in hopeless confusion. Besides, no one can solve it without the key."

"What's got me stung," said Number Four, "is that whoever it was who shot me – and I can't think who it can have been except Standish – must have known about the pen. If he didn't, why did he aim for my hand?"

"That weapon has served its purpose," said Demonico, "though I admit it's very disconcerting. It shows knowledge on their part which is not reassuring. You think it was Standish?"

"Who else could it have been? Darrell and that guy with an eyeglass were both shadowed to their flats: Leyton hasn't left his rooms at all: it can't have been the police. So it must have been Standish."

"Then one wonders excessively why, having incapacitated you, they didn't make you a prisoner."

"Exactly, boss. I haven't stopped wondering about that since it happened. They had me cold, and with the pen found on me I should have been taped direct for Sanderson."

Demonico rose and began pacing up and down the room, whilst the others watched him anxiously. That he was worried was clear, though his voice when he spoke was quite calm.

"You say that Standish has not returned to his rooms?"

"Not when the last report came in an hour ago," said Pendleton, and at that moment the telephone rang on his desk. He picked up the receiver.

"Yes. Sir Richard Pendleton speaking."

The others waited in silence: the message was obviously surprising the listener. At length he replaced the instrument.

"An unexpected development," he said. "Drummond left early this morning for Paris."

"Who was that speaking?" asked Demonico.

"Spackman. Apparently he picked up one of the maids who was having her day out and she told him."

"What can have caused that?" said Demonico thoughtfully.

"Possibly he found that things were getting too warm," remarked Pendleton. "So he came to the conclusion that discretion was the better part of valour."

Demonico shook his head decidedly.

"That is not my valuation of Captain Drummond at all," he said. "In fact, I should not be at all surprised if it isn't true. He may have said he was going to Paris for the benefit of his household staff and possible callers, whereas in reality he has done nothing of the sort. In any event, for the time we must regard both him and Standish as lost and make our plans accordingly. To start with, neither of them has an inkling that you are involved, Pendleton?"

"So far as I know it's impossible that they should," said the doctor. "They were both unconscious when I saw them in Standish's rooms. And yet I must confess that the tone of the few remarks Drummond made to me at a cocktail party where we met yesterday gave me to think a bit."

Demonico shrugged his shoulders.

"We must chance it. Now that the Old Hall is useless, I shall have to stay in London. It won't be for long: I had absolute confirmation last night that it will be Tuesday week. Your yacht will be ready by then?"

"She's ready now," answered the doctor. "Who did you get your confirmation from?"

"One of the chief cashiers," said Demonico, "whom I've bought."

"A difficult thing to do," said Pendleton dubiously.

Demonico laughed cynically.

"Not if you're prepared to pay big enough," he said.

"How can he be so certain?" persisted Pendleton.

"He knows the liner that the stuff is consigned to," answered Demonico. "But if by chance there should be a change he will let me know at once. I had two other interesting visitors yesterday evening," he continued. "Legrange and Daly."

"Good Lord! they know nothing about it, do they?"

"No; though Daly wouldn't mind if he did. I've met some Irish-Americans who are rabid against England, but he wins in a canter. However, don't alarm yourself – they know nothing about our little coup. But they do know a lot about the financial condition of this country, and I was amazed at what they told me. If you want to pick up a packet for the asking – sell sterling short."

Pendleton stared at him.

"Why?" he demanded.

"Because England has either got to go bankrupt or get off the gold standard. That's what they tell me and they should know."

"Well, I'll be damned," said Pendleton. "As bad as that, is it? But why the deuce did they bother to tell you?"

Demonico gave a thin smile.

"It is not the first time I have had dealings with those two gentlemen," he said. "We understand each other – admirably. And our schemes are going to help things a lot. However, to return to more pressing matters – Drummond and Standish have got to be found, and when they are found there must be no further mistake. The more I think of it, the less likely does it strike me that Drummond has gone to Paris. What possible reason could he have for suddenly going there on a Sunday morning? He is therefore either still in his house, in which case he must have a peculiar sort of staff if he can get a maid to say he's left for Paris; or, and this is far more probable, he has left Town and is hiding somewhere."

"In that case it's going to be a pretty impossible proposition to find him," said Pendleton. "In any event, he will have passed on to the police by now all that he knows."

"But what *does* he know? He knows that he was drugged with Standish the night before last by the people who were concerned in Sanderson's death. All the world will know that after the inquest tomorrow. He knows me as I am now, but not as I shall be in half an hour's time. He knows about the Old Hall: that is now empty. He knows that he fought for his life in the squash court, but since he didn't kill his assailant and only stunned him, there will be no evidence to produce there. My dear Pendleton, Sanderson's very necessary death has turned this case into a *cause célèbre* already: anything further that Drummond or Standish may say matters but little. Because they do *not* know what we are here for: they do not know where I am, nor, now that the men are scattered, where any of them are. And, last but not least, they do *not* know, nor will they ever know, the solution of our cipher. Furthermore, our arrangements are cut and dried, and we are only going to be in the country for a few more days. That is the position as I see it, though I frankly admit that I should feel happier if they were both out of the way. And, when they are found, they must be put out of the way, as I said before. Men who can call on a gang of friends to follow up their movements, as those two apparently can, are far more to be feared than the police."

"I wish I felt as confident about it as you do," said Pendleton uneasily.

"Not losing your nerve, are you?" remarked Demonico with a slight sneer. "What is worrying you?"

"The conversation I had with Drummond at that party," said the other. "I can't get out of my mind the feeling that he had his suspicions about me."

"Nonsense," cried Demonico. "How could he have? He could not possibly have seen you in the squash court, and anyway, that was after your party. And when you saw him in Standish's rooms he was drugged and unconscious. As a medical man you could be certain of that."

"He was drugged all right," agreed Pendleton. "For all that I don't feel sure."

"Another thing," put in Demonico. "If he'd had any suspicions of you, is it not more than likely he would have said something when he was in the squash court? He must have known that two men and a woman were looking on, and one of those men he knew was me, because I spoke to him. Surely, if he suspected you, he would have called out."

"Perhaps you're right," said Pendleton. "Anyway, we will proceed on the assumption that he doesn't. And if he doesn't, Standish doesn't either."

"There is still another point which to my mind conclusively proves it," went on Demonico. "If your surmise that he suspected you at the time of this cocktail party is correct, those suspicions must have been aroused before the party took place. So that even if he said nothing to you in the squash court he would surely have said something then."

"Unless he's playing a very deep game," said Pendleton.

"Good God! man," cried Demonico contemptuously, "what's happened to you? If I'm not worrying, why should you? You might just see that the way is clear for me to get upstairs without any of your servants seeing me: I want to make a few radical alterations in my appearance. Then I, too, shall follow Drummond's example, and – go to Paris."

"All clear," said Pendleton, returning from the door, and Demonico, after one swift glance round the hall, went rapidly upstairs.

"I didn't quite get what he meant by selling sterling short," said Number Four as the door closed behind him.

"That's easy," said Pendleton briefly. "If this country got into serious difficulties, and couldn't pay her way, the value of the pound is going to fall abroad. Say it goes down to fifteen shillings. So that if I sell a pound now I get twenty shillings for it, but when I have to deliver it on settling day I only have to pay fifteen shillings. Clear gain of five shillings per pound, and you can work out what that comes to on a hundred thousand."

"But supposing it doesn't go down?"

"Doesn't matter: I can't lose anything except brokerage. It can't go up above twenty shillings: I can't have to pay more for it than I sell out at. Jove! it's interesting. I knew things weren't too good: I didn't know they were as rocky as they evidently are. For Legrange doesn't make many mistakes. And if he hasn't made one this time, there are going to be a good many fortunes waiting to be picked up."

He sat down at his desk, and began glancing through some papers, whilst the other watched him curiously.

"You're an extraordinary bloke, Doctor," said Number Four after a long silence. "You draw a fat income chopping up people's insides: you can live in peace and quiet and the odour of sanctity, and yet you mix yourself up in these sorts of games. Why the devil do you do it?"

"Love of excitement," answered Pendleton at once. "It takes us all in one way or another. To see a horse-race leaves me cold, and I wouldn't cross the road to watch a game of football. But this – this is life. I wouldn't miss next Tuesday or the rehearsal this week for any sum of money you could give me. Hullo! madam, what on earth are you doing here?"

The door had opened, and an elderly woman had entered. Her hair under a fashionable hat was grey: her clothes, to Pendleton's discriminating eye, were exactly right in a woman of her age. And for a space she surveyed him through *lorgnettes*, while he continued to stand by his desk feeling increasingly surprised at this unexpected intrusion.

"Sir Richard Pendleton?" she asked, her survey concluded. Her voice was musical and cultured, and the doctor bowed.

"That is my name," he said. "You wish to consult me?"

"Only to the extent, my dear Pendleton, of asking you to place the trousers I have left upstairs, along with the other male garments, in some safe hiding-place."

The voice was still that of a woman, and for a moment or two Pendleton stared at her blankly. Then the truth dawned on him, and he sat down limply.

"Well, I'm damned," he cried. "Demonico, I congratulate you. It is the most marvellous disguise I've ever seen. No one – *no one* – would ever recognise you. It is magnificent."

Demonico smiled slightly.

"Nor even Drummond."

CHAPTER 8

To Daphne Frensham the whole thing seemed like a nightmare. As Drummond had predicted, she had been accosted on leaving his house, and she had carried out his instructions to the letter. A natural actress, she had had no difficulty in playing the part of a parlourmaid out for the day, and she was convinced that she had completely deceived the man. Moreover, she knew that she had not been followed: the bus going west that she had boarded in Piccadilly had been empty save for herself, and when two hours later she had let herself into her tiny flat the street outside was deserted.

She found her employer in a trying mood when she arrived at her usual time on Monday morning. And there was no doubt that had her devoted following of film fans seen the beautiful Miss Moxton that day they would have received a severe shock. A programme that includes one successful and one unsuccessful murder on two consecutive evenings is not conducive to mental calm, and her features indicated as much.

But it was not the past that chiefly worried Corinne Moxton: it was the immediate future. She lunched with Sir Richard the previous day, and his misgivings had communicated themselves to her. How much did Drummond know? No good to argue that he could know nothing – no good to argue that unless he had positive proof he could say nothing: people with guilty consciences want something more substantial than that. How much did he know, and what was he going to say at the inquest?

Like Demonico she was convinced that he had not gone to Paris. There seemed to her to be no conceivable reason why he should leave the country early on a Sunday morning to go to France. And if that was so, the very fact that he had put up a blind made him the more dangerous. Why should he have bothered to do so?

Corinne Moxton was true to type in that she was utterly and absolutely selfish. So long as no shadow of suspicion rested on her the others might go to the devil. Even for Sir Richard she cared not one whit, except for the fact that if he was dragged in she might be involved also. And although she had not actually heard the conversation between him and Drummond at the cocktail party, it had left a bad impression on his mind.

"Your letters, Miss Moxton."

Daphne Frensham brought them to the side of the bed.

"What are they?" she cried irritably.

"The usual autograph ones," said the secretary, resisting a strong impulse to add that her employer had better write "Murderess" after her signature. "Two luncheons; a line from the publicity agent, and a request that you will say you use Doctor Speedworthy's Purple Ointment for removing blackheads in return for half a dozen tubes of it."

She held the letters out, and the film star snatched them from her hand. What did Drummond know? What was he going to say at the inquest? Damn him. Damn that fool Pendleton. Damn that miserable bungler Number Four for having failed to kill him.

"Say – how do you hold inquests in this one-horse place?"

Daphne Frensham's face registered just the right amount of surprise at such an apparently unusual question: so that was the lie of the land, was it?

"I'm afraid I don't really know, Miss Moxton," she said. "I've never attended one. I believe they have a man called a coroner, and a jury, and then they find a verdict. Why do you ask?"

"Can the public get in?"

"I believe so. I think the proceedings are always open."

"Find out where they're going to sit around on that guy who was killed on Friday night, and his house burned down."

"You mean Mr Sanderson?"

For the life of her Daphne Frensham could not keep a slight tremor out of her voice: there in the bed in front of her was, if not the actual perpetrator of the crime, the woman who had stood by while it was done. And now she was calmly asking about the inquest: proposing to attend it.

"For the land's sake don't stand there gaping, Miss Frensham. Of course I mean Sanderson."

The secretary left the room, and with a vicious movement Corinne Moxton flung the letters on to the floor. Then she sprang out of bed. What did that big guy Drummond know? What was he going to say?

"It is being held in the hall attached to the mortuary in Hampstead," said Daphne Frensham, returning. "At eleven-thirty."

Corinne Moxton glanced at the clock: ten-thirty now. Then she looked at her complexion in the glass: at least three-quarters of an hour's hard work was necessary there. So it could not be done.

"All right," she snapped. "Pick up the mail, and answer as usual."

It was better so, she reflected, snatching a pot of face cream from the dressing-table. It would have looked very curious for Corinne Moxton, the famous film star, to attend an inquest. Almost as if she was interested in it – in the dead man. And suddenly a look of gloating ecstasy came into her eyes: Number Four had not bungled that time. She saw again that deadly pen that was not a pen; she heard again that quick hiss, saw Sanderson crumple in his chair, his head crash forward – dead. If only they could have got him before he had rung up: it was that

that had caused the trouble. But he was too wily. Number Four had no chance; she admitted that. And one thing at any rate was certain: Sanderson had said nothing incriminating over the telephone.

Her thoughts automatically turned to Standish: where did he come in? She had never seen him: he meant nothing to her, but it was him that Sanderson had rung up. A sort of detective, so Sir Richard said; moreover, the man who had shot Number Four. But he could know no more than Drummond, and once again her mind went back to that large individual. What was he going to say at the inquest?

She finished dressing, and went into the sitting-room, where Daphne Frensham was awaiting her with the answers to her letters. Twenty-past eleven: the thing was just going to begin.

"Sign them for me," she said. "I can't be bothered."

"But I can't sign the ones asking for your autograph," protested the other.

"Then throw them in the fire," screamed Corinne Moxton.

What a maddening girl! Couldn't the fool understand that her nerves were all on edge? That she did not want to be worried signing trashy letters to idiots. And then she pulled herself together; Daphne Frensham was looking at her in a very strange way. She must be careful: never do to let her secretary suspect anything. Not that she would, of course: the only person who knew she had been present when Sanderson was murdered was Number Four, and his mouth was effectively shut. And Sir Richard, but he did not count.

"I guess my nerves are a bit on the jag this morning, Miss Frensham," she forced herself to say. "Give me the letters and I'll do them now."

She scrawled her signature at the foot of each, not even bothering to read them through. The clock showed eleven-thirty: the inquest was starting.

"I shan't want you any more today, Miss Frensham," she said. "You can have it to yourself."

"Thank you," said the other. "But I've got two or three hours' work filing your press cuttings which I'd like to do before I go."

Corinne Moxton, as she watched Daphne Frensham methodically gathering the letters together, checked a strong desire to tell her to clear out of the flat: she *must* be careful. Damn the fool woman: could the idiot not understand that she wanted to be alone – that unless she could know something definite soon she would scream? At last the secretary left the room, and Corinne Moxton began pacing up and down.

A quarter to twelve: it had begun. At that very moment the words might have been spoken which would end her career, would brand her in the eyes of the world, would… Great God! she had not thought of that.

"Miss Frensham," she called loudly. "Miss Frensham."

The secretary appeared.

"Say, Miss Frensham," she cried, "what would happen in this country if – if, well, if say someone was murdered by someone and someone else was present at the time?"

Daphne Frensham's face was quite expressionless.

"I suppose you mean, what would happen to the someone else," she said with maddening deliberation, and Corinne Moxton felt she could hit her. Was the girl completely daft this morning? What else could she have meant? And what was that the fool was saying? The someone else would be hanged!

"Even if she had nothing to do with it?" cried the film star shrilly.

"She!" Daphne Frensham raised her eyebrows. "Your someone else is a woman, is it? It makes no difference, Miss Moxton: women are hanged in England just the same as men. And, you see," she continued, "she must have had something to do with it, otherwise she'd have told the police at once, wouldn't she?"

Corinne Moxton bit her lip, and her nails cut into the palms of her hand. She *must* be careful what she said: there was no doubt whatever that her secretary was now looking at her most strangely.

"Thank you, Miss Frensham," she said. "The point comes up in a new film I'm thinking of. Don't let me keep you any more."

Hanged! Great heavens, what a fool she had been to go! Why had not that miserable cur Pendleton told her that she would be hanged? It was not possible; it was not justice: she could not be hanged. She had not done it: you cannot hang a person merely for watching someone being killed.

A frenzy of panic seized her, and rushing into her bedroom she began hurling things into her dressing-case. She must get away: leave the country while there was still time. Hanged! Taken out in the early morning with a rope round one's neck and hanged.

"Are you going away, Miss Moxton?"

Daphne Frensham was standing in the door and with a superhuman effort Corinne Moxton pulled herself together. If only some occult force had struck her secretary dead on the spot she would have danced with joy on the body. But it did not: she continued standing by the door, watching her employer out of a pair of wondering blue eyes.

"I thought you said you were filing press cuttings, Miss Frensham," she cried furiously. "It seems to me, I guess, you're spending most of the morning fooling around the passages."

"I'm sorry, Miss Moxton," said Daphne Frensham sweetly. "The filing is not urgent, and I thought perhaps I could help you pack. Does that come into the film, too?"

She left the room, leaving Corinne Moxton motionless. What did the girl mean? Did she suspect? Impossible: utterly impossible. No one could suspect – yet. No one could know anything about it at all. Unless... God! unless Drummond had said something at the inquest. But what could he have said – be saying now?

A quarter-past twelve: was it over? Anyway, it was too late now to bolt: the police watched the boats, she had been told, in cases like that. Hanged! Hanged! Like that film of Mata Hari in which she had played a small part before she became a star. Only Mata Hari was shot. With snow on the ground.

She bit her thumb to prevent herself shrieking. She had seen a play once – a Grand Guignol play – "Eight O'clock." The last half-hour of a man's life before he was hanged. He had prayed with the chaplain: the sole of one of his boots had had a patch in it – she remembered noticing that as he knelt by the bed. And then suddenly the whole cell had been full of people, and a thin-lipped man in a sort of uniform had come swiftly up to the murderer, and pinioned his arms, and half pushed, half carried him up some stairs behind the cell. Screaming; screaming. And then a dull thud, and silence.

Hanged! That had been acting: in her case it would not be. It would be reality. She would be awakened in the morning, if she had ever gone to sleep. And men would come in and drag her out, and there would be that dull thud, and – silence. But she would not be there to realise there was silence. She would be dead.

The front-door bell rang shrilly. And when a few moments later Sir Richard Pendleton entered he was met by Daphne Frensham.

"I don't think, Sir Richard," she said, "that Miss Moxton is very well this morning. She has just fainted."

"Fainted," he cried. "I'll go to her at once. When did it happen?"

"Just after the bell rang," she said, and as he hurried into the bedroom a little smile twitched round her lips. "I don't think she was expecting you."

And if there was a slight emphasis on the last word, Sir Richard did not notice it: was not the lovely Corinne Moxton unconscious on the bed and in need of professional attention?

"My dear," he said solicitously when she opened her eyes, "what made you do that?"

For a while she stared at him blankly: then she sat up and clutched his wrist.

"Has he said anything?" she cried.

Sir Richard frowned, putting a warning finger to his lips, and Corinne Moxton saw that her secretary was just behind him.

"That will do, thank you, Miss Frensham," she said. "Sorry to have given you the trouble: I suddenly felt queer. Now I want to talk to Sir Richard."

She waited till the door had shut; then she turned on him feverishly.

"Well," she cried, "what has happened?"

"Absolutely nothing," said the doctor gravely.

"Drummond hasn't split?"

"Drummond wasn't there."

"Is the inquest over?"

Sir Richard nodded.

"Yes. A purely formal affair with a formal verdict. And I don't like it."

But Corinne Moxton was paying no attention. The inquest was over and Drummond had said nothing. All her fears were groundless, and she jumped up gaily.

"And to think that I've been worrying myself sick," she cried, "wondering if he was going to say something about you and me. That's what made me faint: when the bell rang I thought it was the police."

"Don't talk too loud, Corinne," he said. "That girl of yours is in the next room. No; he said nothing, for the very good reason that he wasn't there. Nor was Standish. And what I am wondering is, why they neither of them were there. I don't like it, my dear: I don't like it at all."

She stared at him uncomprehendingly.

"What's stung you now?" she cried. "You surely didn't want him to say anything."

"Not about you and me naturally," he answered. "But I can't understand why no mention has been made of other things connected with the case. And I can't understand why two of the principal witnesses have not been called. It looks very suspicious to me."

But Corinne Moxton was in no mood for gloom: the reaction after her previous fears was too wonderful.

"Gee, Richard, your face would turn the butter rancid. Go and shake a cocktail, and then take me out to lunch."

He went into the next room obediently, but he was still looking worried when she joined him.

"Number Nine was present," he said, closing the door. "I've just seen him. And what you don't seem to grasp, my dear, is that a formal verdict such as the coroner instructed the jury to bring in is only possible at the instigation of the police. It means they've got something up their sleeves."

"As long as they haven't got me," she cried. "I guess they can keep what they like there."

"It's not quite so easy as that, Corinne," he remarked, handing her a drink. "Why has no mention been made of the Old Hall? Why has nothing been said about the drugging of Standish and Drummond? They are lying low at the moment, and I should feel a great deal happier if we had a few more of their cards on the table. The fact that no mention was made of those things rather discounts the value to us that no mention was made of you and me."

She put down her glass.

"You mean," she said slowly, "that they still may know we were involved."

"Precisely," he answered. "If some of those points had been alluded to, and nothing had been said about us, I should feel absolutely safe. As it is I don't."

"Well, what are you going to do about it?"

Her voice was shrill: all the old terrors were returning.

"There is nothing to do about it," he said. "All we can do is to hope for the best. It may be all my imagination: Drummond probably suspects nothing at all. But" – he shrugged his shoulders – "I wish I could be certain. Anyway," he continued reassuringly, "I don't think it possible that anyone can have an inkling of the fact that you were present when Sanderson was killed."

Her spirits revived: that was really all that mattered.

"It was very unwise of you to go, as I've told you before," he went on, "and had I had the slightest idea that you proposed to I should have forbidden it. But it's done and there is no more to be said about it. What we've got to do now is to concentrate on the future."

He paused and stood listening: then stepping swiftly across the room he flung open the door, almost colliding as he did so with Daphne Frensham, who was just outside.

"Good gracious, Sir Richard," she said calmly, "how you startled me. There's one letter I forgot to give you, Miss Moxton: will you sign it now?"

Sir Richard watched her closely as she crossed the room. Had she been listening outside? If so, it was a superb piece of acting. Not by the quiver of an eyelid had she given herself away.

He waited until she had again left the room: then he swung round to Corinne Moxton.

"Is that secretary of yours all right?" he said in a low voice. "I could have sworn I heard a sound outside just before I opened the door."

"I guess I was a little indiscreet this morning," she answered, quite humbly for her. "I kind of got nervous, Richard: I kept on thinking over what you said yesterday about Drummond. And I suddenly began to wonder what would happen to me if they did find out I was there when Sanderson was killed."

"My God! Corinne, you didn't say anything about it to her?" he cried, aghast.

"No, honey, no. I just put a sort of hypothetical case."

"Well, if you take my advice, you won't put any more. We've bitten off quite enough already, without adding anything else. And we don't want that young woman butting into things. Now – I've got an appointment which I can't get out of, but I'll meet you at the Ritz for lunch at one-thirty. And don't forget: no more hypothetical cases."

Corinne Moxton watched him go: then she mixed herself another cocktail. She had been indiscreet: she knew it. Especially that insane moment of panic when she had started to pack her dressing-case. Just blind, unreasoning fear had driven her, and now she cursed herself for a fool. But if only they could know for certain.

Suddenly an idea struck her. It could do no harm, and it might settle matters once and for all. She picked up the telephone book and looked up Drummond's number. She would ring up the house, and ask him round for a drink that night. If Paris was a blind; if he was either stopping quietly in his own house or was somewhere in England, she might be able to get at him.

A man's voice answered – Captain Drummond's butler.

"I am sorry, madam, but Captain Drummond is in Paris; I cannot say where. I do not know when he is returning. Can I give him any message from madam? To have a drink with you some evening after he returns. Very good, madam."

She replaced the receiver: whether it was the truth or not, the story was evidently being stuck to. And after a while, when a third cocktail had followed in the wake of its predecessors, life began to look a little better. It must have been Sir Richard's imagination over his talk with Drummond: she was perfectly safe. And even if the doctor was suspected, there was no reason why she should be. Just because she had been about with him a good deal since she had been in London was no justification for the police to get at her. They might question her, but she was quite capable of dealing with questions. In fact, if she handled the thing properly it might prove a good advertisement.

One thing, however, would be a good thing to do: get rid of Daphne Frensham. The girl must have suspected something that morning, even if she was not wise to the truth. And it would be as well to get her out of the flat before *the* night. The rehearsal did not matter, so if she gave her secretary a week's notice it would just be right: she would be leaving on the Monday and it was booked for Tuesday. And it would seem more natural than giving her the sack on the spot.

"Say, Miss Frensham," she said, stopping on the way to her bedroom, "I guess it's customary in this country to give notice, the same as in mine. Wal, I'm quitting early next week, and going to Berlin. So I shan't be requiring you after Monday next. I hope that is convenient to you."

"Quite, thank you, Miss Moxton," said Daphne Frensham.

"It will give you time to look around for another situation, and of course I'll give you a first-class reference."

She went on into her room: that was all right. The girl had taken it quite normally and evinced no surprise, and as she repassed the room on her way to the front door she saw her with her head bent low over the table absorbed in her work.

Daphne Frensham waited until she heard the front door close; then pushing back her chair she lit a cigarette. She was frowning a little; being given the sack was not going to help matters. Had she played her part badly that morning: was that the reason? She did not see how else she could have played it. To have remained quite unsurprised at such an exhibition of nerves would in itself have been suspicious. Or was the woman really going to Berlin?

After a while she went into the other room and rang up Peter Darrell.

"Would you like to give me a spot of lunch today?" she asked.

"You bet I would," he said. "Where and when would suit?"

"As soon as you like," she answered. "And somewhere quiet."

They fixed on a small place off Wardour Street, and a quarter of an hour later she found him there waiting for her.

"I've been followed," he said, as they shook hands, "but that is nothing new during the past few days. My attendant is that nasty-looking mess eating spaghetti in the corner. Well – what news?"

"I've been sacked," she answered as they took a table as far removed from the follower as possible. "Given a week's notice this morning."

"The devil you have," he remarked, staring at her. "However, I don't think it matters: a week will be enough. I've been in communication with Hugh Drummond and a fellow called Standish this morning early, and they think that whatever is going to happen is coming shortly. But why did you get the boot?"

She told him briefly what had happened and he listened in silence.

"The nuisance is," she concluded, "that I've so far found out nothing new, and what is worse, that man Pendleton now suspects me. I only just straightened up in time when he flung the door open."

"Probably it's that that got you the bullet," said Darrell thoughtfully. "For Heaven's sake be careful, my dear: this isn't a bunch to play any monkey tricks with."

"Where is Captain Drummond?" she asked.

"Falconbridge Arms in the New Forest," he answered in a low voice. "They are battling with that cipher, and also lying low for a few days. You see, Bill Leyton and I don't count: we're only the small fry. It's those two the other crowd want."

"What happened at the inquest?" she asked.

"The whole thing was over in about ten minutes," he said. "Bill and I said our little piece, and the coroner literally shut us up if there was any question of us talking out of our turn. The whole thing was run by the police."

"That's what is making Sir Richard uneasy," she remarked. "I could just hear enough to realise that this morning."

"By the way," he said suddenly, "there's no danger, is there, of any of their underlings recognising you?"

She shook her head.

"None of them have ever been near the flat," she told him. "Sir Richard would, of course, but no one else."

"And he doesn't know me," said Darrell, relieved. "And since there is only one of them here, and he's my portion, you can get back all right. But don't forget Drummond's address in case you want him urgently. His telephone number is Brockenhurst 028. But be careful where you 'phone him from."

"How long is he going to stay there?"

Darrell grinned.

"From what I know of him not long," he said. "Vegetating in the country is not his line at all. And it's only Ronald Standish who has persuaded him to do it."

He struck me as being a very determined individual," she remarked.

Darrell laughed.

"He is, as several people in the past have found to their cost. And he is one of the few beings I have ever met who does not know what the word fear means. That is why Standish must have brought some heavy guns to bear to get him to go and hide, because when all is said and done that is what they are doing."

"That reminds me," she said suddenly. "I'd quite forgotten. That woman rang him up this morning."

"What's that?" he cried. "But she doesn't know where he is."

"His London house," she explained. "And it must have been that dear old thing Denny who answered."

"He won't give anything away," said Darrell, relieved. "He doesn't even know where Hugh is himself."

"She was evidently asking him to come round and have a cocktail," she continued. "I heard her say, 'Give him my message when he returns.' "

"Rather amusing that," said Darrell. "I wonder what she proposes to do with him when she gets him there – ask the dear doctor to poison him?"

"She'd love that," remarked the girl. "It would be a new sensation for her."

"She must be a unique case," said Darrell thoughtfully, holding out his cigarette-case. "Think of having her lying about the house permanently."

"My temporary experience is quite enough, thank you," she answered. "She's inconceivably and utterly vile, and I simply hugged myself this morning when I realised that she was in a complete panic."

"She must have been to faint," he said.

"She thought she was going to be arrested, of course," went on Daphne Frensham. "And since I'd pitched it in good and hearty about the hanging part of the business she simply blew up."

"I hope to Heaven they don't think you know," he said anxiously.

"No need to worry about that," she answered decidedly. "They think that quite naturally I am curious over her strange behaviour this morning. I was worried myself to start with, but now I've thought it over I'm sure that's how it stands. You see, to anyone who didn't know the truth she would have seemed like a mad-woman."

"You know," said Darrell earnestly, "we're being most indiscreet."

"How do you mean?" she asked, surprised.

"Well, I can see the follower," he explained, "and he's finished his second plate of spaghetti. Which shows that we've been here some time. Now, don't you realise that he must be wondering what we're talking about."

"He can't hear what we've said."

"True, most adorable of your sex. But he can see our faces. And I ask you – what have our faces registered? Earnestness: grim resolve. Hence our indiscretion. We have made him curious. Why should any man register grim resolve who is lunching with you?"

Her lips began to twitch.

"What are we going to do about it?" she said.

"Well, I have a suggestion to make," he answered gravely. "Supposing – you will, of course, realise that it is only made to deceive our spaghetti eater – supposing you moved your left knee a little nearer my right knee, they would certainly connect. And he would see the deed, and would think that our conversation, which had evidently been concerned with love, was beginning to reach a successful conclusion."

She pressed out her cigarette.

"Conclusion?" she murmured.

"Good God! no," he cried, aghast. "Merely the opening gambit for the next half-hour. The conclusion I alluded to was that of the grim-resolve period."

"And what do our expressions register during the knee-touching spasm?"

"That, Daphne, I leave entirely to you. But don't forget, we've got to allay spaghetti's doubts."

He grinned suddenly.

"You're the most adorable girl," he went on, "and you must never forget one thing, for I never can." His voice had grown serious again. "You saved the life of the man who is my greatest friend – Hugh Drummond."

"Rot," she answered with a smile. "You saved him, Peter. And if you really think we ought to put spaghetti out of his misery, we'd better get on with it, because I must be off soon."

"But you said you'd got a day off," he protested.

"I'm not going to take it," she said. "I might find out something. And after next Monday I shan't be so busy."

"You topper," cried Peter. "What's the matter?"

"Nothing much," she answered. "But you're a very conscientious actor, aren't you?"

"Spaghetti has an eye like a lynx, darling," he said happily. "He'd know at once if we were faking things."

"And is 'darling' included in your part?"

"You bet it is. Spaghetti is a lip reader. But if you prefer sweetheart I have no objection."

"It strikes me, Mr Darrell, that you're a pretty rapid mover."

"Only in times of stress like this," he assured her. "At others I'm a lay preacher."

With which monstrous reflection on a worthy body of citizens Peter Darrell proceeded to concentrate on the matter in hand to such purpose that closing hours for drink passed unnoticed – a state of affairs that speaks for itself.

"I think we ought to meet every day, don't you?" he said as they finally rose from their table. "Just to report progress, you know. Anyway, give me your private address, so that if I feel nervous I can come round and hold your hand."

He scribbled it down in his note-book, and put her into a taxi.

"I'll tell him to drive to Selfridges," he whispered through the window. "You can put him wise when you've started. So long, you angel."

He watched her drive away: then with a courteous smile he turned to the consumer of the spaghetti, who had just emerged from the restaurant.

"Now, sir," he remarked, "I am completely at your service. Let us talk of this and that for a while, and then with your kindly permission I propose to go to my club. You prefer not to? Well, well; as you please. In that case, I will leave you. I shall be dressing for dinner about seven-thirty."

And it was at that hour precisely that the telephone rang in his flat, and he heard Daphne Frensham at the other end.

"Darling," he said. "This is too wonderful."

"Listen, Peter," came her voice a little urgently. "There have been developments this afternoon. I must see you at once. Where can we meet?"

He thought for a moment or two.

"Look here, dear," he said quietly, "the last thing we want to do is to give away where you live. On the other hand, they all know where I live. If I come round and see you I shall be followed: do you mind coming here to my flat?"

"Of course not, my dear," she answered. "I'll come at once."

He put down the receiver thoughtfully: developments, were there? And then for a while he forgot such minor matters in the very much more important question of Daphne Frensham. What an absolute fizzer she was, and where would they all have been without her? But when she arrived a quarter of an hour later he saw at once by her face that something serious had happened.

"Peter, dear," she said without any preamble, "I'm desperately afraid that I've given away Captain Drummond's address."

He whistled under his breath.

"That's a pity," he said. "How did it happen, darling?"

He pulled off her cloak and pulled a chair up to the fire.

"I'd better start at the beginning," she said. "When I got back this afternoon the flat was empty, so I went on with the job of filing her rotten press cuttings to fill in the time till they returned. They didn't get back till nearly five, and they went straight into the drawing-room and shut the door. I'd heard their voices in the hall, and it was pretty obvious that that beast

Pendleton was feeling amorous. And as the last thing I wanted to listen to was the pig making love, I stayed on where I was.

"Suddenly I heard the telephone go, and I crept along the passage. He was answering it, and of course I had no idea what was being said at the other end. Then I heard him say – 'I get you. Ardington: tonight – four o'clock.' That was all I got; in fact, that was all he said, but its effect was remarkable on her.

"She jumped to her feet the instant he'd rung off, and rushed to him.

" 'Tonight,' she cried, and there was a sort of ecstasy in her voice. 'Say, Richard, that's too marvellous.'

" 'Earlier than I expected,' he said. 'It was to have been next Thursday. Is that damned secretary of yours still in the flat?'

"That was my cue, and I was safely back in my own room before he opened the door. Two collisions in the same day would have been asking for trouble.

" 'You really are a model secretary,' he said in that foul, sneering voice of his. 'I thought Miss Moxton had given you the afternoon off.'

" 'I'm badly in arrears with this work, Sir Richard,' I answered, wielding a pretty scissor. 'And I prefer to get up to date, thank you.'

"He went back to the other room, and I heard the murmur of their voices. It wasn't safe to do the keyhole act again, so I controlled my curiosity and went on pasting the wretched notices in a book. What on earth did it mean? I'd never heard of Ardington: I didn't even know if it was the name of a man or a place. What could there be to make that woman get in a flat spin about?

"Then she came along the passage to talk to me, and I took one look at her face. You know I told you, Peter, about the time she saw that street accident, and the episode of the dog. Well, the same expression was in her eyes as she stood by the table, though her voice was under perfect control.

" 'Thank you, Miss Frensham,' she said, 'it's good of you to finish them up. But I guess I'd sooner you didn't come till after lunch tomorrow: I feel like a long morning in. So stay on now, and take your time off tomorrow instead.'

" 'Certainly, Miss Moxton,' I answered, and she went back to Pendleton. Again I didn't dare to try to listen, and there I sat fuming, unable to hear a word of what they were saying. At last the door opened, and they came out, on their way to a cocktail party.

" 'We'd better go, or we'll be late,' said Sir Richard. 'I told Parker to wait.'

" 'But you won't take him tonight,' she cried.

" 'Good God! no,' he answered. 'I'll drive myself.'

"Then the front door shut, and they were gone, leaving me more puzzled than ever. Parker is Sir Richard's chauffeur, and if there is one thing the doctor loathes doing it is driving his car. So why should he be so emphatic in saying that he was going to do so himself tonight? Evidently something is going to happen which Parker mustn't see. Don't you think so, Peter?"

"Sounds like it, my dear, I must say," said Darrell. "But how did you give Hugh away?"

"I'm coming to that," she continued. "I went on racking my brains as to what it could mean, and after a while I rang you up. There was no reply, and I didn't know what your club was. And so, like an idiot, I put through a call to Captain Drummond. The flat was empty, and I knew they wouldn't be returning for an hour at least. I got through to the Falconbridge Arms after a bit of delay, and asked for him. And as I was waiting while they went to see if he was in I happened to look round: standing in the doorway was a woman.

"For a moment or two I stared at her in complete bewilderment: I couldn't imagine where she had sprung from. She was middle-aged, with grey hair and very well dressed, and

I was on the point of asking her who she was and what she wanted when Captain Drummond came to the telephone.

"I should think he must have thought me an absolute idiot.

" 'Is that you, Mr Johnson?' I said, taking the first name I could think of.

" 'Hullo! Miss Frensham,' he answered, 'I recognise your voice. What's the great idea?'

" 'Sorry,' I cried. 'Wrong number,' and rang off.

" 'How annoying it is when that happens, isn't it?' said the woman, coming into the room.

" 'May I ask you who you are and how you got in?' I cried.

" 'You must be dear Corinne's secretary, I suppose,' she said, without answering my question. 'She told me you were very charming.' "

"First good point I've heard about Corinne," said Darrell with a grin.

"Shut up, Peter: this is serious. We went on talking for a while, and at last I discovered that she was a Mrs Merridick, who had known the Moxton woman for years, and had a key to the flat. Which in itself struck me as being very extraordinary. If she was such an intimate friend as all that, why had she never used the key before? To my certain knowledge it was the first time she had been in the flat, at any rate during the day, since I'd been in the job.

"However, I am bound to admit that she was very nice: asked me about my prospects, where I lived..."

"Which I hope you did not tell her," interrupted Darrell anxiously.

"Of course not, bless you: I just said with my mother. But to cut it short, Peter, I didn't hear her open the front door, and so I don't know when she came in. And so I can't be sure how long she had been standing there. Did she hear me ask for Captain Drummond, and did she hear me mention the Falconbridge

Arms? Not a muscle in her face moved when I said Mr Johnson, but that means nothing."

"It does not," agreed Darrell. "And there is no doubt whatever that Hugh must be warned at once. I'll get through to him now."

"Wait a minute, Peter: we must try and think what this Ardington business means. At first, as I told you, I couldn't make out if it was a man or a place or what it was. Now if it's a man why four o'clock? And why shouldn't Parker drive? Of course, Sir Richard may not want to keep him up so long, but I've never known him show any consideration before."

"Is there a place called Ardington?" asked Darrell.

"Yes, there is. I looked it up in the AA book. It's a tiny village with two hundred and fifty inhabitants somewhere up in the Midlands, and it's one hundred and thirty-three miles from London."

"Old Cow Hotel; 13 brms.; unlic.; I know the sort of notice," said Darrell with a grin. "But, my dear," he went on seriously, "what under the sun can be taking 'em to a spot like that at the ungodly hour of four in the morning?"

"Ask me another, Peter: I can't tell you."

"You're sure you got the name right?"

"Absolutely positive."

Darrell shrugged his shoulders.

"Well, I'm beat. But the first thing to do is to ring up Hugh and put him wise to the possibility of his hiding-place having been discovered. Then we'll think about this Ardington business later."

He was walking towards the telephone when she put a hand on his arm.

"Peter," she said, "I've got a hunch. Don't 'phone: let's go down ourselves."

"That's an idea, by Jove!" he cried. "I'll guarantee to get away from any car spaghetti can get hold of."

"Doesn't matter if you can't. I'm certain in my own mind that Mrs Merridick heard, so their address is known. I've tried to kid myself that she didn't, but in my heart of hearts I know she did. Let's go down and tell them: you can't make it clear over the telephone. Let's start at once."

He grinned at her.

"Right, angel; we will. I'll ring up my garage and tell 'em to have the bus ready in ten minutes. Then we'll step on the juice."

CHAPTER 9

They arrived at Falconbridge at ten-thirty, and stopped in the village to ask the way to the hotel.

"First on the left, sir," said the local constable, "but if you and the lady are looking for rooms I doubt if you'll get them there tonight. There's been a terrible accident not half an hour ago."

"What's that?" cried Darrell, a sudden fear clutching at his heart.

"Half the hotel blown up," said the policeman, and paused aggrieved as the car shot away like a mad thing: he was just getting into his stride.

"What's happened, Peter?" cried the girl in a frightened voice.

"God knows, my dear," he answered grimly. "But we'll soon find out. Hotels don't blow up without some good reason. Great Scott! look there."

The Falconbridge Arms had just come into sight, and though it was obvious that the policeman had exaggerated, something was clearly amiss. Numbers of men with lanterns were moving about, and by their light it was possible to see a great jagged hole in the wall nearest them.

"Mind out, sir," came a warning voice. "The whole of the drive is covered with broken glass."

"Is anybody hurt?" cried Darrell anxiously.

"Two gentlemen, sir, who were in the room where the explosion took place."

"Are they dead?"

He forced the question out and waited, sick with anxiety, for the reply.

"No, sir, but how they escaped is a miracle. They're both unconscious."

"Stay in the car, dear," said Darrell, "while I go and make some enquiries. There's been some devilry here."

He made his way through the gaping crowd of curious villagers to the front entrance of the hotel, where a man, who was obviously the manager, was in close conversation with two policemen.

"Excuse me," he said, breaking in without apology, "but what are the names of the two injured men?"

"Captain Drummond and Mr Standish," answered the manager. "Do you know them?"

"Intimately," answered Darrell. "In fact, it was to see them that I have just motored down from London."

"Then perhaps you can throw some light on this extraordinary affair," said the other quickly.

"First I should like to hear exactly what happened."

"I can only tell you what we all heard. It took place about three-quarters of an hour ago. I was in my office, and several people were sitting in the lounge. Suddenly there was a deafening explosion which shook the entire hotel. It came from the private sitting-room which your two friends had. The hall porter at once dashed in to find the whole place blown to pieces. All the windows had gone, and there was a huge hole in the wall. Mr Standish was lying in a corner quite unconscious: Captain Drummond had been hurled clean through the window and was found on the drive outside. May I ask, sir, if they were experimenting with some new form of explosive?"

"Not that I'm aware of," said Darrell. "Where are they now?"

"In their bedrooms. The doctor has seen both of them. Ah! here he is."

Darrell turned on him eagerly.

"What news of your patients, Doctor?"

"This gentleman is a friend of theirs," explained the manager.

"They're both alive," said the doctor, "though how they escaped being blown to pieces is more than I can tell you. Still more amazing, they don't seem to have broken anything. Whether they are damaged internally or not I cannot at the moment say. The bigger man of the two, who was found in the drive, is the one who got off lightest. He's cut his face a bit – probably that hit the gravel first. But I should think that he will recover consciousness before the other."

"And how long will it be before he does?" asked Darrell.

The doctor shrugged his shoulders.

"My dear sir, it is impossible to say. Cases have been known where people have remained unconscious for weeks. But luckily for them they are both of them extremely powerful men with magnificent constitutions, and I hope that that will not be so with them. Has anyone got any idea what caused the explosion?"

"No one," said the manager. "It must have been some form of bomb, I should think. You're quite sure, sir" – he turned to Darrell – "that they were not carrying out any experiments?"

"One can never be *quite* sure of anything," said Darrell, "but I think it most unlikely. What I would like to know is, whether they had any visitors tonight."

"I'll send for the hall porter," said the manager. "Now, Dean," he went on, as the man arrived, "did any visitor go into Number Three this evening?"

"Not that I know of, sir," answered the man. "There ain't been no one come to the hotel at all except the lady after dinner what took a room."

"A lady came after dinner, did she?" said Darrell quietly. "What sort of a lady?"

"Middle-aged lady, sir, with grey hair."

"Is she in the hotel now?"

"I suppose so, sir: she took a room."

"Presumably after that explosion she wouldn't have remained in it. Is she in the lounge?"

"What's the idea, sir?" said the manager.

"Only that I'd rather like to have a look at her," answered Darrell.

"That's easy. Let's go inside. Now, Dean, where is the lady?"

The hall porter looked around: then he shook his head.

"She's not in here, sir. Shall I go up to Seventeen and see if she's there?"

The manager looked questioningly at Darrell, who nodded.

"Make some excuse about hot water," he said to the hall porter. "Now, sir," he continued to Darrell, "it's obvious you know something."

"Let's wait until Dean comes back," said Darrell. "I may be quite wrong."

A few minutes later the hall porter returned, looking puzzled.

"She's not there, sir. And I've made enquiries outside and her car has gone."

"What name did she register under?" asked Darrell.

"We can find that out in the office, sir."

They crossed the lounge, and turned up the book. "Eve Matthews: London" was the entry, and the reception clerk supplied some further information.

"Lady said she was terrified by the explosion and would not stay. So she paid her bill and cleared out."

"Well, I may be wrong," said Darrell, "but I believe that if we could lay our hands on Eve Matthews of London we should catch the perpetrator of this little outrage."

"But what on earth was the object of it?" cried the manager. "Had she a grudge against them? Was it a love affair?"

"I assure you not that," said Darrell with a grim smile. "No: the reasons behind it are very simple. Captain Drummond and Mr Standish were mixed up in the Sanderson murder case which you must all have read about. And they are not at all popular with the gang of criminals who killed him. This was an effort to put them out of the way."

"But we can get hold of this 'ere Mrs Matthews," put in one of the constables.

"I doubt it very much," said Darrell quietly. "She will never be seen again, and even if she is, we've got no shadow of proof. No one saw her go into the sitting-room, and the fact that she left the hotel after the explosion means nothing. Many ladies on their own would do the same thing. Hullo! my dear."

"I got tired of sitting in the car, Peter," said Daphne Frensham as she joined them. "How are they?"

"I'm going up to see them in a moment," said Darrell. "They're both unconscious."

He drew her away, and they sat down in a corner of the lounge.

"I'm afraid your fears were justified, darling," he said in a low voice. "I haven't said anything to those warriors, but I'm convinced Mrs Merridick did this. A middle-aged, grey-haired woman calling herself Mrs Matthews arrived here after dinner and left again after the explosion. Said she was too frightened to stay."

"Peter – I'll never forgive myself," she cried miserably. "What induced me to be such an awful fool?"

"My dear, you couldn't help it. It was just one of those unfortunate accidents that might happen to anyone. And they're not dead: only knocked out. Hugh is not as bad as Ronald, according to the doctor."

"Oughtn't we to tell them about Mrs Merridick?"

"What's the good, dear? We've not got an atom of proof. We've got very strong suspicions but no more. And there's no use getting a couple of village policemen unduly excited when it can't do any good. Now you sit here while I go up and look at the two invalids."

He found Drummond tossing and moaning on his bed. His face was bandaged up and so was one hand, whilst every now and then he babbled incoherently. Standish lay quite motionless: only his faint breathing proclaimed that he was alive. And it was while he was with him that the doctor came in to say that the ambulance was at the door.

"They will be far better in hospital," he said. "In fact, it is essential they should be in a place where they can get skilled nursing."

"Far better," agreed Darrell.

From other points of view beside nursing, he reflected. When it was found that they were not dead it was more than likely that another attempt would be made to finish them off. And then an idea struck him.

"Look here, Doctor," he said, "I'd be very much obliged if you'd do something for me. You said downstairs that you had no idea when they would recover consciousness, didn't you? Well, I wish you'd pile that on as thick as you can when the reporters begin to get busy. Say that you think it may be a question of weeks. We're moving in deep waters, and if the bunch who did this show tonight think that even though they're not dead, they're safely out of the way for some time, it'll be healthier for all concerned."

The doctor nodded.

"Certainly," he said. "And in doing so I shall not be stretching the truth at all. For it is my candid opinion that it *will* be a question of weeks, certainly in the case of Mr Standish. Are you going to remain here?"

"For tonight at any rate," answered Darrell. "And tomorrow morning I'll come round to the hospital to see how they are."

He waited till the two men had been placed in the ambulance; then he rejoined Daphne Frensham in the lounge. A reporter who had arrived on the scene made a bee line for him, but Darrell waved him aside curtly.

"Look here, dear," he said, "we've got to think what we're going to do. If, as I believe, it was the woman who called herself Mrs Merridick who did this, one thing is very clear. You can't go back to Corinne Moxton, for they now know that you're in touch with Drummond. Further, you won't be safe in your own flat, for I assume she knows your address."

"No she doesn't, Peter. She's never asked me and I've never told her."

"Well, that's one good thing, anyway. We must chance your being safe there. But about tonight. I suggest that we should take rooms here in the hope that Hugh may recover consciousness tomorrow. Then if he doesn't, you go back to London and lie low, whilst I get Bill Leyton down here to look after Ronald."

"What are you going to do, Peter?"

"Stay here, darling," he said promptly. "Or perhaps go to an hotel in Bournemouth. I must be on hand the instant Hugh comes to, because there may be something to be done which he won't be fit to tackle. And you see, the doctor can't give me any idea how long he's likely to remain like this. So I'll go and book two rooms, and then I vote for a spot of bed. But for Heaven's sake, my dear, lock your door: with this bunch you never know. I don't think we'll have any of 'em down here tonight, but one can't be sure. Tomorrow, when it's in all the papers, and they know that Hugh and Ronald aren't dead, it will be a different matter. And that's why I think I may go to Bournemouth with Bill Leyton."

"Peter," she cried suddenly. "What about Ardington?"

"Good Lord!" he said. "I'd forgotten all about it. Anyway, my dear, it's too late to get there now. We'll have to let Ardington take care of itself. Now, you pop off to bed: we'll see what luck we have tomorrow with old Hugh."

But they had none, and when they left in the afternoon he was still babbling incoherently.

"It's hell," said Darrell gloomily. "Supposing they have found out something, and don't come round before it is too late. What's the matter, dear?"

For the girl had suddenly laid a hand on his arm.

"Stop, Peter, and go back to that paper shop." Her voice was urgent, and he glanced at her curiously. "There was a poster outside, and I'm sure I saw something."

He backed the car obediently, and then for a while they both sat staring at the placard in silence.

GHASTLY TRAIN ACCIDENT
AT
ARDINGTON
HUGE DEATH ROLL

"Get a paper, Peter," she said in a low voice.

He bought two copies of the *Evening Mail*, and handed her one. And in flaming headlines they read the news.

"APPALLING ACCIDENT TO EXPRESS
TRAIN LEAVES RAILS WHEN TRAVELLING AT
SIXTY MILES AN HOUR

HEAVY LOSS OF LIFE

"One of the most dreadful railway accidents of modern times occurred last night near the little village of Ardington, which for sheer majesty of horror as a spectacle can only have been equalled by the tragic loss of the ill-fated R101 when she crashed near Beauvais on her maiden trip to India. And a further parallel between the two disasters is that in both cases only one person appears to have seen it actually happen. I have just left the spectator of last night's accident, and he is still almost dazed by what he saw. He is Mr Herbert, of Plumtree Farm, where he has lived for the last twenty years.

" 'I had been up all night with a sick cow,' he told me, 'and was just leaving her to go back to bed when I heard the express approaching. It was coming through the cutting half a mile away, and I waited to see it pass. After the cutting there is an embankment on a bit of a curve, and the train came roaring round it. And then suddenly it happened. The engine seemed to leap into the air, and rush down the side of the embankment, followed by all the coaches. There was a crash such as I had never heard: everything seemed to pile up in a heap, and then there was silence for a moment or two. But not for long: such a pandemonium of screams and yells broke out as I wouldn't have believed possible. The lights were still on, though some of the carriages seemed to be telescoped, and I could see the passengers climbing out of windows – those that weren't dead. It was terrible: I shall never get it out of my head.'

"So much for the only eye-witness' account: now for some further details. The train was the night express from Scotland to London. It was travelling at full speed, but, according to the guard, John Harrison of Bexley, who is lying seriously injured in a neighbouring cottage, no faster than usual on that stretch of line. They were up to time, in fact a minute ahead of it, so that the accident took place about 4.15 a.m. And then the inexplicable thing occurred. The wheels of the engine left the rails, and the locomotive, owing to the curve, plunged down the embankment at sixty miles an hour, dragging the heavy train behind it. The driver and fireman were both killed, and up to date there is a death roll of thirty-five with seventy-one injured, several of them very seriously. Unfortunately, these figures by no means represent the total loss. A breakdown gang is at work, but several hours must elapse before some of the coaches can be lifted free of others into which they have been telescoped, and it is a regrettable certainty that when this is done many more casualties will be discovered.

"I had a talk with Walter Marton, the attendant in the sleeping-car, who, by some miraculous stroke of luck, escaped with nothing worse than a shaking.

" 'I was sitting in my seat reading,' he said. 'She was running as smoothly as usual, when suddenly she gave a terrific lurch, and I got flung into a heap of soiled linen. And the next thing I knew was that the coach was upside down. I climbed out through one of the windows.'

"And that is one of the things which increases the horror of the spectacle: almost the whole of the train is upside down at the foot of the slope. Only the two rear coaches, one of which was the guard's van, are still standing on their wheels, and in these no one was killed, though several passengers sustained fractures, and the guard himself was hurled from one end of his van to the other."

LATER.

"The death roll in this ghastly tragedy has now reached forty-nine, and two coaches still remain telescoped. It is feared that the final count will number between sixty and seventy, since no one can possibly be alive in those two carriages. The gruesome task of identifying the victims is being carried out in the little concert hall of Ardington."

"But, Peter," said the girl, and her face was as white as a sheet, "it's unbelievable; it's inconceivable. How did they know that this was going to happen?"

He stared at her.

"Know it was going to happen," he repeated foolishly. "They can't have known an accident was going to happen."

"But was it an accident, Peter?"

"My God!" he muttered. "My God!" And fell silent, still staring at her dazedly.

"What was the object, Daphne?" he said at length. "What can have been the object? My dear, you *must* be wrong. It was an accident."

"So that was why Parker wasn't to drive," she went on, as if he had not spoken. "What are we going to do about it, Peter?"

"What can we do about it?" he said heavily, as he got back into the car. "A sentence heard through a keyhole isn't much to go on. Their answer would be a flat denial that the words were ever spoken, or that they ever went there. And it's impossible to prove that they did."

They drove on in silence, each busy with their own thoughts. Unbelievable; inconceivable, as she had said; and yet it was true. Right from the beginning she had mentioned Ardington: it was not as if she had not been sure and had thought of it after seeing the account in the paper. Even the time fitted in. It was true. For some diabolical reason the Scotch express had been wrecked, and Corinne Moxton and Pendleton had known it was going to happen and had been spectators.

"Don't say anything, Daphne dear," he said, as they drew up at her flat. "You'll do no good by speaking too soon. Our only chance is to let them think they're not suspected. Then we may catch them."

He went round to his club, and the first thing that caught his eye was a headline in a later edition of the *Evening Mail*.

"SENSATIONAL DEVELOPMENT IN ARDINGTON DISASTER
EVIDENCE OF FARM LABOURER

"A sensational development has taken place in the Ardington disaster, where Colonel Mayhew, of the Home Office, has already opened the preliminary investigation. It appears that Mr Herbert was not the only eye-witness of the accident, but that George Streeter, a farm labourer employed at the neighbouring village of Bilsington, also saw it. He states that he was returning after a late dance to the cottage in which he lives, and was walking along the main Towchester road as the train left the cutting. This would mean that he was about two hundred yards from the actual scene of the disaster. And he affirms most positively that just before the engine left the rails, he saw what he describes as a sort of flash right in front of the wheels. Pressed by Colonel Mayhew to be more explicit, he said that it looked like a big yellow spark, and that it happened when the engine was four or five yards away. He heard nothing, but that is not surprising in view of the noise of the train and the direction of the wind. Too much importance should not be attached to his story, though when I interviewed him he struck me as being a reliable and unimaginative man. At the same time the possibilities that are opened up, should his statement be correct, are so inconceivably monstrous that it would be well to await further evidence before jumping to any conclusion. That anything in the nature of a bomb outrage should happen in this country seems utterly incredible. Unfortunately, the permanent way is so badly ploughed up for nearly a hundred yards that some considerable time must inevitably elapse before the final examination is concluded."

He laid down the paper: there was the proof. Naturally the reporter sounded a note of warning over believing such an incredible thing, but he did not know all the facts. Nobody did except Daphne and himself. And ceaselessly the question hammered at his brain – what ought he to do? Then another one took its place: what had been the object of such an apparently senseless outrage? Surely there was no man living, not even Pendleton, who would have done such a monstrous thing merely to gratify Corinne Moxton's craving for cruelty and excitement.

"Hullo! Peter. Seen the latest about the Ardington accident?"

He looked up: Tim Maguire, a Major in the Royal Engineers, was standing by his chair.

"You're a Sapper, Tim," he said. "How could a thing like that be done?"

"Easy as falling off a log," answered Maguire, "if anyone wanted to. You've only got to wedge a slab of gun-cotton or any other high explosive up against one of the rails and then fire it by electricity just before the train reaches the spot. By that means you cut the rail. But surely you don't believe this labourer's evidence, do you? The thing is preposterous."

He strolled away: just so – the thing was preposterous. And that is what everyone else would say if he told them what he knew.

After a while he left the club, and getting into a taxi he went round to see Bill Leyton. He had ceased to care by now whether he was followed or not: everything, even the bomb outrage at the Falconbridge Arms, seemed to pale into insignificance beside this crowning infamy.

He found Leyton in, and plunged into the story at once.

"What ought one to do: that's what has got to be decided," he concluded.

Leyton pushed over the whisky decanter.

"I think what you told Miss Frensham is right, Darrell," he said. "I don't see that you can do anything merely on the strength of what she heard through the keyhole. Besides, it's pretty obvious that even though they were spectators they were not the actual perpetrators of the crime."

"No; but they probably know who they were."

"More than likely; but they're not going to give it away. They will simply say that they haven't an idea what you are talking about, and that you must be mad. And if you persist, or go to the police, they will run you for libel. You see, all your information is second-hand; that's the devil of it. We may know that it is true; but so long as Drummond and Standish are unconscious our hands are tied."

"I suppose you're right," said Darrell moodily. "Well, are you on for coming down to Bournemouth with me so as to be on the spot the instant we're wanted?"

"Sure: I'll throw some kit into a bag now."

And that night found them installed at an hotel in the pine woods, where the average age of the clientele appeared to be in the early eighties. The period of weary waiting had begun. Three times daily did Darrell ring up the nursing-home for news: every evening he got through to Daphne to make sure she was still all right. And with incredible slowness the days dragged by, with No Change the invariable bulletin.

The papers had unanimously discounted George Streeter's statement, and since no confirmatory evidence appeared to be forthcoming from the examination of the debris, the Ardington disaster was universally regarded as simply being the most appalling accident of the century. The death roll had been published, and had reached the ghastly total of eighty-four, with seven more not expected to live.

"And what beats me," said Darrell, "is that they're all absolutely unknown people. Hugh, I know, had an idea that there might be some political significance behind these swine's activities, and it would be within the realms of comprehension if they had wrecked the train to kill one big man, regardless of the others. But there wasn't a big man on the train: if there had been, and he had escaped, we should have heard all about it. But all these poor devils are just common or garden birds like you and me."

"I know," said Leyton. "That point had occurred to me. And there's another thing too: if it was a terrorist action done by Communists or people of that sort to further their own ends, it fails in its entire object if the public believe it was only an accident. So surely, by some means or other, without giving themselves away, the men who did it would have let it be known that it was deliberate.

"Which brings us back to our old starting-point, that the whole thing seems utterly and absolutely senseless."

It was Sunday morning, and they were sitting disconsolately in the lounge. Five wasted days, and nothing to show for them. And then, as so often happens, everything changed when they least expected it. A page-boy came up to them with a message that Darrell was wanted on the telephone by the Falconbridge hospital. And a minute later he was back.

"Hugh's conscious," he said briefly. "Let's get a move on."

They were met by the doctor.

"Captain Drummond came to about an hour ago," he said, "and is seemingly none the worse for it. But go easy with him."

They found Drummond sitting up in bed. He looked pale and drawn, but he grinned cheerfully when he saw them.

"Hullo! chaps," he said, "that was a close shave."

"How are you feeling, old boy?" cried Darrell.

"Damned sore," said Drummond. "And it hurts like hell to laugh. I gather my jaw took the drive first. But I'm still absolutely in the dark as to what happened. All I know is that I was standing by the open window, and there was suddenly a terrific explosion behind me. After that little Willie passed out."

"There's a lot to tell you, Hugh, but before I begin I've got one question to ask. Did a grey-haired, middle-aged woman come into the sitting-room any time during the evening?"

Drummond frowned thoughtfully.

"Now you come to mention it, Peter, one did. Came in, sat down, and when we mildly pointed out it was a private room she apologised profusely and withdrew. Why do you ask?"

"She's the girl friend who did it," said Darrell. "She must have left a bomb behind her. Don't look so surprised, old man: lots of funny things have taken place since we last met. Do you feel fit to listen?"

"Fire ahead, boy. I'm fine."

He listened in silence whilst Darrell told him everything that had happened: then without a word he got out of bed and rang the bell. He was still shaky on his legs, but on his face was the look of grim determination that Darrell knew well of old.

"Sister darling," he said as the nurse came in, "would you bring your baby boy his trousers, please?"

"But you aren't going to get up," she cried aghast.

"Not only that, my poppet, but I'm going to London. And I feel I shall attract less attention if I'm wearing my trousers."

"But it is madness, Captain Drummond," she said. "I'm sure the doctor will never allow it."

Drummond smiled cheerfully as she left the room.

"Is it wise, old lad?" said Darrell anxiously. "I don't quite see what you are going to do when you get there."

"I am going to have a heart-to-heart talk with Sir Richard Pendleton," answered Drummond quietly. "And what I've got to say to him will give that gentleman to think pretty furiously."

"What's this I hear, Captain Drummond? You say you're going to London?"

The doctor had come bustling in.

"That's correct, Doc.," said Drummond. "In a nice fast motor-car. Now, it's no good saying I mustn't, my dear fellow, because I'm going – with or without trousers. There are times – and this is one of them – when trifling considerations of health simply do not come into the picture. By the way, how is my fellow sufferer?"

"Just the same," answered the doctor. "Well, I suppose I can't keep you here by force, so you'd better get his clothes, Nurse."

"Haven't got such a thing as a spot of ale about the premises, have you?" said Drummond hopefully, and the doctor laughed.

"You're a hopeless case," he cried. "I'll see whether there is any."

"If only that damn bomb had gone off five minutes later," said Drummond, as the doctor left the room. "You realise Standish had solved the cipher."

"The devil he had," said Darrell. "That should help."

"Unfortunately it doesn't. He was just going to explain it to me, when up she went. And so until he comes to we're no better off than we were before. Thank you, light of my eye."

"You idiot," laughed the nurse, putting his clothes on the bed. "And matron is sending up some beer in a minute."

"What a woman," said Drummond. "I like it by the quart. Yes," he continued as she left the room, "he'd just said to me 'I've got it' when that blasted bomb burst."

"There haven't been any more messages so far as I know," said Darrell. "None at any rate that have appeared in the papers."

"By the way, Peter, are they watching this hospital?"

"I don't know," said Darrell, "this is the first time we've actually been over here: we've rung up every day."

"The betting is five to one on," remarked Drummond thoughtfully. "Sister, dear," he said, as she returned with the beer, "is there a way out by the back?"

"There is. Why?"

"Because, darling, I want to use it. I feel tolerably certain that these kindly people in London who take such an interest in my welfare have got someone watching this place."

"Funny you should say that. A strange man has been loitering about these last few days. Look – there he is now."

"Don't go to the window, my dear," said Drummond quickly. "Where is he? I see. Peter, do you spot him? When you and Leyton go, make sure he hears you discuss my condition in voices choked with tears. And, Sister, you pass it around the staff that I had a brief moment of consciousness, and have now become completely gaga again. I want that bird to think I'm still here. Then I'll join you, Peter, somewhere down the road."

"We'll just have to pop over to Bournemouth and pay the bill," said Darrell

"I think I'll stop on there," said Leyton. "Ronald may come to just as unexpectedly as Drummond did, in which case I'd like to be close at hand."

"Not a bad notion," remarked Drummond. "And if he does, get in touch with us at once. Now then – are we ready? If so, let's get a move on."

They went downstairs, and ten minutes later Drummond joined them in the car out of sight of the hospital.

"I don't think he suspected anything," said Darrell. "We left him still standing about the place."

"Good!" cried Drummond. "Because I have an idea that the sweet Corinne is more likely to be at home if she doesn't know I'm coming."

"I should think that the chances are that she may be genuinely out on a Sunday," said Leyton.

"Then I'll wait till she's genuinely in," said Drummond quietly. "And that lantern-jawed swine of a saw-bones."

Leaving Leyton in Bournemouth, and stopping on the way for lunch, they reached London at four o'clock, and Drummond went straight to his house.

"I'd like you to come with me, Peter," he said, "but I shouldn't think there is much good arriving before about six."

And it was then that Denny gave him Corinne Moxton's message.

"I heard about that and forgot to tell you," said Darrell.

"Shall we ring her up or not?" remarked Drummond thoughtfully. "Taking everything into account, I think it would be better if we arrived unexpectedly."

"Are you all right again, sir?" asked Denny anxiously.

"Fit as an army mule, old soldier," said Drummond. "I only feel as if I'd been trodden all over by an elephant. Now, Peter – a slight change of apparel, and then we must decide on what line we are going to take at the interview. Also, I suggest that anything we want we have before we go. She'd probably adore to see someone die of a poisoned drink."

At six o'clock they left: point-blank accusation was to be the order of the evening. Only two things had they decided to leave out. The first was any mention of Daphne Frensham, which ruled out the Ardington disaster; the other was the fact that Standish had solved the cipher.

"He *may* come to soon, Peter," said Drummond, "and if so, we don't want him to have another one to solve. And now is luck going to be in?"

It was: they found Corinne Moxton and Sir Richard Pendleton in the drawing-room. And the doctor's violent start and the sudden blanching of the woman's cheeks under the rouge did not escape Drummond's notice. But it was only instantaneous: whatever else she might be she was an actress.

"Why, Captain Drummond," she said, rising and coming towards him with hand outstretched, "this is bully. I'd heard you'd had an accident."

"You heard perfectly correctly, madam," answered Drummond, folding his arms. "And it is about that accident and one or two other things that Mr Darrell and I have come to talk to you. Moreover, it is very fortunate that Penholder, or whatever his name is, is here. Saves the necessity of sending for him."

"What the devil do you mean, sir?" cried the doctor angrily. "You know perfectly well that my name is not Penholder. Are you trying to be gratuitously offensive?"

"Is it possible to be offensive to carrion like you?" asked Drummond languidly. "Great pity I didn't throttle you that night, Penwiper. If I'd known who you were, and one or two other things which I subsequently discovered about your character, I should have done."

Sir Richard lit a cigarette with ostentatious deliberation.

"I saw in the papers, Captain Drummond," he said, "that you had recently been blown up, and sustained concussion. I can only come to the charitable conclusion that you are still suffering from it."

"That you would take that line was fairly obvious from the word 'go,' " said Drummond. "The spot of bother as far as you are concerned, however, is that I was not suffering from concussion on the night Sanderson was murdered by that engaging individual with the fountain-pen, so ably assisted by Miss Moxton's admiring plaudits."

But this time she was ready, and her laughter was admirably natural.

"My dear man," she cried merrily, "you must have been worse than was reported in the papers. Richard, ain't he cute?"

"Cute or not cute: sane or not sane," said Pendleton furiously, "his statement is absolutely monstrous."

"Oh! yeah," Drummond drawled. "Pity I drank beer that night in Standish's room, isn't it? You hadn't doped the beer."

For a moment or two there was dead silence.

"I fear you're a bit of an ass, Penworthy," Drummond continued. "How anybody in their senses can employ you as a surgeon, Heaven alone knows. Incidentally, I don't think many people will by the time I've done with you. And your market value, madam, isn't going to soar through the roof."

"Say, Richard, isn't there some law in this country to prevent this man insulting me?"

Her voice was shrill with anger.

"None; until he does it outside these four walls. Then he'll soon find out one or two truths. I suppose, Captain Drummond, that even you are capable of realising the disgraceful cowardice of coming to a lady's flat and then advancing these preposterous threats. Why, if you are suffering from these delusions, have you not been to the police?"

"I have," said Drummond calmly. "So put that in the old meerschaum and set fire to it, Penturtle."

"And they, I imagine, treated your demented ravings with the contempt they deserve," said the doctor, but to Drummond's keen ear there was fear in his voice.

"But I wasn't demented," explained Drummond cheerfully. "Scotland Yard has known all about you two for a week."

Corinne Moxton caught her breath with a sharp hiss.

"I don't believe you," said Pendleton contemptuously. "If you had really gone with these incredible stories to the police, Miss Moxton and I would have heard from them by now."

"Not of necessity," remarked Drummond. "Rightly or wrongly, Standish and I came to the conclusion that you and Miss Moxton were very small beer. In fact, except for your repulsive habits, you cut no ice at all. The man we want to lay our hands on is that strange individual with a head like a pumpkin, who apparently answers to the name of Demonico, and who I last had the pleasure of meeting at the squash-court entertainment. By the way, I hope you enjoyed it: you had excellent seats."

Pendleton turned to Corinne Moxton.

"It's all right, my dear," he said reassuringly. "I have met cases like this before, though this is a very remarkable one. I don't know what hospital he has been in, but the doctor in charge deserves the gravest censure for allowing him out so soon. And I warn you seriously, Mr Darrell I believe your name is, that unless you take the greatest care of him his reason may be irreparably impaired. As you see for yourself, the poor fellow is talking gibberish."

"My fee is three guineas," remarked Drummond. "Stick to a light diet of porterhouse steak and onions, and don't trip over the mat as you go. No, Pendleton, it won't do: I'm as sane as you are, and you know it."

"May I have a word with you in private, Mr Darrell?" said Sir Richard, ignoring Drummond completely.

"You may not," said Darrell decidedly.

"Then I must say it in front of him. The symptoms are clearly defined, but if proper care is taken of him there is no reason why in a month, or perhaps less, he should not make a complete recovery, and these delusions, which are the direct outcome of his concussion, will disappear like the morning mist. But I again emphasise – proper care. You must get him home, keep him very quiet, and get his doctor to see him. And for everybody's sake, in view of the bent his particular delusions have taken, it would be as well if he saw as few people as possible."

"Peter, hasn't he got a charming bedside manner?" said Drummond admiringly. "A voice at once soothing and firm. Well, Pendleton, as I said before, I thought it probable you would take up this line: when one comes to think of it, it would be impossible for you to take up any other. And yet I am quite prepared to admit that, as far as other people are concerned, it's a very good one. To them it would seem more likely that I was suffering from delusions than that a celebrated surgeon and a well-known film star are a pair of devils incarnate. But I warn you that you are in very dangerous waters, because, as I have already told you, there can be no question of my having had the jimjams at the time when the police were notified that you were in Standish's room on the night of Sanderson's murder. I was not drugged, though you thought I was, and I saw you there."

"And you expect the police to believe such a preposterous statement on your uncorroborated word? I'd never heard of Standish in my life till I saw his name mentioned with yours in connection with the bomb outrage. And I haven't an idea where his rooms are. If you thought you saw me there it was a case of mistaken identity."

"This is beginning to bore me," said Drummond. "So I will deliver my ultimatum, Pendleton, and then go. I have the best of reasons for knowing that some big crime is planned early this coming week. What it is I don't know. But unless the police are informed anonymously as to what it is going to be, in time for them to prevent it, my depositions to them with regard to you will stand. And since they connect you intimately with the gang who murdered Sanderson they will not do you much good. If, however, the police are informed, it is conceivable that I might come to the conclusion that it was a case of mistaken identity. So choose, you damned swine – choose. Come on, Peter."

The front door closed behind them, and then the tension broke.

"Richard," screamed Corinne Moxton, "ring up Scotland Yard now and tell them. It's our only hope."

"Hush, my dear, hush: I must think." His face was grey: his hands were shaking. "God! how did they find out?"

"Find out what?"

Mrs Merridick was standing by the door.

"Drummond has been here, and he knows all about us," said Pendleton. "He wasn't drugged at all that night, and he saw me."

"My dear Sir Richard, for a doctor that seems singularly stupid of you. What do you propose to do about it? Did I hear Corinne say something about ringing up Scotland Yard?"

She bit her lip, as Pendleton flashed her a warning glance.

"No, no," she cried. "Of course not."

"Let us all have a drink and consider the matter carefully," said Mrs Merridick, going to the sideboard, and picking up the cocktail shaker. "You say that Drummond knows all about us. I don't think he can know much about me."

"Perhaps not," said Pendleton. "But there are other people besides you in the world. And he knows that something is going to happen early this week."

"Something. So he doesn't know what that something is?"

"No; he doesn't know that."

"Then am I right in supposing that the object of his visit here was to try to threaten you into telling him what it was?"

"More or less."

"Naturally you didn't."

"Of course not," said Pendleton. "How could you imagine such a thing for an instant?"

A faint smile twitched round Mrs Merridick's mouth; then she turned round with three drinks on a tray.

"Then I don't think we need worry," she remarked. "Let us drink a toast to the successful issue of our plans."

They all drained their glasses, and Mrs Merridick lit a cigarette. And then, quite suddenly it happened. Sir Richard, his face convulsed with agony, clutched at his side.

"You devil," he croaked. "You've poisoned us."

On the floor writhed Corinne Moxton, and Mrs Merridick watched them in silence.

"I have," she said at length. "Your intentions with regard to Scotland Yard did not appeal to me."

A few moments later, without a backward glance at the two motionless figures, she left the room. And it was only when her hand was on the latch of the front door that she remembered something and went back. Into her bag she placed her own glass: to stage what would inevitably be taken for a suicide pact three glasses would be a mistake. Then once again the door closed behind her, and Mrs Merridick went downstairs to her waiting car.

CHAPTER 10

With a frown Hugh Drummond lit a cigarette: then he picked up his morning paper from the floor where he had thrown it. Not that they really deserved any other fate: it was the complete unexpectedness of the thing that had upset him for the moment.

"TRAGEDY IN WEST-END FLAT
DEATH OF WELL-KNOWN SURGEON
AND FILM STAR

"A shocking tragedy occurred last night at Number 4A Barton Mews, the charming residence of the beautiful film star Corinne Moxton. The discovery was made by her chauffeur, who had been ordered to call for her at seven o'clock. When he had waited till eight he began to fear that something was amiss, since he could see the light shining from her sitting-room. At nine o'clock he decided to summon a policeman, and between them they forced the front door. To their horror they discovered the actress lying dead on the floor, and by her side was the body of a man, also dead. This man the chauffeur at once recognised as Sir Richard Pendleton, the celebrated Harley Street surgeon. Their faces were convulsed with agony, showing that they had died in great pain.

"A doctor was at once summoned, who gave it as his opinion that they had been dead between two and three hours. It appears that two empty glasses were on the table; also a cocktail shaker half-filled with liquid. The contents were immediately analysed, and were found to contain a high percentage of a very rare and deadly poison, barely known outside the medical profession. The inquest will be held today."

Drummond put the paper down: so they had taken that way out. And he was just finishing his coffee when the door opened and Peter Darrell came in.

"Morning, Hugh. I didn't think they'd do that, did you?"

"I didn't, Peter. Certainly not her. He must have gone away and got this poison, and then put it in the drink."

"Well, old boy, I don't think you need feel any guilt on the matter," said Darrell.

"I don't. If ever a couple richly deserved to die, they did. But it's a bit of a shock all the same."

"Have you seen the other thing in the paper?"

"No. Anything interesting?"

Darrell turned to the front page, and pointed half-way down the agony column.

AOYSLKEJSSCQOOIEHORJKQSC
AHOSDCVKQSCXJEJOLISTORNY
XDKYDCQOYQATSKJOXYDCSH
XEJBKMMVOXIKTSC.

"A long one," said Drummond. "Hell! if only Standish was conscious!"

"You can make nothing out of it?" asked Darrell.

"Not a letter, old boy. He hadn't time even to give me a hint. And you know what a hopeless fool I am at anything like that."

"We might be able to find someone in London who could do it," said Darrell. "If Ronald could solve the bally thing, there must be someone else who can."

"We'll have a dart at it," agreed Drummond. "But who the deuce does one go to? Is there a cipher department at Scotland Yard?"

"Must be, I should think. Let's go and find out. The sooner we give it in the better."

But the expert they eventually ran to ground held out but little hope. Having at last persuaded him that it was not a betting code, but something really serious, he consented to do his best if he had time. And at that they had to leave it, returning to their club to kick their heels and get through time as best they could.

The late evening papers contained the result of the inquest. Evidence was given to show that the two deceased persons had been on unusually friendly terms, and that Sir Richard Pendleton had frequently visited her in her flat, and not leaving till the early hours of the morning. Further, the chauffeur stated that on the very night of the tragedy his orders had been to take them both out to dinner at a house not far from Henley.

"It is almost certain," said the Coroner in his summing-up, "that the poison must have been obtained by Sir Richard, as a drug of such a rare kind would be hardly procurable by a woman. It is therefore clear that it was he who was primarily responsible for the tragedy. Indeed, we have no evidence before us to show whether the deceased woman knew that the drug had been added to the cocktail ingredients, a point the jury must bear in mind when arriving at their verdict."

Which when given and reduced to plain English was to the effect that Sir Richard Pendleton had committed suicide while temporarily insane; and that Corinne Moxton had either done the same or been murdered by him. But the motives for such an amazing crime were naturally a profound mystery.

"And will doubtless always remain so," said Drummond. "What about ringing up this wench of yours, Peter, and getting her round for a bite of food? She'll be interested to know the truth."

And though it was not the truth, she was: profoundly interested.

"I've been puzzling my brains the whole day, Captain Drummond," she said, "as to what could have made them do it. And even now it is almost incredible, because from what you say you promised them they would get off if they told the police."

"Incredible or not, they did it, and I don't think I shall lose an hour's sleep over the fact. Two nasty pieces of work. Well, I'll join you after dinner. Peter's expression indicates either indigestion or suppressed love, and I can't run any risks after that recent round of mine with a bomb."

He left them in the ladies' side of the club and went into the smoking-room. The conversation was confined almost exclusively to the Pendleton affair, and as he listened to all sorts of fantastic theories being advanced he smiled cynically to himself. And then he suddenly heard a phrase which caught his attention.

"Undoubtedly Pendleton was one of the syndicate."

Hervey, a stockbroker whom he knew slightly, was talking to two or three other men, and Drummond joined the group.

"And it's a damned dangerous syndicate too," Hervey continued, "as far as this country is concerned. They've been selling sterling short by the million abroad this last week."

"Do you know who the others are?" asked Drummond.

"Hullo! old boy," said Hervey. "I heard you'd been blown to bits in the New Forest. Are you all right again?"

"Quite," said Drummond. "Feel a bit stiff still, but otherwise no harm done. But this syndicate Pendleton was in – was it a big one?"

"Did you know the man?"

"Slightly," answered Drummond with a faint smile.

"Never had a vestige of use for him myself, though I believe he was a very fine surgeon. And as far as I know, he was the only Englishman in this crowd. Daly is an Irish-American, Legrange is a Frenchman, and there's another somewhat mysterious individual in it who no one seems to have ever seen. Calls himself Demonico, and I should imagine he might be a Greek. But whoever he is, he's in with this bunch, and if they go on as they have been doing and the country's credit drops they'll get a packet."

Drummond strolled away: would it be possible, he wondered, to get at Demonico through Daly or Legrange? He could almost certainly get their addresses from Scotland Yard, and he was just pondering on the advisability of ringing up McIver and putting the matter to him when another man he knew came up and spoke to him. He was an eccentric individual named Jellaby, whose little peculiarity was that he was always in possession of some secret which had just been passed on to him by some highly placed official, and which only he knew. He had always heard it in strict confidence: with equal regularity he ran round the club imparting it to everyone in even stricter confidence. Generally Drummond avoided him like the plague, but on this occasion he was fairly and squarely buttonholed, and escape was impossible.

"Heard a most amazing thing this afternoon, Drummond." Jellaby's voice sank to a hoarse whisper. "Straight from the horse's mouth. For Heaven's sake don't pass it on: it's a profound secret. It's about the Ardington train disaster."

Drummond's half-suppressed yawn ceased abruptly.

"You remember the evidence given by that labourer, George Streeter, to the effect that he had seen a yellow flash in front of the engine wheels?" Jellaby rarely waited for any answer to his questions. "Now I am in a position to tell you definitely – I got it direct from one of Colonel Mayhew's staff – that that evidence was correct. After exhaustive examination of the torn-up rails, they have discovered one place where the break, according to the experts, must have been caused by an explosive. The disaster therefore was not an accident at all, but a deliberately planned outrage."

"With what object?" said Drummond.

"The very question I myself at once asked," said Jellaby, his voice becoming even more confidential. "And the answer was an amazing one. This country, as you know, is going through a very severe financial crisis, and anything which might help to spread the idea abroad that our reputation for law and order no longer held good would tend to increase the gravity of that crisis. If then it was thought that the condition in England had become such that train wrecking was taking place, confidence abroad would be still further reduced, a state of affairs which would be most advantageous to certain speculators."

"I get you," said Drummond. "Is this new development going to appear in the newspapers?"

"Not at present, at any rate," said Jellaby. "Sooner or later I suppose it will have to, but just at the moment it would be playing straight into their hands. Don't forget – not a word to a soul."

Drummond smiled faintly as he watched Jellaby stalk his next victim: then he lit a cigarette thoughtfully. Things were becoming clearer: what had seemed to Peter Darrell so amazing because of its senselessness had taken to itself a meaning. He went back to the ladies' side of the club and found them still over their cocktails.

"I've been hearing things, souls," he said, "things which have thrown considerable light on matters. And I can summarise them for you in a nutshell."

"So now it is proved that it wasn't an accident," said the girl as he finished.

"According to my friend Jellaby it is," answered Drummond.

"It's almost incredible," said Darrell.

"Not so incredible, Peter, as it was before. Then, if you like, it was unbelievable that anyone who wasn't a maniac should have derailed an express for the fun of it. But now we have got a reason."

"But would a thing like that affect us abroad?" asked the girl.

Drummond shrugged his shoulders.

"On matters of international finance I'm an infant," he said. "But I do know that it's a very delicately balanced affair, and I suppose as Jellaby said that it isn't going to help a country if its neighbours come to the conclusion, rightly or wrongly, that it's got into such a condition of lawlessness that train wrecking is taking place. At any rate it is clear that that is what did happen, and the point now arises as to what we are going to do. Because, as I see things, we, at the present moment, are the only people who are in a position to link things up. Hervey and others in the City know that Demonico's gang of financiers are selling sterling short, and that it is to their advantage to force down our credit abroad. The Home Office, according to Jellaby, know that the Ardington accident was a case of train wrecking. But literally the only thing that could connect and does connect the two together is that Miss Frensham heard what she did through the keyhole. And now the speaker has killed himself."

"I think Scotland Yard should be told all we know," said Darrell decidedly. "I quite see that they can't act on Daphne's unsupported statement, and we haven't a vestige of proof beyond that that Pendleton and that woman ever went near Ardington or knew anything about it. And since they're both dead we can never find out. But in view of the fact that we know some crime is premeditated early this week, we should be grossly to blame if we didn't pass on to the police that vital piece of information which, as you say, Hugh, links up the two things."

"Right," said Drummond. "I'll go down myself at once. Wait here till I get back."

He returned an hour later.

"It's electrified 'em all right," he remarked. "As we surmised, they can't take any action, though Daly and Legrange from now on are marked men. But the trouble is that though they've been combing the country since our information of a week ago for

Demonico he has completely disappeared. Another thing I gathered was this: they do not think that Legrange, at any rate, would lend himself to such an abominable crime as the Ardington one. Of Daly they're not quite so sure, but it is Demonico they believe is responsible."

"So they accepted Daphne's evidence," said Darrell.

"Absolutely: they saw the vital importance of the fact that she mentioned Ardington to you and the time, *before* it happened. By the way, Miss Frensham, they may want to hear it direct from you: if so, they'll let you know."

"I can go at any time they want," said the girl.

"And in the meantime they seem to think there is nothing more to be done. To cross-examine Legrange or Daly would be useless: even with your evidence, my dear, there is nothing to connect either of them with the accident. They were all members of the same syndicate – true – but that's not an offence. So, for the present, the order of the day is wait and see, and all one can hope is that we shan't see some other ghastly crime like Ardington. Are you looking for me, boy?"

A page came up to the table.

"Captain Drummond, sir?"

"That's me," said Drummond.

"Wanted on the telephone, sir: either you or Mr Darrell. Gentleman name of Mr Leyton."

Drummond jumped to his feet, his eyes gleaming.

"By Jove! Peter, it might be news of Standish."

He returned a few minutes later, not quite so jubilant.

"He recovered consciousness for a few moments about an hour ago, and seemed to recognise Leyton. He didn't say anything, but he gave a faint smile. Leyton spoke to him, but he didn't answer, though he seemed to try to. And now he's relapsed again. But apparently the doctor thinks he may come to properly at any time now, and Leyton suggests we should go down there at once in case he does."

"I'm with you, old boy," said Darrell.

"Even if he still can't speak he might be able to decode that message," cried Drummond. "I think we ought to push off immediately, Peter. Will you be all right, my dear?"

"My good man, you don't imagine I'm going to be out of this hunt, do you? I'm coming too. I won't be in the way, I promise."

The two men grinned.

"Emphatically one of us, Peter," said Drummond. "Come along, bless you."

Midnight found them at the hospital, where Bill Leyton met them.

"No luck so far," he said, "though the doctor says that his condition now is more nearly natural sleep than it was. But he holds out no hopes for the near future."

They waited all that night, taking it in turns to sit by the bedside. They waited all the next day, walking feverishly about the room whilst Standish lay there, his eyes closed, breathing easily and quietly.

"Under no circumstances must any attempt be made to awaken him."

Those were the doctor's strict orders, and Drummond, gnawing his fingers, stood by the window watching the daylight gradually fade. In the room Darrell and Leyton were pretending to play piquet, but any devotee of that magnificent game might well have failed to recognise it. And then quite suddenly the girl who was watching Standish spoke.

"Peter, he's awake."

In an instant the three men were by the bed. That Standish knew them was obvious: he looked at each of them in turn and grinned feebly.

"How are you feeling, old man?" said Drummond.

But though the sick man's lips moved no sound came from them.

"Can you hear what we say, Ronald?" asked Leyton.

The other gave a barely perceptible nod.

"Listen, Standish," said Drummond quietly. "I wouldn't worry you, old son, but it's urgent. If I got you a pencil and paper do you think you could decode a message in that cipher?"

Gradually, like a very old man, Standish moved his right arm as if to try it: then he nodded. It took him some time to get the pencil in his hand, but at last he succeeded and with the block in front of him he began to write.

"Here's the message," said Drummond, but Standish shook his head, and the three men crowded round him. It was hardly possible to read what he had written, but at last they managed to.

"What is the day of the week?"

"Tuesday," cried Drummond, and Standish nodded again, and once more began to write. And they saw that with infinite difficulty he was writing out the alphabet.

ABCDEFGHIJKLMNOPQRSTUVWXYZ

They waited breathlessly: he had begun to write another line of letters underneath it.

YADSEUTBCFGHIJKLMNOPQRVWXZ

"By Jove!" cried Drummond suddenly. "I see. The day of the week backwards comes at the beginning, and if there are two A's in it like Saturday you leave out the first. Now the message, old man: here it is."

He put it on the bed beside Standish, who again began to write, putting the correct letter under the code one:

AOYSLKEJ
BSADPOEN

Standish paused, staring at it, and sick with anxiety the others watched him. He had got it wrong somehow: the translation was gibberish.

"My God!" said Drummond heavily, "they must have altered the code."

And still worse was to come. Suddenly the pencil slipped from Standish's fingers, and he fell back on the pillow: he was unconscious once more.

For a while no one spoke: to have got so near, and then to fail was a bit of cruel luck.

"The devils must have altered the code," repeated Drummond. "What an infernal piece of bad joss."

He picked up the piece of paper and studied it.

"You see, the old lad had got the other one: found it out from that clue we discovered in Sanderson's desk. What's stung you, my dear?"

For the girl, her eyes shining with excitement, had gripped his arm.

"Captain Drummond," she cried, "it's Tuesday today, but that came out of yesterday's paper. Let's try Monday."

"You fizzer," shouted Drummond.

Feverishly he seized a pencil and wrote out the new code.

ABCDEFGHIJKLMNOPQRSTUVWXYZ
YADNOMBCEFGHIJKLPQRSTUVWXZ

"Now then – where's the message?"

He laid it in front of him and started to translate.

AOYSLKEJSSCQOOIEHORJKQSC
AHOSDCVKQSCXJEJOLISTORNY
XDKYDCQOYQATSKJOXYDCSHX
EJBKMMVOXIKTSC

BEATPOINTTHREEMILESNORTH
BLETCHWORTHYNINEPMTUES
DAYCOACHREARBUTONEYACHT
LYINGOFFWEYMOUTH

" 'Be at point three miles north Bletchworthy nine p.m. Tuesday. Coach rear but one. Yacht lying off Weymouth,' " he read out slowly. "That's tonight."

"Coach rear but one," said Leyton. "Merciful Heavens, you fellows, it can't be another train outrage, can it?"

"That," remarked Drummond grimly, "is what we now propose to find out. Come on, both of you, we'll have to drive like hell. Get hold of Standish's torch, and his gun. Also that compressed-air rifle. That was a brainstorm of yours, Daphne, but this time, my dear, you cannot come. Sorry, but it's out of the question."

"Easy for a moment, old boy," said Darrell. "We ought to ring up the station-master at Bletchworthy."

"That's true," said Drummond. "But it means delay, Peter. Daphne can do it – can't you, my dear? Ring up the station-master at Bletchworthy and tell him to have the line three miles north of the station patrolled at once. Tell him there is a possibility of an attempt to derail some train – I don't know which – tonight round about nine o'clock."

They dashed out of the hospital and fell into the car. And then began a race against time which Bill Leyton, seated in the back, will never forget to his dying day. Drummond drove all out, with Darrell map reading with the help of a torch beside him. It was a cross-country run which hindered them, and once Darrell made a mistake which took them three miles out of their way. But they did it: the clock showed ten minutes to nine as they roared through the tiny village of Bletchworthy.

And now Drummond went cautiously: it was clear from the map that the road and the railway ran close together at the point they were making for.

"Almost certain to have cars in the neighbourhood," he said, "and we don't want to be spotted."

It was a narrow road, and after they had gone about two miles they saw the red lights of the signals gleaming on their right. As at Ardington, the line was on an embankment, and as they drove along a train roared past above them, going towards London.

Suddenly Drummond checked and switched off his head-lights: his quick eyes had picked up two cars standing in the shadow of some trees in front of them.

"We'll stop here," he said, "and get on to the line. Here's a Fanny for you, Leyton: use it in preference to a gun."

And Leyton found a heavy loaded stick pressed into his hand. Then scrambling up the embankment he followed the other two. They paused at the top: two hundred yards away was a signal box. The signalman's head and shoulders could clearly be seen, and suddenly Drummond started to race towards it. For the door had been opened, and a man with his arm upraised was silhouetted for a moment against the light. The signalman sprang round, even as the arm descended, and they could almost hear the crash as he fell. And a moment later a red light in the distance turned to green.

Drummond stopped, his eyes searching the darkness feverishly. And then to the surprise of the other two he began to run in the opposite direction.

"I see 'em," he muttered. "Half a dozen at least on the track. Into 'em, boys: shoot, kill, murder 'em."

He let out a bellow of fury, and Leyton for the first time in his life had a glimpse of Hugh Drummond going berserk. He split one man's head open like a rotten pumpkin: lifted another with his fist clean over the edge of the embankment, and then waded in on the other four. Revolver shots rang out, and one train wrecker, screaming like a stuck pig, rolled over and over till he reached the ditch below. Then they were alone: the others had bolted. And from far off they heard the rumble of an oncoming train.

Drummond flashed his torch on the line, and a bullet spat past him into the night. Off went his torch: they had seen all they wanted to. Lashed to the inside of the rail was a packet from which protruded two wires stretching right across the permanent way and disappearing into the darkness.

"Cut one of them," said Drummond between his teeth, and just coming into sight saw the lights of the train.

The wire was insulated and stout, but Drummond that night would have split a steel rope with his hands. And his knife went through the lead as if it had been string. Came a whistle, and rocking and swaying slightly the heavy train roared past them and was gone. And as Bill Leyton watched the red tail-lamp vanish in the distance he found his forehead was wet with sweat.

"A close shave," said Drummond briefly, and as he spoke they heard the engines of the two cars in the road start up.

"Let 'em go," he continued. "We're after bigger game than that scum. Only we must do something first about that signalman, and this little packet of trouble."

The cars had gone, and he flashed his torch on the bomb, which was lashed to the rail with string.

"Cut it loose, Peter, and we'll throw it into that pond we passed a short way back. I'm going to the signal box."

He found the signalman looking dazed and sick, sitting on the floor.

"Well, my lad," he said, "you got a nasty one, didn't you? How are you feeling now?"

"What 'appened?" mumbled the man.

"An attempt was made to derail that train that has just gone by," said Drummond. "And before doing so they knocked you on the head."

"Derail the Northern Flier," muttered the signalman foolishly. "Gaw lumme! Wot did they want to do that for?" He scratched his head. "So that's why Bletchworthy rung up to say as 'ow I was to keep my eyes skinned."

"Well, are you all right now?" said Drummond. "I can guarantee that the people who did it won't come back."

"I'm all right now, sir," said the man. "My 'ead's a bit sore – that's all. I'll get on the telephone to Bletchworthy and tell 'em what's took place. Derail the Northern Flier! Well, I'm danged. And she had gold aboard too."

Drummond paused in the door and stared at him.

"Gold!" he said. "How do you know that?"

"Thought everyone did, sir," answered the signalman. "Them there repeyrations to America was on her. Bars and bars of gold, they says, with an armed guard. Lumme! I wonder if that was why they wanted to wreck her."

"I wouldn't be surprised," said Drummond quietly. "I suppose you don't happen to know which coach the gold was in."

"Why – yes, sir. It's allus the same. The rear coach but one: next the guard's van."

A grim smile flickered round Drummond's lips as he left the box and went back to the car. And it was still there when he answered Darrell's question – "What now, Hugh?" with the one word "Weymouth."

"This thing is going to be finished one way or the other, Peter," he said after they had turned the car. "This globe isn't big enough for Demonico and me. And he and I will have a final settlement tonight. There's the pond: bung that damned bomb in."

The moon had risen, and by its light they watched the infernal contrivance sink: then with their noses turned south they started on the last lap of the hunt. To Leyton it seemed nothing short of madness to seek the man out in his own yacht, surrounded by his own people, but he realised the futility of saying so to Drummond. If Darrell and he did not go, Drummond would go alone, and that was unthinkable. But when four hours later they drove along the deserted front, and saw the yacht riding at anchor a quarter of a mile out, he sincerely wished that the last sentence had not been added to the cipher message.

Moored alongside the jetty was a motorboat, and as the car drove up a man stepped out of the shadow of a shed.

"Are you for the yacht?" he said.

"We are," answered Drummond.

"Where are the others?"

"They will be some time yet," said Drummond calmly. "We will go off now. That saves a lot of bother," he whispered to Darrell as they followed the man down the steps of the boat.

They got in, and then for the first time the man took a good look at them.

"Good God!" he muttered. "Who are you?"

"A point of academic interest, laddie," said Drummond pleasantly, catching him by the collar. "Cold, I fear, for bathing, especially in these chill northern waters, but you won't have to swim far."

He flung him into the sea and turned to Darrell.

"Start her up, Peter, and let's hope the blighter can swim."

They shot out from the landing-stage and made for the yacht. Her decks were deserted, but lights were shining in a big saloon aft, towards which they made their way. And reaching the entrance they paused: seated at the table was a middle-aged, grey-haired woman who stared at them with fear in her eyes.

"So, madam," said Drummond at length, "we meet again. Mrs Matthews, I think, was the name under which you registered at the Falconbridge Arms, and your other *alias* I understand is Mrs Merridick."

The woman had recovered herself.

"Presumably you have some idea what you are talking about, sir," she answered coldly, "but I have none. Nor do I wish to have. What is the meaning of this monstrous piece of impertinence?"

"Shall we cut all that out," said Drummond languidly. "Let us even pass over your kindly attention to my friend Standish and myself with that bomb. The hour is late, and I am weary. Where is that swine Demonico?"

"This is intolerable," she cried, rising to her feet. "Demonico! Who on earth is Demonico? I have never heard of the man in my life."

"You lie, madam," said Drummond quietly. "You are in with him, as you were with Pendleton and Corinne Moxton. And I intend to pay my score with him tonight. If he isn't on board now he will be soon. For there are some crimes which are so utterly beyond the pale that they cannot be judged or punished by ordinary standards. And wrecking that train at Ardington was one of them."

"I can only assume that you are insane," she remarked. "But whether you are or not I find your presence here insufferable."

"Fortunately, we were able to frustrate the attempt on the Northern Flier tonight," continued Drummond, "though that does not mitigate the monstrous criminality which caused that attempt to be made."

And then he paused suddenly and his eyes dilated.

"My God! Peter," he shouted, "look at her hands."

For a moment there was silence: then two shots rang out together, while Darrell and Leyton looked on dazedly. They saw Drummond stagger and then recover himself: they saw Mrs Merridick collapse and pitch forward on her face.

"The hands, Peter," repeated Drummond. "There couldn't be two people with those nails and those rings in the world."

He bent down and seized the dead woman's hair: then he gave a tug. And as the wig came away a gleaming, hairless head shone white in the electric light.

"Demonico himself," said Drummond, and suddenly leant against the table.

"What's up, old man?" cried Darrell anxiously.

"He got me through the shoulder," answered Drummond with a grin. "But I guess it was cheap at the price."

So ended the hunt, in a manner very different to its conclusion had Ronald Standish not had that brief interlude of consciousness. And possibly the only other point worth recording is Drummond's remark to him three weeks later as they sat doing a mutual convalescence at Bournemouth.

"This excitement is driving me mad, old boy. Peter is sick with love, and the wench aids and abets him. Bill Leyton has now told me five times how he got a birdie at the fourth. And the hour being what it is, we cannot obtain ale. Let's hire two bath chairs and have a race."

SAPPER

THE BLACK GANG

Although the First World War is over, it seems that the hostilities are not, and when Captain Hugh 'Bulldog' Drummond discovers that a stint of bribery and blackmail is undermining England's democratic tradition, he forms the Black Gang, bent on tracking down the perpetrators of such plots. They set a trap to lure the criminal mastermind behind these subversive attacks to England, and all is going to plan until Bulldog Drummond accepts an invitation to tea at the Ritz with a charming American clergyman and his dowdy daughter.

BULLDOG DRUMMOND

'Demobilised officer, finding peace incredibly tedious, would welcome diversion. Legitimate, if possible; but crime, if of a comparatively humorous description, no objection. Excitement essential... Reply at once Box X10.'

Hungry for adventure following the First World War, Captain Hugh 'Bulldog' Drummond begins a career as the invincible protectorate of his country. His first reply comes from a beautiful young woman, who sends him racing off to investigate what at first looks like blackmail but turns out to be far more complicated and dangerous. The rescue of a kidnapped millionaire, found with his thumbs horribly mangled, leads Drummond to the discovery of a political conspiracy of awesome scope and villainy, masterminded by the ruthless Carl Peterson.

SAPPER

Bulldog Drummond at Bay

While Hugh 'Bulldog' Drummond is staying in an old cottage for a peaceful few days duck-shooting, he is disturbed one night by the sound of men shouting, followed by a large stone that comes crashing through the window. When he goes outside to investigate, he finds a patch of blood in the road, and is questioned by two men who tell him that they are chasing a lunatic who has escaped from the nearby asylum. Drummond plays dumb, but is determined to investigate in his inimitable style when he discovers a cryptic message.

The Female of the Species

Bulldog Drummond has slain his arch-enemy, Carl Peterson, but Peterson's mistress lives on and is intent on revenge. Drummond's wife vanishes, followed by a series of vicious traps set by a malicious adversary, which lead to a hair-raising chase across England, to a sinister house and a fantastic torture-chamber modelled on Stonehenge, with its legend of human sacrifice.

SAPPER

The Final Count

When Robin Gaunt, inventor of a terrifyingly powerful weapon of chemical warfare, goes missing, the police suspect that he has 'sold out' to the other side. But Bulldog Drummond is convinced of his innocence, and can think of only one man brutal enough to use the weapon to hold the world to ransom. Drummond receives an invitation to a sumptuous dinner-dance aboard an airship that is to mark the beginning of his final battle for triumph.

The Return of Bulldog Drummond

While staying as a guest at Merridale Hall, Captain Hugh 'Bulldog' Drummond's peaceful repose is disturbed by a frantic young man who comes dashing into the house, trembling and begging for help. When two warders arrive, asking for a man named Morris – a notorious murderer who has escaped from Dartmoor – Drummond assures them that they are chasing the wrong man. In which case, who on earth is this terrified youngster?